For Jane
With
my friend!

love
jinx

JUST PARDON MY FRENCH
by
Jinx Schwartz

jinx schwartz

OTHER BOOKS BY JINX SCHWARTZ

The Hetta Coffey Series
Just Add Water (Book1)
Just Add Salt (Book 2)
Just Add Trouble (Book 3)
Just Deserts (Book4)
Just the Pits (Book 5)
Just Needs Killin' (Book 6)
Just Different Devils (Book 7)

Other Books

The Texicans
Troubled Sea
Land of Mountains

Boxed Sets

Hetta Coffey Boxed Collection (Books 1-4)

Boxed set of three novels: 3 Mexico Mystery Masters
(with Carmen Armato, John Scherber, and Jinx Schwartz)

JUST PARDON MY FRENCH
Published by Jinx Schwartz
Copyright 2016
Book 8: Hetta Coffey series
All rights reserved.

ACKNOWLEDGEMENTS

As always, my first reader and hubby Robert "Mad Dog" Schwartz is my rock. His patient tackling of techie stuff that has me screaming at my computer is invaluable. Maybe I should give him a raise?

Holly Whitman has been the editor of every one of my books, and she keeps me out of the ditch when my story heads there. The last eyes on the book before I hit the "publish" button, are Donna Rich's. Thanks Holly and Donna.

I have some amazing beta readers! And here they are, in no particular order: Karen Kearns, Sara F. Howe, Loretta Fairley, Lela Cargill, Frances Moore, Bonnie Julien, William Jones, Mary Jordan, Dan O'Neill, Jeff Brockman, Stephen Brown, Jenni Cornell, Lee H. Johnson, Fran Knowles, Brenda Lynch and Dottie Atwater.

Also, we have to thank **Tycho Biard:** Champion, Canine Good Citizen, and Therapy Dog. He's a fun-loving boy who hangs with his friends, goes sailing and paddle boarding and hiking. He cheers up patients in the hospital, and during the school year enjoys listening to classroom kids read to him. He also was kind enough to suffer the indignity of wearing a beret for this book cover shoot.

And for the cover composition we have Karen Phillips to thank.

JUST PARDON MY FRENCH

Every damn fool thing you do in this life you pay for—*Edith Piaf*

Don't care what people say. Don't give a damn about their laws—*Edith Piaf*

Ditto—*Hetta Coffey*

Want to hear Edith sing, with an English translation? Check out the website below.
http://lyricstranslate.com/en/non-je-ne-regrette-rien-no-i-have-no-regrets.html

Chapter One

Ever try varnishing a teak rail with a big ol' furry critter attached to your leg?

Po Thang planted a cold nose-nudge to my bare thigh and grumbled.

"Okay, okay, you win. Fetch your leash." A second after I said this I realized using the F word can mean many things to him, but miracle of miracles, the L word must have overpowered the *fetch* thing, for he bounded onto the dock, leash-in-mouth. I just *have* to learn to give one-word commands other than NO.

Tossing a deteriorating foam paintbrush into a bucket graveyard holding many of its recently deceased relatives, I peeled off latex gloves, wiped sweaty hands on my tee shirt, and hurried down the boarding steps to the dock to that impatient golden retriever. I wanted to get to him before he decided to return to the second deck and sideswipe my morning's labor. As it was, I'd still spend way too much time later on tweezing about a bajillion fine red hairs—none of them mine—from my otherwise perfectly varnished rails.

Po Thang twirled and whined while I clipped the leash to his harness. "Jeez, you'd think you hadn't already had a walk today. This pitiful act is gonna be good for exactly one more day, then you gotta get over it, you hear?" He showed me a retriever smiley face before jerking me down the dock toward the gate.

"And that's another thing," I said in a warning tone while giving his leash a firm tug. He immediately obeyed and gave me a sheepish look before I could finish my threat of more doggy obedience training. I swear, that dog can read my mind.

"Good dawg. For that, there is a breakfast burrito in our immediate life. You got any money?"

He leaned against my leg while I searched his saddle pack and pulled out a hundred pesos. "We're rich! Brekkies it is. Before or after our walk? Your choice."

We split the diff. I took him out for a quick whiz in a vacant lot next to the marina before we grabbed an outdoor table at the Dock Café.

Several boaters I knew gave my dog a pat and greeted me with, "*¡Hola!* Hetta." A single-hander dude, who obviously drank enough breakfast beer to derail any good judgment remaining in his booze-and-weed besotted gray matter, tried giving me a pat as well but was intercepted by a slobbery muzzle and a soft growl. The growl was mine.

The sailor quickly jerked his arm back, downed his beer, and staggered away to a chorus of hoots from those familiar with my notoriously less-than-patient reputation.

Po Thang, after acknowledging his adoring humans at other tables, sat on my feet and put his head in my lap. This needy thing was growing old fast, but I knew where he was coming from; we were both suffering from an acute case of separation anxiety.

Within the past few days, Jan, my best friend, drove back up the Baja to her sig-other's Pacific Coast whale camp a little under four hundred miles to the north, and then Jenks, *my* long-distance significant other, left for Dubai. Too many suitcases, backpacks, and goodbyes had my dog in a dither and glued to me lest I disappear as well.

"I'm not going anywhere soon," I whispered in his ear. He'd been abandoned for real before, left to die on a desolate Baja roadside where I found him. He'd settled into boat life well and, up until now, remained fiercely independent. I guess all this leave-taking was just too much of a threat.

My eyes prickled as a momentary twinge of my own self-pity washed over me, but when an egg and chorizo burrito, refried beans, and a fizzy, overly sweet *lemonada* arrived, Jenks and Jan became a distant memory.

Po Thang and I are easily distracted by food.

Our section of the café cleared out and we were left to stuff our faces and enjoy what I call magic time in the Sea of Cortez. A slight breeze off La Paz harbor's still-warm water—a gift from a strong El Niño event touted as the most intense in fifty years—made for perfect weather. Even in late October we were still wearing shorts during the day and running a fan some nights.

Brilliant blue skies, clear turquoise water, and hundreds of boats bobbing on the bay painted a Chamber of Commerce poster kind of day. Po Thang nosed my elbow and eyed the refried beans left on my plate. "Oh, no. No *frijoles* for you, Podner. Our boat ain't big enough for *your* farts."

As if in protest he let one and a couple preparing to sit at the next table fled. Po Thang has a way of ensuring privacy.

"Good dawg. Now for that walk, then back to work."

We dawdled along the *malecon*, the wide waterfront sidewalk stretching over three miles from Marina de la Paz to the other end of town, admiring the oversized bronzes of pelagic critters both real and mythical, a gigantic bronze and chrome black pearl, and even a statue of Jacques Cousteau.

My badly leash-trained buddy dragged me a mile or so before I turned around; *some*one was in for retraining and, according to dog whisperer Cesar Milan, it was me.

As we approached a mermaid playing with a dolphin sculpture, Po Thang sat and stared. I wondered if he was remembering his dolphin gal pal, Bubbles. We hadn't seen her for a while, so I hoped she'd found more suitable friends. Like the kind who live in water? Anyhow, she—like Jan and Jenks—was also gone, so perhaps my dog and I should put in some time boning up on our social skills?

Unable to justify the dog-walking excuse to evade the inevitable and very long list labeled 'STUFF THAT NEEDS DOING BEFORE BOAT FALLS APART' any longer, I reluctantly returned to my self-imposed boat projects. For almost two years in the Sea of Cortez I'd managed to avoid boat work. When I was working long billable hours I used that as a reason to let things slide. During the hot humid summer, well, it was too hot and humid to work outside when I had a perfectly good air-conditioned yacht, *Raymond Johnson,* in which to hole up. Now that I was unemployed and the temperature just about perfect, it was time to pay the piper and put some TLC into my forty-five foot motor yacht.

After tweezing seemingly never-ending hairs from the last coat of Cetol, a resin coating I decided to use instead of my regular varnish, as it touts UV protection far better suited to Baja's varnish-eating rays, I threw down the tweezers and pushed Po Thang out of my lap. "What the hell, maybe a little fiber will help it last longer? Right?"

Po Thang wagged tail approval, headed for his dog bowl and barked at its emptiness. I grabbed a wine glass and did likewise.

Dog fed, wine in hand, I stretched out on one of my back deck lounges to enjoy my daily afternoon entertainment: watching other yachties fight a combination of stiff breezes and opposing swift tides to get into the marina.

One might surmise my social life sucks.

At the moment my professional life wasn't so hot, either.

I am Hetta Coffey, CEO, CFO, president, and sole employee of Hetta Coffey, SI, LLC. The SI is my little inside joke on the phonetic pronunciation of Civil Engineer. A single woman of forty—yes, I can actually now say that without requiring a heart defibrillator—I'm an engineer by degree who stays somewhat employed thanks to a penchant for engaging in, shall we say, much less than run-of-the-mill endeavors. BFF Jan says I tread heavily upon the felonious side of life, but what does she know? She's a CPA who's flipping tortillas for her honey at a whale camp. At least I get paid.

Perpetually single, I actually have a wonderful—but too often absent—man in my life. Jenks Jenkins works in Dubai and I live in Mexico. When we are together, all is well, but left on my own, I teeter on the brink of blowing the best relationship I've ever had because I'm bullheaded and as temperamental as any Texas redhead. I prefer to think of myself as self-governing.

My friend Jan says I'm stubborn, incorrigible and morally corrupt, which is why she likes me so much.

One can clearly see why Jan and I are practically like sisters.

Po Thang and I were parked at the dock in La Paz, Mexico, but that was not the usual case. I'd spent most of my time in the central Sea where I managed to stay employed. Not always exactly safely or legally employed, mind you, but I'd made enough to keep us in kibble and refrieds. Back when I worked as a project engineer for large corporations, I traveled the world, stayed in five-star hotels, and ate and drank high on the hog, thanks to a fat expense account.

Those days are but a memory.

These days it's boxed wine and a dog for company.

The light was fading and the air cooled, so I pushed myself up to grab a sweatshirt when I heard, "Ahoy, *Raymond Johnson.*"

Po Thang scrambled to the bow and woofed friendly, so I stayed put and yelled, "Permission to come aboard, but only if you have wine."

Chapter Two

My visitor wasn't bearing wine, but just stopped by to remind me of an upcoming event or two.

So, I wrote that titillating bit of information on my calendar, as though by doing so I proved to myself that I actually had something to do besides walk the dog and varnish teak: Mexican Train on Wednesday, Baja Rummy on Friday. I added a footnote on a sticky label: SHAPE THE HELL UP. PS, buy more sticky notes.

I've lived alone most of my life and rarely felt lonely, but Jenks being around and then gone left a void and I was reduced to playing dominos or cards with the ladies at a nearby restaurant twice a week. I knew I'd settle into doing my own thing quickly, but there are always those first few days of ennui after Jenks leaves.

I considered cruising out to the islands, but there was a tropical disturbance promising to become a hurricane down south and those spaghetti-line predictions showed a possible track threatening everything from a category three direct hit to just a bunch of wind and rain. I'd weathered enough crap to know better than to leave port in a storm.

"Maybe we should go to Texas, Po Thang. I'm a little homesick for Mama and Daddy, chicken fried steak slathered in cream gravy, and Shiner Bock beer And you can chase deer to your little doggie heart's content. Ooh, it's deer season, so make that chicken fried venison with cream gravy, whaddaya think?" He wagged his approval, although I doubt he'd ever even seen a deer. You just gotta love a guy that agrees with almost anything you say.

The more I thought about it, the better a road trip sounded. I could drive north to the border and then over to Texas. Or, take the ferry to the mainland and up. Or...the phone rang. Caller ID told me it was Wontrobski, and my heart stuttered. Both he and Jenks were in Dubai and, since I inherited the worry gene from Mom, I generally think the worst.

"Yo, Trob," I said, doing a mental calculation of the time in Dubai: Eight in the morning. "What's wrong?"

"Nothing wrong. Job."

Fidel Wontrobski is a man of few words. I pictured him at his desk, wild black hair, beak nose, and the posture of a buzzard sitting on a cactus. Probably dressed in his signature all black clothes despite the heat in the

Middle East. Figuring I didn't look so hot myself, I was grateful he refuses to use Facetime.

"Who do you want killed?"

Not even a chuckle. The man is a genius but missed out on the humor gene. He knows I'll take on just about anything, but for the record, he really never *asked* me to off anyone. Honest. Collateral damage? Out of my control.

"Courier."

"Wontrobski, I am a highly trained professional. An engineer who fakes it as an expert in engineering stuff. Not a babysitter."

"France."

"France?" I gasped. "*Mais oui!*"

"Email. Details."

I hung up on this dazzling conversation, so dazzled the cabin spun. Either that or some jerk threw a wake in the marina.

Selecting my favorite Edith Piaf song, I turned "*Non, Je Ne Regrette Rien,*"—my theme song—up loud and serenaded Po Thang, doing my best to imitate France's most famous *chansonnière's* torch tones while declaring, "No, I don't regret anything." He covered his ears with his paws and whined. Everyone's a critic.

The ding of fate saved my dog from more of my singing. I rushed to my laptop and quickly read the Trob's email, summarizing for Po Thang as I went. "Okay, here's the deal, Dawg. Baxter Brothers is opening a satellite office in Lille, a French city on the Belgian border, and they want me to accompany a shipment of technical equipment and documentation from San Francisco. Lille? Hey, where's the Paris part?"

The phone rang again and without checking caller ID I spluttered, "Hey, where's the Paris part?"

Jenks's deep laugh warmed me to my toes, leaving a smolder in an unmentionable spot on the way down. "That would be me, Hetta. After you get the load to Lille, we'll meet in Paris, if that's okay with you."

"Okay with me? Are you friggin' kidding? How long can we stay?"

"How's a week in Paris? Then I'm working on a surprise you."

"I hate surprises."

"Not this one, you won't."

When I hung up the phone I was stoked. A job! An easy one for a change. All I had to do was accompany some Baxter Brothers stuff to France in a private plane, and then comes the good part: meet Jenks in Paris. *Oh là là!*

Paris! I love Paris. I even lived there once upon a time. I was a student, living on the Left Bank in a cockroach-infested hovel with a gritty bathroom down the hall, but I was, at least in my mind, *une vraie Parisienne*—a true Parisian—living my dream, soaking up culture and wine. And now I was leaving Mexico for a few weeks of paid vacation in a country I loved.

What could possibly go wrong?

In those days, over twenty years ago, I spoke French like a native and frequented sidewalk cafés where I smoked fat, unfiltered Gauloises while looking blasé. I tried dressing the part, but my body is very un-French, so I went for Bohemian French, which is no easy task. I even mastered the Gallic sniff of disdain for American tourists who talked too loud and dressed in baggy clothes, the Barbarians.

Clothes! I'd been living on a boat for three years. What the hell was I going to wear in Paris? Panic set in, so I took a few deep yoga breaths before my heart jumped out of my chest. A bit calmer, I called Jan, who is a clotheshorse of the highest order. Even in that gawdawful fish camp she manages to look stylish. But then again, she'd make a burlap bag look good, so just maybe she could do something for me.

She answered almost immediately and heard me panting. "That you? Or Po Thang? And what's wrong? Never mind, I don't even care because—"

I cut her off. "I need you to come get Po Thang. Like tomorrow. I'm going—"

She cut *me* off. "I'll be there by four."

"Don't you want to know—"

"Naw. Even getting dragged into one of your harebrained schemes sounds good right now. Whatever it is, surprise me. I'm bored to tears up here in this godforsaken camp. Hell, the whales haven't even shown up yet. Jeez, would you listen to me? I *want* whales? Just harpoon me. See you *mañana*, Chica."

"But—" She hung up.

Sleep wasn't in the cards, so I gave up trying at two in the morning and raided my hanging locker, throwing piles of rejects onto my bed. This sifting through clothes thing worried Po Thang, who sat on a pile of ratty sweats and whined.

"Sorry, sweetie. I know I told you I wasn't going anywhere, but as you should know by now, I lie. I mean, we're talking *Paris* here. You'll go home with your

Auntie Jan." His ears perked up at her name. "And chase seagulls and pelicans as much as you want. Also, you know how you love going out in the boat with Doc Chino," tail thump, "on the whale count."

Doctor Brigido Comacho Yee, aka Chino, is Jan's very handsome, world-renowned Mexican marine biologist boyfriend. The Yee part came from a Chinese shipwreck survivor whose Manila Galleon washed up onto the Baja in the late 1500's, thus the nickname, Chino.

Po Thang dearly loves Camp Chino, what with all those lovely dead fish to roll on, so at least I didn't have to worry about him while I was gone.

Suitable clothes for me? Now, *that* was a worrisome matter.

I gave up finding anything other than sweats, shorts, moldy Nikes, and mismatched flip-flops and made a cup of coffee before printing out the Trob's emailed itinerary and a blank calendar for my own notes. Not one usually cowed by tight schedules, I tackled the seemingly insurmountable timeline. "I can do this, Poochster. It's list-making time."

Jan arrived early; she'd caught a ride with one of Chino's assistants who had to make a three o'clock flight out of Cabo. They'd left before daylight, so she was tired and hungry. We headed for the Dock Café.

As usual, she seemed unaware of the male, and some female, attention she draws. On her worst day her five-eleven, legs-for-days, blonde haired, blue-eyed, Meg Ryan-like looks still turned heads.

My close proximity to her and Po Thang, a superbly handsome fellow in his own right, allow me to live a vicarious life of popularity.

We settled at a table and I dug my schedule and to-do list out of a pocket, while Jan ordered the beer she insisted she get before hearing one word of why she was summoned to La Paz.

Chugging a cold Tecate in record time, she banged down the bottle and gave me a come-on hand signal. "Okay, hit me. What the hell have you gotten us into this time? Is there a possibility of prison time involved? The way my life is right now, a Mexican jail sounds inviting."

"Sorry, no chance of arrest *this* time. But...wait for it...wait for it. I'm going to Paris!"

She signaled for another beer.

Chapter Three

"Gawd, can my life get any worse?" Jan moaned, then turned to the hovering waiter—waiters always hover around Jan which is another reason she's the perfect friend. "More beer, *por favor*. *Pronto*."

"Me too," I added.

Jan sighed a grand sigh. "Here I was, hoping for a typical Hetta Coffey misadventure on the high seas, and you tell me you're leaving for Paris? Just drive a stake into my heart." Po Thang put his head on Jan's leg, somehow sensing her gloom. She hugged him. "Looks like it's you 'n' me, Furface. And the freakin' whales."

"Hey, I'll be back in three weeks. A month tops. Then I promise to get us tossed in the hoosegow, okay? Besides, you should be happy for me; I'm meeting Jenks in Paris and he says he has a surprise."

She sat up straight and grinned. "A surprise? You think he's gonna..." she waggled her ring finger.

That wasn't something I'd considered. "Crap."

"Whaddaya mean, crap? You're in love with the guy. What's the problem?"

"I'm not sure. I guess I never really considered getting *married*. I kinda like my life."

"Hetta, your life is an exercise in brinkmanship. In the name of making a living, you teeter-totter on the very edge of disaster and, by the way, take me along for the fall. Hey, now it's my time to say crap. What on earth will I do if you up and get hitched? I have no talent for getting into trouble on my own. I need your expertise."

"I ain't anywhere near getting married."

"Yabbut you might if someone was crazy enough to ask you. Oh, wait. That's never happened."

"Thanks for the reminder. Anyhow, I'll come home and get a job and everything will be back to normal."

"Ha! Normal, as in *your* normal. You could take a job as a Walmart greeter and cause an international incident. As a matter of...oh, never mind me. I'm just jealous. Paris? Cool beans." She gave me a critical once over. "Do we have time to *do* something with you?"

"Oh, come on. I'm not that bad."

She raised an eyebrow. "Have you perchance glanced into a mirror lately. You need some TLC. Meanwhile, tell me the whole story."

"The Trob has hired me as a courier to accompany some equipment and data to Baxter Brothers' new office in Lille. Then I'll meet Jenks in the City of Lights."

"Courier? You gonna have a briefcase handcuffed to your wrist? I brought mine if you want to borrow them."

A guy at the next table perked up.

I gave him a dirty look and lowered my voice. "Don't think so. What with all the industrial espionage happening, they just want someone besides crew on board the plane."

"And they chose *you*? Hetta Coffey, the one-woman disaster, as the safe-keeper of *anything*?"

I let the barb go, because it was all too often true.

"I'll bet you a peso to a tortilla that Jenks convinced the Trob to hire me to keep me out of mischief here in Mexico. And we've talked about going to Paris for ages, and here's our chance. Anyhow, I have to catch a plane from San Jose del Cabo tomorrow."

"For?"

"San Francisco, then I'll fly to France on a private plane."

"Private plane? How very chichi. So, how much free time will you have in the Bay Area?"

I checked the Trob's schedule. "I leave Cabo tomorrow at three pm, arrive SFO six-thirty, have a dinner meeting at the Sir Francis Drake, where I'm staying, with some Baxter Brothers minion. He'll fill me in on details, but the way I understand it, my plane will leave in the late afternoon the next day."

"Oh, man. I loved it when we went to the Drake every Christmas season for lunch."

We reminisced about our very own holiday tradition at Union Square. We'd put in a few hours at the Red Door, ogle the Macy's window displays, try on every mink coat at Needless Markup, then go to the Drake for a late lunch and oodles of drinks. "I do miss it, but then again, our first Christmas in the Sea of Cortez we got to blow up a meth factory."

"You're such a sentimentalist," I quipped, giving her a high-five.

"Yep. Hey, maybe we can do the San Francisco thing this year? Depends on when you get back from France, I guess."

"Great idea. If the schedule works, we'll do it. Go to the City, stay at the Drake, do our thing?"

Jan clinked her beer bottle against mine. "You got it. Hell, we have some money put away, thanks to your shenanigans down here. We might as well spend some of those ill-gotten gains. Okay, now I feel better about you running off to Paris and leaving me to the whales."

"See? Always a silver lining."

"Back to this trip of yours, Hetta. Looks like you have a full day to kill in the City. Let's go to the boat, cuz we have important appointments to make."

By Happy Hour, Jan had pulled in some favors and I was booked into Elizabeth Arden's Red Door Spa, Union Square, for a major tune-up, which would put a large dent in whatever profits I'd hoped to make from this courier gig. For just under a grand—Jan so dearly loves spending my money—I was in for a mani, pedi, facial, waxing just about everywhere, haircut and color, and a massage. They throw in lunch. Probably something chic and healthy.

Even though I was excited about my trip, and seeing Jenks, I boarded the plane in Cabo with still-teary eyes after hugging Po Thang and Jan goodbye. When we took off, my forehead was glued to the window as the plane made a wide turn and actually passed over La Paz harbor, where I spotted my boat, which squeezed out another sniffle.

In the time I'd been south of the border, I'd formed a bond with a stray dog, really learned what living on a boat and loving it was all about and gained an appreciation for what a crazy and wonderful country Mexico is. As frustrating as some of the laws and customs can be, they add an aura of capriciousness, an unpredictability that keeps life interesting. And as far as living on your boat in one of the most mysteriously beautiful settings in the world—where the stark desert meets turquoise seas—I don't know of many places within shouting distance of the States where a boater has the freedom to roam at will. Certainly not in regulation-happy California.

In a word, I was hooked.

After two days of non-stop activities to secure *Raymond Johnson*, arrange for someone to watch her, pack up all of Po Thang's paraphernalia and quickly stuff a duffle bag with what few clothes met with Jan's approval, I was plumb worn to a frazzle. I downed two Bloody Marys and slept solidly until we touched down in San Francisco.

The valet at the Sir Francis Drake graciously picked up my ratty duffle bag as though it were a Louis Vuitton, but I pictured a raised French eyebrow at any Paris hotel. Note to self: Get one of my name brand suitcases from Jenks's Oakland apartment.

My Baxter Brothers contact in San Francisco was a nice enough Human Resources type who, judging by his barely disguised wariness, was probably wondering why the BBs would trust the likes of Hetta Coffey with, as Jan said, anything. My previous fall from grace was hardly a well-kept secret in the hallowed halls of one of the largest engineering and construction companies in the world, and even though headquarters had relocated to Dubai, I was sure the people in HR were fully acquainted with my history. When I was employed there, I was a royal pain in their side, neck, and other regions. Running end-plays around company bureaucrats has always been, and remains, one of my favorite recreational activities. Right up there with a day at the shooting range.

So when Mr. HR, whose name I quickly forgot, asked if I would like dinner on the company (and was obviously hoping I'd say no) I accepted. "Sure, but I'm not all that hungry. Why don't we go up to the Starlight Room for something light? Best view in town."

He readily agreed.

He'd never been there.

He probably figured the company was getting off light.

He was sooo wrong. Spending OPM—Other People's Money—is art, and am an artiste.

Since my host was unfamiliar with the Starlight, I volunteered to order for us, waving away the offered menus before he got a gander at them.

"Two Gang of Mules, please. Bourbon. Wild arugula salads, prawn cocktails, chicken wings, and an order of your fabulous chocolate truffles for dessert. Oh, and a bottle of Cristal. The sommelier can pick the year, but tell him we aren't Rockefellers here. Please hold the food and champers until we finish our drinks, okay?"

Chapter Four

The Baxter Brothers flunky was mighty dismayed when our waiter at the Starlight Room presented him with a three-hundred-and-eighty-dollar dinner bill, but nowhere nearly as disheartened as the Liz Arden staff was when they caught sight of yours truly the next morning.

Two years of sun, salt, haphazard slapping on of face cream and sunscreen, as well as incinerated hair and my own haircut jobs, had taken a toll. I do try to wear a hat most of the time, but let's face it, boat life is tough on a gal.

Four hours of under-the-breath tsk-tsks later, I exited the Red Door a new woman. My skin glowed, my hair shone, the makeup artist took ten years off me...okay, five... and I'd spent an extra three hundred dollars on multiple dabs of creams, hair gloss, and makeup to ensure my new look didn't fade too quickly.

With three hours left until I had to meet my plane at Oakland airport, I instructed my driver—I'd ordered a limo on the Baxter tab—to swing by Jenks's Lake Merritt apartment to pick up some clothes stashed there in fashionable suitcases. I was sure one of them contained a warm coat and a few sweaters to ward off the early November Paris chill. All I had with me was an "I Heart Baja" sweatshirt.

Jenks's apartment, so rarely used anymore, was in need of a dusting and airing, but I didn't have time for that, thanks to a pileup on the Bay Bridge. Running late for my plane, I quickly went to the walk-in closet where I'd stashed my non-boating gear when Jan and I took off for Mexico on *Raymond Johnson*, pulled down two suitcases labeled GOOD STUFF and WARM STUFF, and hustled back to the limo.

Jenks had taken me on a couple of flights in a plane he uses from his flight club, so I knew the way to the general aviation gate at Oakland airport, but the limo driver was already familiar with dropping wealthy clients at their jet-fueled tax write-offs. However, when we got there I didn't see a Baxter Brothers jet anywhere on the runway. Maybe they were late?

I asked the driver to stand by in case of a change in plans and headed for the office. A man behind the desk, dressed in a military-style flight suit, was on the phone and gave me a nod and a "hold on" finger, told the party on the other end he'd call them back from Nebraska, pointed the finger at me like a pistol and said, "Hetta Coffey?"

We shook hands. "That would be me," I looked at his name on his suit, "Joe."

"Then I guess we're almost good to go."

He was giving me a head-to-toe once-over, which I might have objected to had I not known I looked so fabulous. I straightened my posture and sucked in my gut, certain he was admiring my spiffy new designer self. Not only was I fresh-from-the spa aglow, I'd taken a fast shopping run through Neiman's and sported a new Gucci jacket, silk turtleneck and scarf, linen Armani slacks and soft leather Michael Kors flats. I'd rejected the pointy toed, high heels suggested by the dresser, fearing that after wearing almost no shoes for so long I'd break my stupid neck. But rather than admiring my sleek new look, Joe was sizing me up. Literally.

Reaching under the counter, he threw me a one-piece, drab-green canvas flight suit. "This oughta fit ya. You can change in there," he pointed to a nearby bathroom, "and then we'll grab your bags and boogie. Your plane's all loaded and ready to go."

"I don't think I need to change."

"Okay by me. I'll put the jumpsuit on board in case you change your mind."

"Don't bother. What time do we get into Lille?"

He pulled his iPhone from one of his many pockets and tapped on it. "Looks like your ETA Lille is around oh seven hundred hours French time, twenty-two hundred hours, California time. Maybe sooner if you catch a tail wind."

"Wow, that's great."

"On November three."

"Gimme those freakin' overalls."

"Wontrobski," I yelled into the phone over the loud whine of the engines winding up. "Pick up. I know damned well you can hear me. Pick. Up. The. Phone. Right now, or your courier shuts down this behemoth and walks."

"I was on another line. You're on the plane?"

"If you can call this fat winged guppy a plane, yes."

I looked around the cockpit of the C-130J Super Hercules and had to admit it beat the heck out of the old military C-130 I flew on years ago when I spent a summer working at Prudhoe Bay, Alaska. At least this one actually had a toilet instead of a curtained-off cubby hole complete with the bucket they'd added for my convenience back then; for the guys there was still a funnel that seemed to dump directly overboard.

"You sound upset."

"You have a knack for nailing the obvious. Have you *seen* the flight plan?"

"Yes."

"And you didn't think to let me in on the details? Like that I'm stuck on this tub for over two freaking days, with three different crews?"

"No."

"How long have you known me?"

He hesitated, probably considering an answer like *too long*, but being the Trob, he answered, "Nine years, two months and —"

"Never mind. Long enough for you to realize this inconvenience to my precious self is going to cost you, right?"

Joe, who turned out to be my pilot du jour, caught my attention and indicated I needed to terminate my call. I ignored him, he shrugged and fired up another engine, wiping out any chance of me hearing the Trob's answer.

I hung up, clamped the headphone set over my ears, and strapped myself into the surprisingly comfortable loadmaster's seat for takeoff. The last time I was on one of these planes all I had was a bench located below an air vent spewing a fine spray of frozen mist. I was told this cushy seat was mine until Reykjavík-Keflavík Airport in

Iceland, where we'd pick up a loadmaster for the final leg of my part of the trip. Once in Lille, he would oversee the unloading of the equipment and files I was babysitting, and then the plane would continue on to Dubai.

The lights of the city and the fast-looming Bay Bridge snagged my attention as we roared upwards, then executed a sharp, climbing turn. Evidently, my pilot had spent way too much time dodging hand-held rocket launchers in the Middle East.

Or maybe flying too low over Oakland gave him the heebie-jeebies.

Chapter Five

I settled back into my seat, closed my eyes, and mentally calculated what this piece of crap job was going to cost Baxter Brothers. The Trob and I play this game with every project he throws my way. I demand about twenty-percent more than he offers, he agrees, then later I ding him for extras and he graciously gives me what he intended to in the first place.

All that brainstorming—along with a long day of primping and shopping—added to the throbbing and thunderous drone of the four turboprop engines, lulled me off to sleep until my earphones suddenly came alive. "Hey, Hetta?"

Starting upright, I yelped, "Hey, yourself! You scared the crap out of me."

"Sorry. We're at cruising altitude, so just wanted to let you know you can talk to us now and also move around the plane. See that desk next to you?"

"Yes."

"If you want, go ahead and set up your computer there. I'll turn on the Wi-Fi."

"Great. Where's the bar? I could use a gin and tonic or three."

He laughed. "No booze. But that fridge you saw when we boarded has soft drinks and bottled water. Coffee's already made. If you're hungry, there's a bunch of microwavable guy food. All the comforts of home, so enjoy. We'll be in the air for a while."

"What's a while?"

"About four hours. Less if we—"

"I know, pick up a tail wind."

He grinned. "You're learning."

"So, where'd you stow my bags and computer?"

"Next to the bunks I showed you in case you want to stretch out. You'll find pillows, sheets, and blankets in a locker under the bottom bunk. Anything else you need?"

"I didn't see a shower and I'm gonna be stuck on this friggin' plane for-*ever*."

"Sorry, no luck there. They have them in the crew quarters at the terminals where we refuel."

"Just peachy."

I unstrapped and carefully walked to get my PC, making sure to hold on to something. So far the going was smooth, but you never know when you're going to hit a bump. Living on a boat teaches you to always secure yourself when you're underway, and that doubles on a plane.

Putting my luggage on the bunk, I decided to see what I had since I didn't have time at Jenks's apartment to open the suitcases. Also, I wanted to repack and empty the faded duffle so I'd be down to my computer, briefcase, and two chic suitcases. I was, after all, headed for France.

The first suitcase, tagged WARM STUFF, held a designer jogging outfit that still had its over-priced sales tag attached. Obviously, this was just another of many things I used to buy in anticipation of some new exercise program Jan talked me into and I talked myself out of. I consider shopping a form of cardio.

Under the snazzy suit were a couple of cashmere pullovers, leather gloves, and some of those warm and fuzzy chenille socks, which would certainly come in handy. I laid everything out on a bunk for repacking.

The second suitcase, the one with the GOOD STUFF, revealed three pairs of tailored trousers, two silk blouses, camisoles to go under them, my favorite Calvin Klein blazer and jeans, and best of all, a hand tooled pair of vintage red-leather Tony Lama boots. It was like Christmas morning.

Since I now wore nothing but underwear under my jumpsuit, I grabbed the warm-ups, a pair of socks and the boots, pulled a curtain across the hatch opening, and shed my overalls. Each layer went on like a little slice of Heaven in the chilly plane, and when re-covered with the overalls, felt like a luxurious cocoon of warmth. Funny how, just hours before, I expected to arrive in France looking like a million bucks, and now I was gonna resemble Bibendum—the Michelin Man—in commando cowboy drag. Oh, well, at least he's French.

Sighing, I put on a pair of the socks, tried to pull on a boot, and stubbed my expensively pedicured toe.

"Ow!" I yelped, quickly removing my foot. "What the hell?"

Snaking my hand into the boot, I felt cold metal and the familiar pistol grip of my PT 738 TCP. Pulling out the little Taurus .380, I cooed, "Oh, Taury, there you are.

I wondered what I did with you." Reaching into the other boot, I found an extra clip and two boxes of hollow points.

When Jan and I left for Mexico on the boat, I left my considerable arsenal at Jenks's place, lest the Mexican government throw me in the *cárcel* for possession.

Later on, while *Raymond Johnson* was laid up in dry dock with blisters on her bottom, I took a job on the Arizona border, rented a house there, and asked my friend and veterinarian *extraordinaire*, Dr. Craig Washington, to bring me my guns and some clothes from Jenks's closet. Now the rest of my guns are at Craig's home he bought in Arizona. His house is my legal address in the States, and I am an official Arizona resident of Cochise County, rumored to have the most heavily armed citizenry in the world. I felt right at home.

I still have to keep my weaponry at Craig's house in Bisbee due to some silly law in Mexico about folks not being allowed to have personal protection south of the border. Back when the *new* guys in charge overthrew the *old* guys in charge in the Mexican Revolution of 1910, they quickly outlawed guns to the general population, just in case the ungrateful wretches someday took a page from their own "how to throw a revolution" book. It's a lot easier to stay in control if a disgruntled populace doesn't have a way to overthrow *them*.

So, while I knew my Taurus wasn't at Craig's, I'd forgotten where I'd stashed it, *et voilà!* here it was, appropriately nested in one of my red Tony Lamas. My luggage hadn't gone through any kind of security check as far as I knew, and now I was on a plane with a gun. Headed for *two* foreign countries, Iceland and France. *Merde alors!*

"Hetta, you okay in there?" Joe asked from the other side of the curtain.

My heart jumped into my throat as guilt oozed from my forehead. After a moment of panic, I stuffed the gun under the bunk mattress and answered, in the most normal voice I could muster, "Yeah, sure, Joe, just putting on some warmer clothes and repacking my stuff."

"I'm gonna make popcorn if you want some."

"Great," I choked out. "I'll be out in a minute."

For lack of a better idea, I removed the gun from under the mattress, jammed it back into the suitcase, zipped it shut, and closed the curtain. The irresistible aroma of butter-laced popcorn hit my nose and my stomach growled.

Guns, schmuns. We're talking popcorn here.

Back at my computer, I crammed a fistful Orville Redenbacher Ultimate Butter into my mouth while using the non-greasy hand to cruise the Internet for the legalities involved in smuggling a gun onto an airplane. Since the TSA hadn't nailed me yet, and the likelihood of getting busted while refueling in Omaha was small, I figured it was going to be up to either Icelandic Customs or the gendarmes to ruin my vacation.

Figuring I was safe from discovery in Iceland if I left the gun on the plane, another hour of Googling—with a break to pop more corn—informed me that if I were caught with an unauthorized gun when deplaning in France, I could face a three-year maximum sentence, plus a fine.

I had expected a dire form of punishment, like death by guillotine, so three years didn't sound *too* bad; I could brush up on the lingo, and the food in a French prison should be good, right? They probably, like the Frenchified McDonalds, serve wine.

Next, I asked my legal counsel, *monsieur le* Google, if I *do* get a pistol through French Customs, what are my chances of getting caught in the country packing said heat?

My cyber-*avocat* had zero information concerning that possibility.

Chapter Six

Like a dog trying to hide a bone, I moved the pistol several times during the flight from Omaha to Iceland, all the while stuffing my worry with more popcorn, before our descent into Reykjavik.

My plan *had* been to use the terminal's crew facilities there to take a shower and get prettied up for Lille, but that went down the tubes. There was no way I was leaving the plane with the gun so, just in case someone like a gunpowder-sniffing Islandic German Shepherd Customs agent came nosing around, I stayed on board with hopes of diverting his attention with a handful of popcorn. Not that I really expected a Customs raid, but nevertheless I sat tight.

We were on the ground for four harrowing hours before the new crew, including a loadmaster, boarded. Had they questioned my decision to steadfastly refuse leaving the plane, I intended to plead an overabundance of company loyalty. As it was, they didn't seem to care what I did, but at least they sent me a big fat cheeseburger and fries.

During the nearly eighteen hours since I boarded the C-130J in Oakland, my formerly shiny, bouncy hair had lost all pep and sheen. My makeup, so perfectly done by the Red Door pros, was now fear-sweated into blotches. I probably didn't smell too hot, either, and by the time I arrived in Lille I'd have been stuck on the plane at least twenty-seven hours, and the odds of reeking less by then were nil to none.

I fidgeted as the crew took forever with their pre-flight safety checks at Reykjavik—something I normally appreciate because safety is a really good thing on a plane—willing them to just get us the hell off the ground. Flight time into Lille was at least another nine hours, giving me even more time to stew and stress.

What to do? What to do?

Hide the gun in with the cargo headed for Dubai? Should have thought of that before the loadmaster came on board. Now if I tried sneaking into the cargo hold he might get suspicious.

Smuggle it off the plane in my panties? Hell, I already looked guilty, and any self-respecting Frenchman would surely finger me just for the crime of wearing such mundane cotton knickers. Wait, that didn't come out right.

Or I could throw a perfectly wonderful weapon into the trash along with the increasing pile of empty popcorn bags? Nah, just goes against my nature and is probably illegal in Texas and Arizona.

All this thinking gave me a headache, so I popped an Advil, grabbed a pillow and blankie, and curled up on a bunk. Six hours later I awoke with a start, not knowing for a second where the hell I was. Getting my bearings, I rinsed out my mouth and worked my way back to the main cockpit.

Hunched back over my computer, I surfed Facebook to get my mind off my looming incarceration while sharing witty stuff about wine, cats, dogs, cats and dogs drinking wine, and my favorite: sarcastic anything.

"Miss Coffey?"

I practically levitated as the loadmaster leaned in and called my name loud enough to be heard over my headset. "What?" I yelped.

"Sorry, didn't mean to scare you. We're two hours out, so if you care to freshen up you might want to get started."

"You think it'll take that long?"

He grinned. "Naw, but I thought you might want me to include your bags on the cargo manifest to avoid having to go through customs. I'll need to have them in about an hour. You'll still have to pass through Immigration to get your passport stamped, but that'll be fast. I understand a Baxter Brothers rep is meeting us at Lille, and the two of you can sign off on your part of the load."

Did he just say I didn't have to clear customs?

I wanted to kiss him, but doubted he'd appreciate getting that close to my stinky self.

By the time I turned my bags over to the lovely loadmaster, I'd spiffed up some.

I managed a paper towel and bottled water sponge bath, applied a dab of perfume and a lot of deodorant, smeared on face and eye cream, wiped old mascara smudges away, put on new makeup, and did what I could to perk up my hair. There wasn't much I could do with that butter-stained jumpsuit.

I was totally calm and in control by now, thanks to discovering a bottle of Valium I'd stashed in the same boot with my gun. There's probably something Freudian there.

Further Internet searches revealed sketchy information about entering France without a copy of the original prescription of a controlled substance, which there was no way in *hell* I was gonna dump. In for a penny, in for a Euro, I figured—after popping 10mg of pure courage and stashing the rest next to the .380.

We international arms and drug smugglers lead a stressful existence, ya know.

The loveable effect of a tranquilizer is that you are, well, tranquil. No longer did I care that my hair looked like a grease mop. I was resigned that no amount of wet paper towel could overcome all those hours on a cargo plane. No longer did the prospect of three years in a French jail have my cotton knickers in a twist. Nope, I was confident I'd sail through Customs and beat feet to a hotel, unscathed by the French judicial system.

In my euphoric state, none of those things mattered anymore. I was invincible. Undaunted. Fearless. Right up until the moment I deplaned and spotted Jenks waiting for me on the tarmac, his strong arms held wide for an expected embrace.

I stopped dead in my tracks as almost all of the pill-induced serenity disappeared, leaving me in a sudden state of paranoia. What would Jenks think when I was hauled off in cuffs? Or worse yet, just how bad did I smell? I was torn between rushing into his arms or turning tail for the plane to give myself a good spray of the Lysol air fresher I'd seen in the head.

Jenks closed the distance between us before I could make a decision—another side-effect of tranquilizers is the inability to act very fast—and actually lifted me off my feet (no easy task) for a kiss. At least I'd brushed my teeth. If he thought the rest of me reeked, he sure didn't let on.

Putting me down, he held me at arm's length and said, "Wow, you look great."

I should have been flattered, but wondered what kind of hag he encountered when he visited me in Mexico if he thought I looked good now.

"So do you," I mumbled, and I meant it.

Jenks grabbed my brief case and computer, put his arm around me, and guided me toward a hangar. "Immigration guy is over here and once we sign off on the manifest we can head for the hotel. I'll bet you're ready for a drink and a hot bath."

So he *did* notice.

"Hey, if you'd just spent a jillion hours on that nightmare of a plane, you wouldn't smell so good yourself," I growled. Oh, great, Hetta. Two minutes on the ground and you're picking a fight?

He stopped walking and turned to face me. "Whoa, there, Red. Are you okay?"

"Nuh, no, not really." Tears filled my eyes. Crap, men hate it when women cry.

I wiped my face with a buttery sleeve and took a deep breath. What was I supposed to say? That I was scared to death of getting busted with a gun that I had stupidly and stubbornly decided not to throw away? "I mean, I'm okay. Just dog tired. And you are so right, a hot bath and a couple of drinks will make me a new woman."

"I don't want a new woman, I want you."

Is he wonderful, or what?

"I guess you have me to blame for your crappy flight. When Wontrobski said we needed a courier for a shipment of sensitive documents I suggested you, thinking they'd use a company jet. But then at the last minute, they added all that equipment for Dubai and switched to the C-130. I didn't know that until you were already in the air. I told the Trob there would be hell to pay."

"Oh, yes, he'll pay, all right, of that you can be sure."

"He's already doing so. I booked us into the George V in Paris because you've talked about it so much."

My jaw dropped. "The Zhor-zuh Sank?" I blurted, using my best Parisian accent. "Holy crap. Dang why didn't I think of that? Well, I know the Trob can be generous, but it never occurred to me to stick him for a fifteen-hundred-buck-a-night hotel room. I do have some ethics, you know. Bad ones, but ethics nonetheless. You are my hero."

"Well, we got a family discount."

"Huh?"

"Prince Fauoud's cousin owns the hotel now."

"Ah. How is the prince? He getting tired of you as a permanent house guest at the Al Buri Dubai?"

Jenks shrugged. "He's never there. And I do pay rent, you know."

"How much?"

"Five grand a month."

"Ha! A penthouse at Al Buri probably runs that a day."

"It pays to have friends in high places. He sends his love."

"Where is he these days?"

"Yachting."

"Of course he is. Wow, the George V. How long can we stay?"

"I figure," he looked at his watch, "four days? We need to be in the South of France after that."

"We do? Why?"

"It's a surprise."

I opened my mouth to say I hated surprises when my phone rang.

"Hetta honey," Mom drawled, "I had this really funny feeling that I needed to call you and tell you not to mess up with Jenks. Enjoy your trip and we love you. Bye."

I stared at the dead phone, then turned to Jenks and grinned. "Great! I love surprises. I can't wait."

He looked a little alarmed.

Chapter Seven

After Jenks and I shared another hug and a nice long kiss—thank the Lord for those Listerine pocket strips—he pointed to the hangar where my cargo was now stashed. As we walked, I asked him what he'd been working on, but really wasn't registering what he said as we neared my date with Destiny. Yes, the loadmaster told me my bags needn't clear customs, but that guilt thing went to work, and what was left of my deodorant began to fail.

When I saw the loadmaster and a very Gallic and glum official type with their heads together looking over what was probably the manifest, I put on the brakes so suddenly, Jenks, who was walking close behind me, almost knocked me over. I yelped, Jenks steadied me, said he was sorry, and both men inside the hangar turned towards us.

Striding forward, Jenks stuck his hand out to the French official. "Henri! Great to see you again!" then turned to the loadmaster and introduced himself.

I held back as Henri turned and pegged me with what my guilties perceived as accusatory eyes, then broke into a wide smile. "Ah, *mademoiselle* Coffey. We have heard much about you from *monsieur* Jenkins. *Bienvenue en France!* You must be *très fatigué* after such a journey, so if you will just," he held out the clipboard with the manifest attached, "sign here," he tapped a line, "the formalities will be done."

Guilt and sweat flowed as I dredged up a polite, "*Enchantée,*" even though I was far less than delighted to meet someone who could dump me into the slammer. I took the pen with shaky fingers and scrawled something that resembled my signature to what might end up being a confession. Jeez, I wouldn't last two minutes under police interrogation.

"Hetta, are you sure you're feeling all right?" Jenks asked, putting his arm around me again. "You look like you're about to pass out."

"*Je suis très fatigué.* Yeah, that's it, I'm just very tired," I eked out.

All three men surrounded me, expressing concern. Within minutes me, my luggage, and Jenks were ushered past an immigration official who had quickly stamped my passport, and welcomed me to France. Before you could say, *contraband*, Jenks and I were in his rented Fiat Cinquecento.

With my gear stashed, Jenks put the snazzy little car in gear, and just like that the airport gates were behind us. I melted into the car seat. With the dreaded Customs agent in our rearview mirror and my unlawful goodies riding nicely in the backseat—the Fiat 500 is cute and sporty, but my suitcases wouldn't fit in the trunk—I chugged a bottle of Evian and sighed.

Dang, if I'd'a known that fainting female thing worked so well, it could have saved me so many years of pissing people off!

"Better now, Hetta? If not, we can stay here in Lille for the night and drive to Paris tomorrow."

"Nah. As I remember, it's only a couple of hour's drive and I'd rather just get myself—make that both of us—immersed in a hot tub of bubbles at the George V. They used to have these old, deep bathtubs suitable for two. Hope they still do."

"I'll drive faster."

"My kinda guy."

"I've been wondering why a hotel in France is named for King George the Fifth of England. If that's the story, anyhow."

"Funny you should ask, because I know the answer."

He grinned. "Of course you do."

Ignoring that he just intimated I'm a know-it-all, I grabbed a second bottle of water from his small cooler before launching into tour guide mode.

"The George V was unimaginatively named for the street it's on, which was named for King George the Fifth in appreciation for the UK's support during World War I."

"That was probably the last thing they were appreciative of. Way I hear it, the French are just about the most ungrateful bunch in Europe."

"Not so. Okay, the Parisians might be, but once you get away from the city and talk to people in the countryside, you get a whole different story. You should visit Normandy sometime. You'll see a whole lot of gratitude there."

"Maybe we'll do that."

I don't know why, but every time Jenks says something about "we" doing something in the future, it makes me happy. I leaned over and smooched his cheek.

He smiled. "Was that for me? Or because I got us into this special hotel you are *so* in love with?" We were pulling up to the tollbooth entrance onto the autoroute, and he added, "Uh, which lane should I take?" before I could answer his first question.

"Safest thing to do is look for a Euro sign above the booth so you can pay cash, but for this one you just take a ticket from the dispenser and we pay when we get off in Paris."

"What if you lose your ticket somehow?"

"Into the Bastille with you. Or worse, you get to do verbal battle over a talk box with some nasty broad in Paris who has the ability to hold you captive. The worst that can happen is you have to pay the maximum, whatever that is. And you lose twenty minutes arguing with her. Hang onto that chit."

"Don't worry, I will. Okay, so what's the big deal with this George joint of yours? Besides the ridiculously big price?"

"For starters, it's just off the Champs Elysées, near the Arc de Triomphe, and all that good stuff. But I like it because I feel like Marie Antoinette living at Versailles."

"You know she came to a bad end."

"Well, yes, but man oh man, did she have a good time getting there. Speaking of, you didn't by any chance ice down some champagne in this buggy did you?"

"Sorry, I didn't have time to shop. I only have water because it was an option at the rental agency. As it was, I barely made it to Lille, rented this car, and attended a meeting before you arrived."

"You flew in from Dubai this morning? You gotta be pooped, too."

"I was on a company jet and slept most of the way. So, I'm not at all tired."

I leaned forward so he could see my face, pooched out my lips, and cooed, "Ooooh, zat is very good for me, *non*?"

My attempt at playing the coquette just made him laugh. "You look like Lucille Ball mimicking a Parisian sex kitten."

That made me giggle. "I'll take that as a compliment, I think."

"You should. I like you the way you are, Loocy."

I squeezed his knee. "So, back to why you're here early. "What was the meeting about in Lille? I thought your gig was in Dubai."

"Wontrobski wanted me to meet with security here in France and eventually make suggestions for the new office setup. Besides, it was a good excuse to meet your plane and whisk you off to Paris a day early."

"And what is your take on the Lille operation? I was kind of surprised Baxter Brothers would open an office in France. I'd think Brussels would be the better location."

"Belgium is having problems. It's always been a hotbed of mercenaries, arms dealers, counterfeiters, and the like, but now there're suspected terrorist groups proliferating. I guess BB figured Lille, being right on the Belgian border, was the better choice."

"But close enough to Belgium to warrant having a security expert, namely you, to check things out. Too bad I'm on their S list. I'd love to live and work in France again."

"Hey, they hired you as a courier for this trip and keep throwing work in your direction, so maybe they'll have a change of heart. However, I can't quite see you towing the company line. Maybe you could be their in-house terror."

"Very funny."

He hit the brakes and slowed. "Hell, looks like an accident or something ahead."

Flashing lights rushed up behind us, a distinctive French nee-eu, nee-eu siren blasted, and a police car passed us and worked its way through stopped traffic before joining what looked like a sea of official vehicles ahead. I crossed my fingers and thought, *Please, please, not a cop blockade*.

Chapter Eight

It was a blockade all right, one crawling with uniforms and paramilitary equipment.

After an hour in stop-and-go traffic we approached a lineup of flashing lights, official-looking vehicles and armed services types who looked to be singling out some cars for a secondary inspection. They were actually removing the seats in one vehicle while a couple, she in full burja, looked on.

"What's this? Possible profiling in the land of *liberté*, *égalité*, and *fraternité?*" I quipped, mostly to hide my nervousness.

"Private car. She's allowed to wear it in the car, but otherwise, not in France. I've had to bone up on customs and French law."

Probably a good thing, there, what with the illegality of my present situation. Swiping my damp forehead and upper lip, I hoped I didn't fit whatever data they were using to single out the blameworthy like, say, *me*. What if they pulled us over and discovered that blasted gun? Or, more importantly, why had I put the bottle of Valium out of easy reach? "Crappola."

"What's wrong, Hetta?"

"Uh, gotta go to the bathroom."

"Wanna pull out of the line? They might have some porta potties or something."

"No!" I screeched, causing Jenks to look at me like I was losing it. Which I was. I took a deep breath. "What I mean is, we're almost through and we'll be in the hotel in no time. I can hold it."

"Okay then. Wonder who or what they're looking for?"

Texans smuggling arms into France? But I said, "I have no idea," as innocently as I could manage. *If they find the gun will they arrest Jenks, as well as me?* I could just hear Jan saying, "And, Miz Hetta, you didn't think that getting the man you love busted for gun runnin' just *might* put a chink in your relationship?"

We inched forward toward uniformed officers flanked by what looked like riot police, who were giving each car a long look. The flashing lights made them look like alien robots. I attempted more deep Yoga breaths. Rolling down a window, I strained to hear what the *gendarmes* ahead were asking other drivers, but a dog was barking in the Peugeot next to us, rendering even my legendary hearing useless.

I was shooting the dog dirty looks when I heard Jenks's window whir and a man asking, "*Monsieur*, is this your car?" in French.

Jenks doesn't speak French, so I leaned over and answered, "It is a rental, *monsieur*. We are tourists."

He held out his hand. "Passports, please."

We handed them over—mine was somewhat damp—but before opening them he looked at the covers and sneered, "*Américains*." He said it like a curse.

"Yes, we are," I said in French. "And we are looking forward to our vacation in your beautiful country, *monsieur l'agent.*"

He looked surprised that I spoke the lingo and knew to address him as *officer* in French. "You speak excellent French, Mad…" he looked inside my passport, "*Mademoiselle*, Coffey."

"*Merci monsieur l'agent*. I studied French in Paris many years ago."

He gave me a roguish smirk. "As a child, of course. Welcome back to France." He handed Jenks the passports and waved us through.

I refrained from letting loose with a "Yee Haw!"

Jenks gave me my passport. "You said you spoke French, but I had no idea you could use it to charm the pants off a police officer."

"Trust me, charming the pants off any Frenchman ain't all that hard. They are natural-born *roués*."

"I shall refrain from query or comment."

Another thing I love about Jenks Jenkins is his total incuriosity about my louche past.

Most of it's self-storied anyway.

Entering Paris, catching that first glimpse of the Eiffel Tower and a whiff of a boulangerie, made my heart flutter. I rolled down the window and took a deep breath, only to be reminded that Paris also reeks of open urinals, hordes of smokers, and warm mounds of dog crap.

That odiferous overload was quickly forgotten when I entered the hotel George V's lobby and took a journey back in time, before both the revolution—and that nasty old guillotine toppling aristocrats' heads by the numbers in such rude fashion—and when I was last in the hotel.

Marie Antoinette and King Louis XVI, before being relegated to the Bastille, would probably have felt quite at home surrounded by such splendiferous opulence. It makes one want to check one's pompadour in any of the numerous gilt-framed mirrors to see if perhaps one's head has gone missing.

Scads of mirror-finish marble, luscious silk damask, sparkling crystal, and rich *trompe l'oeil* effects might be considered *de trop* by some, but I love the dazzle of over-the-top.

The palace at Versailles was exactly what the original builders had in mind in 1928 when they opened this ode to the lavishness of another age. A recent re-do into a Four Seasons hotel had enhanced the glamour and romanticism even more than when I staggered through that lobby so many years ago. On that night, however, I hardly noticed the original tapestries and glittering chandeliers; my champagne-besotted eyes were blinded by the *objet d'art* waist-steering me to his suite, Jean Luc d'Ormesson.

Or, as I later dubbed him, Jean Luc d'Rat—I pronounced it "DooRah": not particularly the proper French pronunciation, but it had a nice ring, and a rat is a rat in any language.

That twenty-year-old bittersweet memory hit me like a bolt of lightning, making me sad, mad, nostalgic, and embarrassed at how really stupid I'd been back then. Jan might say nothing has changed.

She might be right, for the Jean Luc DooRah affaire wasn't to be the last time I'd be led down the garden path by a smooth dude, but it was my first real heartbreak. Until then, I thought the word meant you were sad about something, but I *did* learn one thing; true heartbreak involves physical pain.

My sudden discombobulation at being smack dab at the scene of the crime stopped me short as my chest constricted. I glommed onto Jenks's steady arm, hanging on to remind me that those days of uncertainty were over. Sort of. I made a noise and Jenks asked me if I wanted to sit down while he checked us in.

"No, I'm fine, just tired. All I need is a hot bath, a glass of something cold and bubbly, and a lovely evening with you." I gave his hand a squeeze and got a badly needed hug in return.

In the elevator he asked, "So, Red, you think you're up to eating at the Cinq tonight?" While I knew he was hopeful I'd say no, I also knew he'd brave that touted restaurant to please me.

"No way. Besides, I know you don't like French food. And although I'd bet my last centime the chef here at the Le Cinq could change your mind, I'd much rather order room service and spend our first night in Paris alone. Just us two."

He tried hiding his glee, but wasn't very good at it. I sometimes wonder how he is such an accomplished poker player yet so obviously readable where I'm concerned. Even on the rare occasion when he tries telling me a fib, he gives himself away with an ever-so- slight-and-shy grin and an eye twinkle.

Before I could tease him about his lack of guile, a knock on the door announced our bellhop and luggage. I had been reluctant to let my bag of contraband out of my sight, but there was no way in hell the staff at this hotel was gonna let me tote my own suitcase.

Right behind the bellhop was a room service valet with a tray of canapés and a bottle of chilled champagne. Jenks, champers, and Paris! Such a deal. And throw in a room decorated in extravagant white and gold silks and brocades from a period before the one dubbed The Age of Enlightenment? Let them eat cake.

I know, I know. She never really said it.

Reunions are grand.

And sexy.

And fattening.

Our stay at the grand George V was über lovey-dovey and worth a minimum of two pounds a day.

After three days of rich food, great wine, slow strolls around the City of Love, and all that romantic stuff, I longed for my dog, my boat, and cheese that wasn't white. Jenks wanted bacon and eggs for breakfast. It was time to get the hell out of Paris.

"But where to?" I asked.

"South."

"Won't get any argument here. Where south?"

"Well, we have a couple of days to kill, and then there's the surprise I promised you."

"Jenks, you're killing me here. Give me a little hint, at least."

"Lemme think about that. Meanwhile, where in the South of France would you like to go?"

"Well, Monaco ain't really in France, but it might be fun. Have you been there?" I knew he liked casinos, so why not hit the premier joint in all the world?

"Was there years ago, played a little Baccarat."

This guy never ceases to amaze me. "Baccarat? Did you order a bourbon, shaken not stirred, Agent Bond?"

He shook his head and grinned. "No, and I didn't wear a tux, either. I guess I'm just a Vegas kinda guy."

We discussed other places, then I suggested Gruissan which, this being off-season, might be a good spot to land and spend a couple of days on the beach.

"Where is it?"

"Hold on. I'll put it into the GPS."

We drove south from Paris, making our way through mile after mile of France's picture-perfect countryside, with its meandering rivers, historic architecture, vineyards, and fields I knew would be lush green in the spring. The farther south we traveled, the less the chill in the air.

Gruissan is on the Mediterranean Sea, about five hundred miles from Paris and, via high-speed autoroutes, only an eight-hour drive. With stops for gas, lunch, and the like, we wandered into Gruissan late in the afternoon, and I was stunned to see what had become of the little fishing village I remembered.

The center of Old Town is a ring of streets called a *circulade*, encircling the tower ruins of a castle constructed at the end of the tenth century as a fortress to guard the nearby city of Narbonne against sea raids by pirates and Berber incursions. Built on a steep, rocky hill, the castle crowned the fortified village, which was back then surrounded by salt marshes and, therefore, commanded an unobstructed view for spotting marauders. Now the swamp has been drained and a "new" town has evolved that caters to tourists from around the world. Hotels, vacation homes, and condos abound, but the town still holds its charm. Legend has it some villagers are descended from the seven families who settled Gruissan in the thirteenth century.

I pictured them heating up cauldrons of oil to repel us barbaric Americans.

We zeroed in on a chic hotel room with a glass-enclosed balcony overlooking the marina, but then I remembered that just out of town, at the *plage,* was a colony of quaint beach cottages on stilts directly on the Med. So, the next morning we drove around admiring the more than thirteen hundred houses until we found one for rent. It was tiny but available, and by noon we had rented it for three days.

A trip to a nearby super-store with an outdoor launderette in the parking lot, and we were caught up on clean clothes, eats, and wine in time for a late afternoon stroll on the beach. For early November the weather was amazingly nice, especially on the Med, where the winds can be fierce this time of year.

There were a few other walkers out, and just for fun I greeted each one with a hearty, *"Allô!* or *"Bonjour!"* taking delight when the French cringed or frowned, Germans looked away, and Brits smiled and nodded politely. One couple obviously had mixed reactions; she responded with an American-sounding, "Hello," while he glowered.

The sullen man with a mop of beautifully-cut blonde hair, piercing green eyes, and buff bod could have just stepped out of a Ralph Lauren advertisement. I was pretty sure disapproval of my bumptious greeting and the woman's response in kind, had plenty to do with his crappy attitude. Some days are just better than others.

As we continued walking, I mulled over the couple. The friendly woman was, well, on the frumpy side. Not that she was totally unattractive, but, compared with her GQ friend, a definite BEFORE. He was decked out in a cable knit sweater with a jaunty cravat and looked *tres* French. The woman, wearing baggy sweats, had hair that hadn't seen a stylist in perhaps *ever* that was held off her face by a headband probably left over from long ago high school days. She looked like an all-American soccer mom who was dashing to the grocery store after dropping off the kids. Under her sweats, my discerning eye detected an extra twenty pounds, and her overall look suggested she had a few years on her companion. Not older, like she could'a been his mother older, but they were still an odd pair.

Even though they were walking arm-in-arm, one might wonder if they were just friends, but when I looked back over my shoulder, they were sharing a kiss.

I know I'm opinionated and judgmental, but when I see such an improbable couple it makes me ponder. Probably like people do when they see tall, lanky Jenks and short, chunky Hetta together?

"Four out of ten," I said to Jenks.

"Four out of ten what?"

"Ten people. Four friendlies."

"Maybe they think you're going to try selling them something. One thing for sure, some of those people seemed intimidated that you spoke to them."

"It's a gift, bringing out the worst in people. I do the same thing in Florida and other places where Yankees hang out."

He laughed. "You do remember that I'm a Yankee, right?"

"Yep, but you're a *recovering* Yankee."

Chapter Nine

Jenks and I shared a laugh at my quip about him being a *recovering* Yankee as we strolled farther down Gruissan's sandy beach. Judging by a disapproving sniff from a passing elderly Frenchman walking an equally-grizzled standard poodle, we were much too foreign in our loudness.

The man—short, a little round, and probably in his eighties—had a snappy spring in his step. Under his beret, gray hair curled out in all directions and at least a week's worth of white stubble bewhiskered his deeply lined face. Dressed in a tan knit sweater under an unbuttoned, rumpled canvas jacket and corduroy trousers—all of them maybe a size too large—he was saved from looking like a bum by a bright red silk cravat and natty, highly shined ankle length slip-on leather boots. His pants were a bit too short, revealing red-checked argyle socks. He and his pooch personified everyone's archetypical image of: *Frenchman, walking dog.*

The handsome light gray standard poodle, obviously less discerning about strangers than his owner, waggled his butt and strained on his leash in my direction when I squatted down to his level, held my hand out for him to sniff, and spoke doggie stuff to him in French.

The old man visibly softened, stepped forward so I could scratch the dog's ears, and answered the question I'd put to his dog: "Charles." He pronounced it, Sharls.

I looked up into the old man's surprisingly clear, bright blue eyes and returned his sweet, snaggle-toothed smile with a view of my own perfectly bleached chompers. "*Merci, monsieur*, for allowing me to pet your Charles. I miss my dog so much." I hugged the poodle, stood, and held out my hand. "I am Hetta and this is Jenks. He doesn't speak French."

"But *you* do, quite well for an American."

"Why, thank you. But how do you know I'm American?" I asked him, fearing I'd fall victim to French prejudice.

"Your teeth. The English, they have teeth like mine," he said, taking my hand in a two-handed embrace, "I am René Classens, and I am very fond of the Americans."

"*Enchanté, Monsieur* Classens."

"Please, you must call me René. And I am 'appy to meet you, as well," he answered in heavily accented English. "We do not meet many Americans here in Gruissan. Mostly English and," he frowned, "*Bosche*."

Okay, so he liked Americans, didn't seem to mind the Brits, but was definitely no Teutophile. Frenchmen in his age group are rarely enamored with anything German. Just on a whim, I nodded at his dog, "He is named after Charles de Gaulle?"

René beamed and coughed out a laugh made gruff by a lifetime of Galois smoke, judging by the pack in his pocket. "You are a very clever girl, you know. You and your 'usband must join us for a glass of wine. Charles and I live simply, but we do have a decent cellar."

Anyone who calls me a *girl* and has a wine cellar is an instant new BFF. I looked at Jenks, he nodded, and I said we would be delighted. "When and where? We are only here for a couple of days."

"Why not now? I am nearby."

As we walked together chatting in both French, and when he could, broken English to include Jenks so I wouldn't have to constantly translate, the odd pair I'd seen earlier had doubled back. As they approached, René hissed under his breath, "*Beur.*"

Butter? Why would he say that while glaring at the couple?

I waved gaily at the woman and said, "Hello, again," just to get her dude's goat, but this time he put his arm around her, pulled her closer, smiled, and nodded at us. Which, by the way, transformed him from just good-looking to drop-dead gorgeous.

"Gee, Hetta, aren't you just a regular peacemaker today?" Jenks teased.

"I guess that honey versus vinegar thing really works. Who knew? Grandmama was right."

"Grandmothers usually are."

And she also told me, what with my mouth, I should always pack a pistol. "I sure hope so."

"Huh?"

"Never mind."

We stopped at our cottage to grab warm jackets and a bottle of wine on our way to René's place, which he told us was in the oldest part of Gruissan, a couple of kilometers away. Jenks stuck the wine into a deep pocket at my request; I had no idea of René's economic status and didn't want to be a burden. On the other hand, I didn't wish to embarrass him after his generous invitation.

His building, larger than its neighbors, was a weathered salmon-colored affair with multiple French balconies, faded blue shutters, and window boxes overflowing with flowers. I loved it at first sight, but having lived in France, I knew the interior might prove dank and dark. As he pushed open a heavy blue door and waved us into a large, black-and-white checkered marble foyer, an older woman rushed forward, took his coat, and unhooked Charles from his leash, all the while fussing at René for being gone so long.

René chuckled. "She worries too much. Celeste, please tell André we have guests for drinks." Then he looked at us and raised an eyebrow, "And, perhaps for dinner?"

The tiny woman beamed and nodded. She typified French-chic and would be hard to peg, age-wise, had her close-cropped hair not been white. Dressed in a high-end sweater and slacks, she hardly looked like a housekeeper.

After proper introductions were made, I said, "We don't wish to impose." We really hadn't planned anything past canned soup, salad and a baguette back at the cottage, and dinner with René sounded great, but one must be politely French when offered an impromptu invite, giving the inviter an out.

Celeste spoke up. "Oh, please, I insist. I am tired of cooking for two old men and a dog."

René barked a laugh. "You see, Hetta, you must stay or Celeste will be cross with me. It is never good to have a bad-tempered chef, *n'est-ce pas*?

I looked at Jenks and he raised his hands in a classic French gesture. "Why not?"

Celeste bustled out, Charles hot on her heels.

"Obviously we do not get many visitors. Please, take off your coats while I consult with Celeste as to what she can pull together for our dinner. I will meet you in the library," he pointed to a pair of huge beveled glass French doors, "right in there."

We dumped our coats onto a foyer bench, careful to hide the bottle of wine that was not worthy of such a setting, and entered a cozy room complete with wall-to-ceiling books, leather chairs, and a blazing fire.

"Jenks, I think I've died and somehow landed on a cloud. This place is a dream. Okay, so the George V was sumptuous, but next to this? This is the real deal. No decorator involved, just years of very well made stuff handed down through the generations."

René returned, followed by a tall thin man bearing a silver tray with two bottles of wine, an assortment of glassware, an ice bucket, and a bottle of Chivas Regal, which I was certain was added for Jenks. The man was dressed in much the same garb as René, but was wearing white gloves.

"This is André, and you 'ave already met his wife, Celeste. They stay with me for sentimental reasons and have chosen to take on household tasks we could easily hire others to do, but they refuse. André here is my cousin and we have been together since we were boys. He wears many hats, including choosing the wine. Since my wife died, we have relaxed our ways in the household, but some," he grinned and patted the gloved hand, "are slow to change."

While Celeste prepared dinner, René talked of the history of Gruissan, told us of his war experience when, as a boy, the Germans occupied France and he and his father sent his sister and mother to England. André, a few years younger, also went to the UK with his mother, but his father stayed.

"We were fortunate, for my father and uncle were fisherman and, therefore, of use to the Bosch. With our fishing vessels, we spied on the 'appenings along the coast, and passed information to the exiled de Gaulle regime across the Channel in England. We like to think we contributed to the safety of the allies who liberated us." He crossed himself and added, "And apologize to those who perished."

"So," Jenks said, "you were in the French Resistance."

"French Resistance," René scoffed in English. "To 'ear some tell it now, everyone in *France* was in the resistance. But I tell you right now, I can name many in this very village who kissed any filthy Bosch *cul* for a day of rations. *Vrai*, real, *La Résistance française* lived in *extrême* danger. Some would have starved but for my father's fish, but you never 'eard *them* brag about what they did. I was a boy, so with my bicycle, I was able to deliver food and messages right under the German's noses." He then chortled and winked. "When *ma mère* 'eard about that after she and my sister returned after the war, she almost killed *Papa*."

André entered to announce dinner, heard René's comment, and deadpanned with a British accent, "Your mother was far more dangerous than the Bosch."

We moved into yet another lovely room with a smaller fireplace and fire, and a huge crystal chandelier hanging over a round table that could easily sit twenty, but was set for six: five people and one dog.

Celeste's "pulled-together" dinner was divine. *Sole meunière*—melt-in-your-mouth sauted filet of sole in a butter, parsley and lemon sauce with a few capers added—served with *riz soubise* which, she explained, was thin ribbons of onion cooked with rice, cream, and Gruyère cheese. The pencil-thin asparagus were steamed to perfection. Jenks eyed the rice doubtfully, but once he took a bite, he was all smiles.

What with the ubiquitous baguettes, a lightly-dressed butter lettuce salad, a cheese plate, *crème brûlèe*, coffee, and brandy, I was enamored with René's idea of living simply. And after tasting his wine selections, I wanted to toss that bottle hidden in Jenks's jacket pocket into the nearest cesspool.

André drove us back to our beach cottage in a vintage limo straight out of a movie. Although he still wore somewhat rumpled clothing similar to that of René's, he'd added a chauffeur's cap and leather gloves. Before he ushered us into the elegant black and gray car, he showed it off, explaining it was a 1966 Austin Princess, which made me feel like one just riding in it.

We slept late the next morning, only to be awakened by a banging shutter.

I'd warned Jenks about the infamous mistral, a seasonal wind much like the winter northers in the Sea of Cortez, and now it had arrived with a vengeance. The cold blow is accompanied by clear blue skies, and usually drops during the night. I turned on the television and learned this one would howl for at least two more days, with winds into the forty-knot range. The sea in front of our cottage was already whipped into a white frenzy. Luckily, our cozy beach house had a fireplace, so we planned to hunker down for a day of reading and hanging out.

Putting on every warm thing I had with me, I braved a fast beach walk to counteract the previous evening's food and booze, but got sandblasted for my efforts. When I returned, Jenks, bless his heart, had braved the cold to go into town for a baguette for him and a *pain au chocolat* for me. So much for trying to repair the calorie damage from the night before.

I prepared *café au lait,* which we drank from heavy earthenware bowls at my insistence; I was determined to re-embrace the French experience and drag poor Jenks along, albeit kicking and screaming.

"I have to say," Jenks commented as he downed a piece of bread smothered in butter, "this is the best butter I have ever tasted. Why?"

"It is," I said with a French accent, "zee *terroir."*

"Zee what?"

"*Terroir*. Literally, it means the history of the soil. Lots of rain, lots of green grass, happy cows, great tasting butter. Oh, and about two to five percent more butterfat than ours."

"Where do you learn all this stuff?"

"I took a cooking class in Paris. Nothing fancy, but fun. Another thing I learned about was *agneau de pré-salé*."

"Okay, what's that?"

"Lamb from a salt meadow. Once again, the *terroir* thing, in Normandy. The sheep eat this grass that grows in salt water and the meat is pre-salted. I ate it in a restaurant near Mont Saint-Michel and it was fantastic."

"I'll take your word for it," he said dryly.

"Your tastes are sooo pedestrian, you know," I teased.

"That's not true. I never eat pedestrians."

Just as we finished breakfast and were discussing what to do on such a windy day, Jenks's phone chirped. His end of the conversation was suspiciously cryptic but I couldn't lean in to listen to the other end without being obvious. When he hung up, he announced, "Our ship has come in."

"What ship?"

"My surprise for you."

"Come on, tell me."

"Nope, not yet. However, the surprise is a day early, so we need to get on the road tomorrow."

"Jenks, I invited René for a good old-fashioned American breakfast tomorrow morning."

"Does that mean we get to use good old-fashioned coffee mugs?'

"Not *that* American. So, how far away is this surprise of yours?"

"Not far. Plenty of time for breakfast with René, because we don't have to be there until two."

"Where at two?"

"Me to know and you to find out."

It wasn't easy pulling together the ingredients for an artery-clogging American breakfast, but after hitting three markets in town, I found bacon and those wonderful farm-fresh eggs so hard to come by back home. I struck out on *lait fermenté* and had to fall back on my old make-your-own-buttermilk trick for the biscuits. Using whole milk, mixed with a little yogurt and lemon juice, I was able to almost duplicate my grandmother's recipe, but mine were not as fluffy as hers because French flour has a lower gluten content than ours.

For the sausage gravy I found some smoked links, took the meat from the casing, fried it up, and made cream gravy.

René loved the food, and asked for the biscuit recipe. I could envision one disgruntled Chef Celeste at Chez René.

We bid *à bientôt*, not exactly good-bye, but more like until we meet again. I promised to let him know where we were and what we were doing, as I still didn't know. I got the feeling Jenks took him aside and shared his secret because René said he would be stopping by for a glass of wine. Stopping by where?

We loaded up the car and headed for the autoroute towards Toulouse. "Okay, Jenks, just where are we going now?"

"Grocery store."

"Gosh, what a wonderful surprise. I've always wanted to go there."

"Smarty."

"Okay, I must surmise we are not headed for a resort if we gotta buy food."

"Yep."

"Oh, come on! You're killing me here. So, what are we going to buy?" I figured maybe I'd get a clue.

"Lots of stuff. We need to provision as if we were going to the islands outside of La Paz for two weeks."

"That I can do, but we might need a bigger car."

I don't think we could have gotten another bottle of wine into that Fiat. When we bought things that required refrigeration and cooking, I did learn we would have a fridge and a stove. Not much of a hint there.

About twenty minutes later, we arrived in a small village, crossed a bridge, turned into an unpaved drive, and pulled up next to a funny looking boat.

Jenks swept his arm at the boat and announced, "Your yacht in the South of France, mademoiselle, and ours as long as you want to cruise the Canal du Midi."

"Oh, Jenks, this is wonderful, but there's something missing to make it even more perfect."

"What?"

"Can we maybe rent a dog?"

Chapter Ten

As we walked down to *Villepinte*, Jenks told me the rental fleet was named after local villages and towns on the Canal du Midi. "I hope this boat's okay with you. Heck of a lot smaller than your *Raymond Johnson,* but I think we can manage for a couple of weeks or so. What do you think?"

I was still gawking at my surroundings. My eyes were misty when I turned to Jenks. "Okay? Okay? It's more than just *okay*, Jenks. This is absolutely the most wonderful thing anyone has ever done for me."

"Uh, you aren't going to cry, are you?"

I wiped my eyes. For someone who hardly ever lets anyone see me cry, this past week had been an emotional roller coaster that threatened tears on a regular basis. "No, I am not, but if I did they would be tears of joy. It's just that I'm a little overwhelmed. How on earth did you know I've dreamed of barging on the canals and rivers in Europe for years?"

"Jan. I called and asked her how to make up for getting you stuck on a cargo plane, and she told me the George V was a good start, and she'd heard you talk about taking this canal trip for years. She said I could win your heart, then she warned me that might be dangerous for my future well-being."

"Ha, sounds like her. But, believe me, you already had my heart. I think you just touched my soul. Thank you."

He kissed me, then said, "Okay, enough mush. Let's get this show on the road. We start our trip here, head east," he pointed behind our boat, "and end up almost back at the Mediterranean. Let's unload the car, open a bottle of wine, and toast our voyage. The marina staff are on lunch break until one-thirty, then they'll show us how to drive this tub."

"No one's here?"

"Nope."

"Then I guess I have time to show you my appreciation."

"Bad girl."

"Oh, you have no idea."

Log of the *Villepinte*, Canal du Midi: Day 1

Our "barge" is actually a boat, but called a "penichette" meaning a low and small barge. This baby we rented is definitely not a seagoing vessel, but designed for cruising in protected waters like the Canal du Midi and going under very low bridges. At a little over thirty feet long, and about ten feet wide, it is small, but efficiently laid out. And evidently meant to bounce off lock walls, as the entire boat is surrounded by inflated fenders and resembles a nautical bumper car. There are several large, privately owned barges tied along the dock here, but they are unoccupied right now. Even they are fortified with giant fenders. I have a feeling we're going to be fending off a lot.

The driving lesson this afternoon was probably under the worst possible conditions, with fifteen-knot winds whistling down the canal. Jenks did better than I, as I've never handled a single engine boat of this size. I've deemed him the designated driver for the locks ahead; I'll handle the lines.

Ours is the smallest vessel available for rent, with one master sleeping cabin, a combination toilet/shower compartment, and an extra bunk bed we're using as a wine cellar and storage. The largest cabin is in the aft of the boat and is surrounded by windows. There is a galley and a large dining table surrounded on three sides with a cushioned settee. A small refrigerator, stove, and sink form the galley. It sure ain't no *Raymond Johnson*, but Jenks felt we'd give it a try, and then if we want we can upgrade later. He's booked it for fifteen days, so we'll see how it goes.

I am loving this idea of meandering through the French countryside in a boat. We spent the afternoon stowing food and gear, then tomorrow morning, since the wind is due to blow one more day, Jenks is going to move the car to Argens and stash it at the marina there. We figure by the time we get that far, we are going to be in dire need of a major grocery run. I've made up flash cards for Jenks to show train personnel and taxi drivers, so I think he'll be fine.

Our evening meal was made up of all those pre-prepared goodies they have in the super *marchés*— shrimp cocktails, chicken Kiev, potato soufflé, and a mixed salad vinaigrette—accompanied by a fresh bagette, of course, and that wonderful sweet butter only the

French seem to have and, *naturellement*, red wine. For dessert, an éclair for Jenks and crème brûlée for me. *Fantastique!*

Luckily this barge comes with a bicycle.

Tomorrow the adventure begins! H

Log of the *Villepinte*, Canal du Midi: Day 2

While Jenks took the car to Argens this morning, I read the brochures, studied charts, and beefed up on the rules and regulations for boating on the Canal du Midi. Most of the regs involve simple boating common sense, but since the literature also boasts, NO BOATING EXPERIENCE REQUIRED, I can see why the humorously illustrated brochure warned captains about such things as: Do not roll the mooring line around your arm or ankle. The drawing showed a person stretched out between the bank and a boat four feet away, with a foot tangled in one end of the line and the other around his wrist.

Another warned: Do not try to stop the boat with your feet or hands. Evidently that's what all these fenders are for.

Jenks made it to Argens and back with no problem, so we decided to get underway.

We left the dock at three.

And again at 3:15.

And again at 3:30.

The wind was still howling and we couldn't get the boat's bow to turn. *Villepinte* doesn't have the power or rudder response to overcome the wind, so every time we weren't heading into it, or with it, the wind turned us broadside and we sailed down the canal sideways.

Luckily, except for a couple of ducks, there were no witnesses to such a debacle by two experienced boaters. H.

When we were back at the dock for the third time, I said, "Jenks, I have an idea."

"Turn this boat in for one with bow thrusters? Or at least twin screws?"

"Well, there's that. But that last maneuver you made gave me an idea. Ram the grass bank bow first and give it power. We'll turn one way or another, for sure. And all those bumpers will keep us from doing the boat harm."

Jenks shook his head. "Goes against my nature to ram something on purpose."

"Think about it. She'll pivot."

He grinned. "Aha. Professor Coffey's theory of fulcrum dynamics, as applied to boating. What the hell. Not my boat."

Worked like a charm, and soon we were on our way to the a lock.

By the end of the first day of cruising the canal we ran out of time and energy because we couldn't get to the next lock before it closed at five. We tied up at a wait dock and spent the night next to the *éclusier's* charming home that looked to have been there for at least a hundred years. The wind had died and sun glimmered through the trees, so we went out on deck and had drinks as we watched children playing in the home's small yard, and greeted bikers and walkers on the path along the canal. A large goose paced and honked nearby, looking as though he was expecting a treat, but I knew better. They bite.

We had an early dinner of spaghetti and meatballs and went back out for a nightcap.

"Ah, this is what I expected it to be like. Thank you again, Jenks, for making this happen. I can't believe how worn out I am. Last of the big time party animals here."

He gave me a hug. "Getting dark, want to move in? We're on battery power tonight, but if you get cold I'll start the engines so we can run the heater."

"Nope, you'll keep me warm."

"Oh, yes, I certainly will."

Oh là là.

Log of the *Villepinte*, Canal du Midi: Day 3

Locks, or *écluses*.

Yesterday we cleared our first three, all doubles and quite the trial by fire, mainly because I was nervous. Even though I'd done my homework, I was worried I'd screw something up. Luckily, a very friendly *éclusier* helped us at the first one, showing us the ropes, literally, while complaining about too many commercials during NASCAR races he live-streams..

By the time we got through the next two sets we were worn out.

I am *le* donkey.

It is my job to handle the lines and open the locks when they are automated. By the end of the day, I'm plumb done. Luckily, Jenks bought both of us gloves from the rental office, because they've saved my poor hands from being a hot mess of blisters. My shoulders and arms are sore from hand-over-handing the lines as we go up and down with the water level.

I've been humming Sam Cooke's, "Chain Gang" and trying to remember the words. I do pretty well on the, "Uh! Ah!" parts.

All that said, I am loving it! And, with all this exercise, I won't end up rolling back to Mexico. Oh, and we learned all those fenders were not so much because of kamakazi captains—although we're sure to meet some—but protection from ancient stone walls lining the locks and bank-rammers, like us. H

Log of the *Villepinte*, Canal du Midi: Day 4

After spending our first night off the grid, we were delighted to cut the next day short and tie up in a marina at the Port-Lauragais. We were early enough to wander around, and even have lunch in town. H

With much more knowledge of what we could expect our days of canal cruising to involve, we set a more leisurely pace, stopping by mid-afternoon.

Jenks lost his footing and came close to sliding into the canal while he was pounding long aluminum mooring stakes into the slick grass and slimy mud on the bank. I managed to snag his jacket collar right before he went in, then we both scrambled backward on heels and butts until reaching the hard-packed path, where we were almost plowed into by a bicyclist.

Jenks gagged and sucked air, I giggled, and the departing biker cursed, but we were successfully, if less than professionally, tied up for the night. We granted ourselves a well-deserved shower and nap.

Happy Hour was getting earlier each day, as was sunset. When twilight's chill arrived, we moved inside and played cards or dominoes before cooking. Pretty tame stuff, but it was a cruising life we had grown used to over the years.

After dinner I always checked out the charts, did some calculations as to how far we'd go the next day, how many locks we had to clear, and whether there was a village within walking distance we wanted to explore, even though we found most of them devoid of people and stores.

I told Jenks I was ready for a real town, so we agreed that when we reachcd Castelnaudary we'd stay for a few days. "From everything I read, this place is going to be right up my alley."

"And what alley would that be?"

"Historical, and chock full of *boulangeries*, *pâtisseries*, and markets."

Jenks threaded our boat through a narrow arch festooned with flowers, under a low bridge, and right into the pure charm of Castelnaudary. It was only two in the afternoon, so we nailed a coveted side-tie right by the harbor master's office, just two blocks from the center of town.

After we checked in and hooked up to water and electricity—the first we'd had in days—I headed up a cobblestoned street to a plaza fronted by those promised *pâtisseries and boulangeries*.

After a late lunch of cheese, bread, fruit, and wine, we napped. I hadn't realized how really tired we were until we could totally relax for a couple of days without worrying about basically dry camping. Without a way to charge our computers, it was becoming a worry. The boat generated DC power while the engine ran but no AC power. I anchor out a lot on *Raymond Johnson*, but my boat is equipped for it with a generator, solar panels, inverter and a water maker. *Villepinte* had none of those, so we had to run the engine to charge batteries and heat the cabin. I was used to conserving water, so no problem there.

"You know, Jenks, how much I love being anchored out in the Sea of Cortez. But I gotta say, I'm happy as a clam being back to modern conveniences and fresh food."

"Then we'll stay here as long as you like. We can even go out for dinner tonight. I spotted several promising restaurants in town, and they were open."

"Open? What a concept." One of the things we'd learned since getting to France was that the most frequently used word other than, "*Bonjour*," was FERMÉ: CLOSED.

We'd been surprised at the number of McDonalds in a country famed for its food, and they were jammed with French people. Then we figured it out: THEY. WERE. OPEN.

"Lemme get this straight, you found restaurants that are not only open, but will be so tonight before eight o'clock? And you say they held promise. What did they promise? No French food?" I teased.

"Very funny. I just like what I like, without the frills."

"Then you, *monsieur*, are in zee luck. Chef Hetta will prepare for you, this very evening, *biftek servi en baguette avec haché du oignons grillés*.

"Uh, maybe we'll go out, after all."

"What? *Monsieur* does not trust Chef Hetta to please him? *Monsieur* does not desire my hamburger on a baguette with grilled onions for his *dîner*?

"On third thought, let's eat in."

"I figured you might say that—uh, Jenks, about that baguette I just bought?"

"What about it, other than it's almost gone."

"Nope, it's all gone. A swan is eating it."

He spun around, yelled, "Hey!" and a long, white, graceful neck pulled back from our open galley window, what was left of our baguette in its orange and black beak. "Oh well, that bread was three hours old anyway."

"*Monsieur* is becoming very French, in spite of his barbarian American tastes. Next thing you know, you'll buy a beret."

"I don't think so. Shut that window and sit tight. I'll go get us a fresh baguette. You need anything else from town?"

"Bag of swan food?"

Chapter Eleven

I went out on deck to people-and-swan watch while awaiting Jenks's return from the *boulangerie*. I named the swans Siegfried and Odette, after the hapless lovers in Tchaikovsky's Swan Lake. Not all that familiar with the big birds, I was fascinated with their beauty and size, but after reading up on them in my local guide, I didn't fall victim to their panhandling ways. I didn't want to give them what they *should* eat, which was my lovely bread and butter lettuce. Besides, they already copped half a baguette, which is a big no-no according to the Internet. I considered us even for now.

The sidewalk and street bustled with walkers and cars, a far cry from our last five days along the canal banks. It was a nice change, sort of like getting back to a dock after being at sea.

Much to my surprise, I saw two people who looked familiar. Where had I seen them before? I hate it when this happens. As they passed, hand-in-hand, I suddenly had a flashback to the beach at Gruissan and the odd couple we passed and greeted just before we met René and his stately poodle, Charles.

Once again my curiosity, something known to get me in trouble occasionally, was aroused. They strolled slowly along the quay, not paying any attention to me, leaving me free to stare. She, slightly dumpy and frumpy, and he—rock star gorgeous—just didn't jell in my never-so-humble opinion. The man, by my guess, was a few years younger than she, but it was hard to tell since the woman had let her hair go to gray streaks, while his seemed suspiciously salon-streaked. I missed having Jan around as a sounding board for such things.

As they passed, I couldn't resist tracking them with my eyes. When they boarded a rental boat much larger than ours, parked a few spaces back, my feet followed. I was almost abreast of the boat when I heard Jenks call out.

Turning, I burst out laughing.

Jenks, baguette in hand, was wearing a beret and cravat.

We spent the next day wandering around Castelnaudary's historic streets and waterfronts, playing tourist, gawking at gaily-painted narrow boats—barges much larger than ours but still designed for canals and low bridges. Most of them were over fortyish feet long, and through lacy curtain-framed windows I noticed they boasted a level of domesticity rarely seen on a regular yacht like mine. These were certainly floating homes, complete with regular sofas and furniture. I made a mental note to educate myself on owning and living on one of these babies some day.

I snapped a few photos of the more whimsical ones and those brimming with flower boxes overflowing with colorful blooms. One even had an outdoor garden on the roof with a crop of big red tomatoes, lettuce, and herbs.

We also walked the half-mile to the next set of locks to check them out for the day we departed, although leaving Castelnaudary wasn't on my radar yet. I dearly loved this town.

Since going out after eight every night—when the restaurants finally opened—didn't appeal to us, we cooked dinner on board after having drinks on deck most evenings. We had no outdoor grill on the boat, so I cooked our filet mignons the old-fashioned way: pan seared with tons of butter. As I was deglazing the skillet with brandy and adding a dollop of cream, I spotted the woman from the odd couple walking by alone, carrying what looked to be her grocery bag. "Wonder where dreamboat is?" I mused aloud.

"Who?"

"Remember that couple we saw on the beach at Gruissan the day we met René?"

He gave me the look; the one that says, *"What? I'm supposed to remember stuff like this?"*

"Never mind. Anyhow, I thought they were oddly-matched, and René said something about butter."

"You might want to cut back on the wine, Hetta."

"Very funny. Well, I saw those two again yesterday afternoon here in Castelnaudary. Matter of fact, they're on a rental boat parked right back there." I nodded my head behind us since my hands were occupied adding calories to protein.

"And?"

"Nothing. She just walked by alone."

"For God's sake, call Interpol!"

"Just forget it. You're not nearly as much fun as Jan."

He sidled up behind me, pulled me close and nuzzled my neck. "Really? Can Jan do this?"

"Jan who?"

Jenks's phone chirped, rousing me from a deep sleep.

A one-eyed peek at my travel clock informed me it was 2:00. Jenks left the cabin so as not to disturb me with his call, but it was too late. By the time I pulled on a sweat shirt and pants and stumbled into the main cabin he was saying, "Okay, what time?" He listened and nodded. "I'll be ready."

"What? What is it?" I asked, fearing the answer.

"I am so sorry, Red, but I have to leave for a few days. There's been a massive terrorist attack in Paris and I'm needed in Lille. Wontrobski is sending a car here for me, and then I'll fly out of Toulouse."

"What kind of terrorist attack?" I wasn't quite awake yet, but what I meant was, did someone fly a plane into the Eiffel tower like they did the WTC in New York?

"ISIS kind. Firing into crowds last night. Reports of hundreds shot or killed. I don't have the details yet and I doubt anyone else does, but Wontrobski is pretty sure you'll be safe staying here. Once I assess the situation, I may move you to another location, but for now, you should stay put. Just keep a low profile for the next couple of days until we know whether other attacks are in the works. Probably are, but a place like this wouldn't get them enough publicity."

"Why can't I come with you?"

"Not to northern France, Hetta, until we know more. You'd just be stuck in a hotel all day while I work. It'll be safer here. But now that I think of it, maybe it's a good idea for me to send in a bodyguard, just in case?"

"I don't need no stinkin' bodyguard."

"I was thinking for the protection of the innocent citizens of Castelnaudary."

Jenks grabbed a leftover éclair on his way to the waiting car, gave me a last kiss and, just like that, he was gone. Again.

I'd planned to send him off with a stomach full of good old fried bacon and eggs, but we somehow ended up back in bed and lost track of time.

The minute he left a pall descended on my previous joy at being in France with Jenks, and on a boat, to boot. Long-ago memories, bad ones, crept in. Maybe returning to France had been a rotten idea. The George V revived a twinge of the gut-wrenching pain of abandonment I'd experienced all those years ago when, after the steamy month-long whirlwind romance, Luc DooRah dumped me like a hot *pomme de terre*.

That fateful summer—I call it fateful because I truly believe the events changed me in a way that colored my dealings with men for the next two decades—I was still a student in Brussels. I was thrilled to be chosen to participate as an intern with a large French engineering and construction company. My classes at ULB— *Università Libre de Bruxelles*—wouldn't start until late August, but I was too broke to fly home. I was getting by on a few bucks saved from past summer jobs, holding workshops in lithography, and interest earned on a small inheritance that paid the rent, but money was tight.

In Paris I wasn't officially put on the company payroll, but was given pocket money and the use of a studio apartment on the Left Bank, within walking distance from work.

Five days a week we were fed a large lunch that entailed leftovers we could schlep home for dinner, even though taking a doggie bag home is frowned upon by the French as showing you can't afford to waste food. I never understood this attitude and evidently, someone is seeing the light because France recently passed a new law making it illegal for supermarkets to throw away perfectly good food that can be donated to charity, or at least to pig farmers for their stock.

I guess they finally ran out of cake.

As an intern, which is what they called my status as an unpaid glorified gofer, I was assigned to the restoration project of the Pont Neuf. The bridge, spanning the River Seine, was getting a facelift in celebration of its upcoming 400th anniversary. Just in time, in my opinion, because it was in dire need of repair, as well as structural shoring, but what wouldn't be after four hundred years?

Our intern team of fifteen came from all over the world, and I think I was chosen because I'd actually worked in construction; I'd spent a summer at Prudhoe Bay, Alaska, when the pipeline was getting a spiff-up. I sincerely hoped that after I graduated I'd finally get to work on a project building something new instead of fixing someone else's old stuff.

Meanwhile, I lived the Left Bank dream, perfecting my French while drinking wine in St-Germain-des-Prés, where the likes of Hemingway and Jean Paul Sartre drank theirs while debating deep, philosophical ideas. Unless someone else was fronting drinks, my budget didn't cover getting whacked enough to wax too philosophical; instead, I sipped one glass of over-priced house red over a couple of hours, but hey, that's also *tres* French, *non*?

The highlight of the summer came with an invitation to attend a fellow student's wedding at the legendary George V Hotel on Bastille Day, July 14. I spent an entire week's food allowance on a secondhand gold silk Yves Saint Laurent frock that was obviously designed for someone with no boobs. It was a good thing I couldn't afford much food for the two weeks before the event because I barely squeezed into the designer's creation as it was. I sincerely hoped that no one from YSL was invited to this society "do"; they'd probably tear his creation from my bod. Just in case, I wore fancy black silk underwear.

I never knew if it was my red hair, my being a Texan—considered by the French as exotic for some reason—or the amount of leg and décolletage escaping golden silk, but the best looking guy in the room, who turned out to be one of the bridegrooms, honed in on me like a duck on a June bug.

Jean Luc d'Ormesson wove such an irresistible web of sophisticated nonchalance—after all the French invented the word, did they not?—and charm around me, I was powerless to reject. Not that I tried, mind you. I was a fish out of water, totally ignoring all the warnings I'd heard about Frenchmen when it comes to matters of the heart.

When I later asked him why he picked me over a bevy of dazzlers vying for his attention, he said it was my Texas sense of humor. I took it as a compliment at the time, but wondered later if he couldn't have at least mentioned my dress.

A few years older than I, and obviously completely at ease in such opulent surroundings, he had no problem whisking me to his suite for an after-reception party he hosted. More bubbly flowed as I yukked it up with all my new BFFs, then when we were finally alone, Jean Luc and I went for a tipsy stroll through damp Paris streets gilded with the early morning light.

I fell head over heels in love.

For all my travels during my twenty years of life, I was still pretty naive when it came to men like him. I'd never dated anyone close and was totally unprepared when after a month of hot nights in more ways than one, he dumped me.

Just flat disappeared.

While I fell hook line and sinker for his charm, I didn't realize he was more interested in the art of catch and release.

Jean Luc's unceremonious dumping of my precious self was the reason I'd visited the beach city of Gruissan before; I was trying to track him down.

By the time I made another bowl of coffee after Jenks left for Lille, another damp dawn tinged the sky. Fiddling with the crappy boat radio's dials, trying to learn more of the Paris attack, I finally found one station, but it was too scratchy to make anything out. I decided I'd go to a nearby *brasserie* later, despite Jenks's warning to stay on the boat and away from the plaza or anywhere else people might gather.

He needn't have worried, as Castelnaudary no longer bustled. The normal morning foot and car traffic was nonexistent. I could see the brasserie from the boat, but judging by the lack of the usual outdoor tables, they hadn't opened yet. No surprise there.

Oddly enough, I saw the woman from the other boat strolling down the quay alone, apparently unaware anything at all was amiss. With her head down and purse loosely hanging over her shoulder, she personified what I call a walking victim: someone wholly unaware of their surroundings.

I stepped out on deck and called out in French, "*Bonjour, madame.* Have you any news of Paris?"

She stopped dead in her tracks, frozen like the proverbial deer in the headlights. "What?" she blurted in English.

I switched to English myself. "I asked if you had more news from Paris. My radio reception is terrible, and I don't have a television."

She walked over to my boat. "What *about* Paris?"

"There was a major terrorist attack there last night."

She turned so pale I thought she might faint. "Oh, no! Rousel is in Paris."

I jumped off the boat and grabbed her arm before she hit the cobblestones. "Whoa, there. Hang on to me and let's get you inside before you conk out."

Holding her arm tightly, I steered her into my galley settee. "Sorry I startled you. Uh, I'm sure whoever Rousel is, he's fine. Want some coffee?"

"Sure. Uh, is that brandy over there?"

Brandy at dawn? I was gonna like this broad.

Chapter Twelve

After I guided Rhonda inside and poured her a bowl of brandy-laced *café au lait*, she cupped it and sipped slowly, hiccupping back tears while staring at her ominously silent cell phone on the table.

To distract her, I tried to lighten her stress. "You know, don't you, that a watched phone never rings?"

She did manage a wan smile.

"I surmise this Rousel is your boat mate? You know, I saw you two on the beach at Gruissan last week. What a coincidence we are both cruising the Canal du Midi. I've dreamed for years of taking a barge on the canal and rivers in Europe."

"You saw us in Gruissan? Isn't that just a super place? I'm sorry, I don't recall...oh, maybe I do. You were with a poodle?"

If Charles weren't such a handsome hound, I might have taken exception. "Yes, he is a fine-looking dude, that Charles. Your Rousel, by the way, ain't no slouch. No wonder you didn't pay much attention to me and Jenks, my boyfriend. Ugh, that *boyfriend* thing sounds silly at my age, huh?"

She shook her head and smiled. "Not to me. Want to hear *really* silly? Rousel is my first boyfriend since high school, and I'm pushing forty. Well, I guess that's more pitiful than silly."

I didn't want to agree, but it was, indeed, pitiful. "Some of us are late bloomers."

Rhonda snorted. "Late bloomer? I never budded."

For some reason this cracked us up, and when she laughed I could see she was actually pretty, just worn beyond her years. Jan could do wonders with this gal.

"So, you two rented a boat on the canal. Spur of the moment, or a long planned-for trip? I think—"

My phone rang. Jenks said he was in the air on the way to Lille, and I asked him about the latest from Paris. He filled me in about the stadium attack and the hits on restaurants and bars, and told me the president of France was closing the borders, and that Paris was in lock down.

Rhonda sat quietly, listening to my end of the conversation, and after Jenks and I said our *love you's* and *goodbyes*, I told her what I'd learned.

She picked up her phone and hit redial. "All I get is a beeping sound."

"My guess is the phones are jammed with people trying to talk with loved ones in Paris. But what are the odds Rousel would be in the stadium or any of those restaurants and bars during the attack? I'm sure he's just fine and can't get out on his phone."

"You're probably right, but I wish he'd call."

Her statement took me back to the weekend when DooRah told me he had to attend a family reunion in Gruissan, but he'd call me when he returned. I didn't have a cell phone in those days, but the studio apartment came with a land line. I'm embarrassed to say I sat by that phone, not even leaving the apartment, for five days. I called in sick to work and had a friend drop off food and a lot of wine. That call from Jean Luc never came and, three weeks later when my project ended, I took the train to Gruissan.

"Hetta?"

Jerked back to the present, I said, "Huh? Sorry, I was daydreaming. What did you say?"

"I asked if you wanted to have lunch with me today on my boat. I mean, since we're sort of on self-imposed house, uh, boat arrest."

"Sure, why not? I'll bring the wine."

"Good. I don't have any on board. Rousel doesn't like me to drink."

Hooboy.

She'd pulled together a large platter of cold cuts and fruit for us, and we got better acquainted while eating lunch and doing in a bottle of wine I brought.

When she told me she'd only known Rousel for three very intense weeks, warning bells went off. Been there. However, I was trying very hard not to say anything to rain on her parade. Maybe hers would be all sunshine and light, but something she said earlier ticked a box. Three weeks into the relationship and he's telling her she can't drink?

"So, where did you meet Rousel? In Gruissan?"

"Not exactly. Well, technically, I guess. My friend Rhea, who came with me to Europe for the summer, and I were playing lounge lizards on the beach at Cannes when I first spotted him coming our way. What with that beautiful hair, great tan, and a loose white shirt and pants setting it all off, he was hard to miss. Rhea and I sighed and speculated whether he was a movie star or something. He and a friend, another good-looking guy, took a table right by us, but never even gave us a glance. Not that we were surprised, you know?"

I did know, but felt it impolite to agree. "I would've figured they were gay."

She giggled. "It did cross our minds, but Rhea and I are perfectly aware we aren't exactly dude magnets. Anyway, we went back to picking out our next stop in France and agreed, after some discussion, on visiting Gruissan."

"So, is your friend Rhea still around here somewhere?"

"Oh, no. She left Gruissan a couple of days after I met Rousel. We'd both taken a leave of absence from the charter school where we teach and skipped the first half of the academic year, but she had to go back to work."

"And you stayed here. Because of meeting Rousel?"

"Well, that certainly sealed the deal. That day on the beach when we decided on going to Gruissan, I also told her I'd just about decided to stay in France at least through Christmas, because I didn't have to return now that I had a bundle of money. I lost my mother this year, and wasn't looking forward to the holidays back in that empty house."

"Oh, sorry."

"It's all right. At least now it is."

"So, how did you finally meet Rousel?"

"It was the weirdest thing. There Rhea and I were, once again sitting on the beach, this time at Gruissan, and I did a double take when Rousel walked by."

"What a coincidence." I said it sarcastically. I do not believe in coincidence, but my sarcasm went right over her head.

"I know. We were surprised at first, then stunned when he stopped, looked at us and asked, 'Haven't we met?' in that sexy accent of his. I mean, Rhea and I, well, we look like what we are: middle-aged school teachers."

While I wanted to object to that middle-aged thing, since I was a little older than Rhonda, if anyone fit the bill, it was she. "So, what happened then?"

"We spent a little time, the three of us taking in the sights, with him as a guide. Turned out he was staying in our hotel and knows all these great little restaurants in Gruissan."

Hmmm. I'd spent time on Mykonos witnessing Greek pretty boys—I dubbed them all Yanni—working flocks of summering American teachers.

After Yanni worked his charm for a couple of days, he'd escort the woman to the ferry landing, and when she got into the departure line, he'd peck her cheek, and trot over to the incoming pigeons and, like a wily fox, zero in, pluck out the weakest and neediest one, and turn on his seductive act. The chick ends up dumping a bundle on an upgraded hotel room so she and Yanni can be alone—away from her nosy friends—and wining and dining in the most expensive places in town, with maybe even a side trip or two to a couple of upscale clothing establishments for men. She gets a goodbye kiss and he gets a kickback from enterprising local business men.

Summer is short, so the Yanni's have to work their prey fast.

These thoughts inspired me to take a nosy tack. "I really liked Gruissan and want to go back one day for a longer stay. Which hotel did you stay at?"

She named the same one Jenks and I zeroed in on for the one night before we rented the beach cottage.

"That's where we stayed. Nice, huh? How did you pick it?"

She mulled a moment. "We asked a waiter in Cannes for a suggestion."

Perhaps within hearing distance of Rousel and his friend?

"Were the restaurants in Gruissan very expensive? We never ate out there."

"I don't know. Rousel insisted on paying for all of us."

Hmmm, *there's* a twist. But then again, Jean Luc never cost me a *centime*, either. Just my heart.

"So, your friend Rhea left for the States and you stayed in Gruissan."

She blushed. "Like a love-sick teenager."

"Hey, it happens to us all if we're lucky. You've definitely decided not to teach this year?"

She nodded. "I called and told them I wouldn't be returning. I had intended to stay on another year, but I'd been taking care of Mom for so many years, and when she died...well, now I have real money. When I met Rousel...."

"Carpe diem, and all that stuff. I'm glad your mother was able to leave you enough so you can make that kind of decision now," I said, but I was thinking: *the old lady is probably spinning in her grave.*

"She was a needy, stingy, manipulative woman, but she was my mother. Little did I know, after scraping by on my salary for all those years, she had a bundle in the bank. Imagine my shock when the lawyers told me she was worth several million dollars, and it was now all mine."

I almost choked on my wine. "Holy crap!"

She smiled and raised her glass, and once again I realized what Rousel probably saw in her; she had a wonderful smile and beautiful eyes hidden behind those bottle glass lenses. Oh, man, what Jan and Elizabeth Arden could do with this one.

However, a dark thought crept in. Did Rousel overhear Rhonda and her friend talking on the beach at Cannes and follow them to Gruissan? And did she and Rhea discuss her windfall within his hearing distance? Call me cynical, but...okay, just call me cynical.

Rhonda broke into my distrustful thoughts by raising her wine glass. "To Mom!" she toasted.

I clinked my glass against hers. "Indeed, to Mom."

"You got any more of that wine?"

"Is there a grapevine in France?"

Jenks called again late in the afternoon, waking me from a Merlot-induced nap. I have just *got* to learn not to drink at lunch. And keep drinking after lunch.

"Wha..."

"Hetta? Are you all right?"

"Uh, yes, I guess I fell asleep. What time is it?"

"Five."

"A.M. or P.M.?"

"It's evening. Little early for your bedtime, isn't it? What have you been up to?"

"I was visiting a sick friend."

"Huh?"

"Just kidding. I spent the afternoon with that woman on the other boat, you know, the one we saw on the beach at Gruissan? Her guy upped and left her here, as well, so we're hanging out."

"Hetta, you know I didn't want to leave you."

"Oh, sorry, I didn't mean it that way." *Oh, yes you did, Hetta.*

"Well, I'm glad you have someone to keep you company. Where'd *he* go?"

"Paris, of all places. The day before the attack. Rhonda hasn't heard from him and she's worried, but what are the odds he'd get caught up in the assaults?"

"One in twenty-five million."

"Leave it to you to know. He'll call when he can. Uh, they're starting to release the names of victims if you want to give her the link to check." He gave me the name of a website. "Some of our employees are using it…they haven't heard from relatives, either."

"What a mess. When Rhonda tries calling Rousel all she gets is a fast beeping sound."

"Things are starting to settle down, but I don't think he'll be back in Castelnaudary anytime real soon. I hear they've shut down the train system in order to catch the bad guys still on the loose. My guess is most of them are already dead by suicide, but the ones who do the planning? They're holing up, plotting a new attack."

"How about Lille? Would that be a target?"

"The whole country is on high alert, so we've beefed up our perimeter."

"Perimeter? I love it when you talk military, Sailor."

He chuckled, then sighed. "Hetta, I may be here longer than I thought. The State Department has notified American companies doing business in Europe to take extreme care. No one knows yet how extensive these attacks might get. I'm glad you're in the south. According to my sources, you should be safe, but don't go hanging out in bars, okay?"

"*Moi*? Hang in bars?"

"Yes, *toi*. I don't want to have to worry about you. Just stay close to the boat, and keep your head down."

"Aye, aye, *mon capitaine*!"

He laughed. "You know what I mean."

"Okay, I really didn't want to tell you this, but if it'll make you feel better, I have my .380 on board."

Silence.

"Did you hear me?"

"Oh, I heard you, all right. I'm just trying to figure out how and why that happened."

Expecting to get chewed out, I told him about picking up the suitcase from his apartment and not realizing until I was in the air that the gun was packed inside. I left out the part about the Valium.

He absorbed this news and surprised me with a loud snort. "Well, of course. I mean, doesn't everyone pack a pistol in their boot?"

"Maybe just us Texans?"

"I should be pissed off, but the truth is I'll rest a little easier knowing you have heat on board. Just please, Red, try not to start World War Three down there, okay?"

Chapter Thirteen

After my talk with Jenks, I had the whole night in front of me and a two-hour nap behind me. With no television and no desire for another drop of wine or bite of food, I turned to my inner thoughts. This is rarely a good thing.

Okay, so here I was in the South of France, on a boat, parked at one of the coolest cities in France, but with little to do. With Jenks gone, I was left to my own doings and historically, when left on my own with no purpose, I invent one.

But first, I had to send a bunch of emails letting everyone know I was okay, as was Jenks. I also posted the same info on Facebook. I wanted to call my mother, but after I talked with Jenks, I couldn't get a signal again. I opened a bottle of water and turned on the computer to surf the Net for news of Paris and the rest of the world, but a photo of the Eiffel Tower suddenly took me on a mental trip back in time, to that Paris fling with Jean Luc d'Ormesson years before.

Curiosity being my strong suit, I Googled the family name, d'Ormesson—I figured Jean Luc DooRah wouldn't get me anywhere—not really expecting to find much, but I was so wrong. Not only did I find Jean Luc, I landed on his family tree going back to the early fourteen hundreds. They even had a family coat of arms, with a dark blue background and three tiger lilies. Now head of his father's world-famous architectural firm, DooRah was all over the place. Matter of fact, at least five pages worth of hits.

I started at the top and found a recent photo of Jean Luc looking even more debonair with the passing years—how unfair is that?—and his bio said he was married with three children.

Moving down the line, I hit a bombshell: He and said wife were married *one week* after he so cavalierly shattered my soul!

Stunned, I traded my glass of water for wine, but even a whopping gulp did little to assuage my rising fury. I literally saw red, and it wasn't wine.

This seeing red is not good and has caused me to do great damage to others in the past.

Since it was so early in the evening, I took a forbidden walk into town in an effort to settle my nerves. I needed someone to vent to, but it was certainly not going to be Jenks, and Rhonda, quite likely headed for a similar disaster in her own life, was not the best sounding board.

I found a park bench and got a dial tone, much to my surprise. Jan answered immediately.

"Hetta! I've been trying to reach you. Got your email and called your mom. Uh, are you all right?"

"That sonofabitch was planning his wedding while screwing my brains out!"

"What? Jenks got married?"

"No, DooRah. Oh, forget it."

"Who? Are you drunk?"

"Not yet, but I think I'll go find a friendly bistro and get that way."

"Calm down and let's start over. Hello, Hetta, where are you?"

"On the boat on the Canal du Midi. Where are you? And what's that noise?"

"What noise?"

"Are you running a generator?"

"Oh, *that* noise. Yeah, that must be it. Wanna talk to your dog?"

"Put him on."

I heard a rustling as she put the phone to Po Thang's ear. "Hi, baby. How's my furry, wurry, widdle baby doggie?"

"Whine."

"I miss you so much."

"Woof."

"Okay, put your Auntie Jan back on."

"Woof!"

That last woof was an eardrum banger. "Ouch! Jan, you back?"

"Yes. Now what in holy hell has you throwing such a tele-tantrum?"

"Nothing, really. Old history. I'll tell you all about it one of these days. I guess I'm in a snit at getting left here by myself, not that it's Jenks's fault. Damned terrorists."

"Don't go after ISIS on your own, okay?" she teased. "Wait for me."

"Ha. Thanks for the laugh. I really miss you guys."

"Us too."

After I hung up, I felt much better. Why get in a dither over something that happened twenty years ago?

Talking with Po Thang and laughing with Jan reminded me of how lucky I was to have my life, and it took the edge off my anger. Temporarily, that is.

Back on the boat, though, I was soon on my computer, irresistibly drawn to delving further into Jean Luc's life *apres* Hetta.

Moth to the flame.

Eyes drawn to a freeway pileup.

And all of those other clichés for being dragged toward something certain to derail me.

Cyber-delving further into Jean Luc's life, I found those posed wedding shots were by professional photogs and staged after the wedding press releases. Captioned, "Love on the Med," they were shot on the beaches of Gruissan. Most were of the bride, radiant and stunningly beautiful, although I searched for moles or crooked teeth in the grainy newspaper photos. And then the two of them, the rat dashing in full morning suit gear complete with top hat. Other shots had them flanked by an entourage of attendants and family.

I recognized one of the men. I'd met him in a bistro Jean Luc took me to one night. After Jean Luc disappeared, I'd gone back to that dive and actually found DooRah's friend. His buddy denied knowing anything about Jean Luc's whereabouts, the lying sack of crap. Here he was, barely a week later, smiling for the camera at the wedding. My potential victim list grew by one.

Another article took up half a page in the society section of *Paris Match*, with gaga wording about "the wedding of the year." Pictures galore showed Jean Luc DooRah fawning over his tall, willowy bride, who was draped in a jillion miles of designer silk, lace and what I hoped were fake diamonds. And speaking of that, one showed her perfectly manicured finger barely able to hold up a rock the size of Gibraltar.

Part of my career over the years has involved research, and now I put all those skills to the bad. Deeper and deeper I dug, torturing myself with Luc's perfect life, wife, kids, achievements, and then, poof, there was nothing for the past five years.

This was very upsetting. If he was dead, I wasn't going to have the pleasure of killing him.

Then I found him on Facebook.

La vengeance est un plat qui se mange froid.

Revenge is a dish best eaten cold.

Rhonda banged on the hull around ten the next morning, waking me from the huddle I'd collapsed into on the narrow settee by my computer.

I slid the door open and saw she had a big smile on her face as she waggled her phone at me. "Rousel called! He's fine, but has to stay in Paris for a few more days. I guess the attacks affected the family business."

"Probably a family *wedding*," I grumped under my breath.

"Huh?"

"Never mind. Want to go for a walk? I need major caffeine to clear the cobwebs."

"You do look a little…fuzzy. I'll go get a sweater and we'll find a nice *brasserie*."

I brushed my teeth, ran a comb through my frightful hair, pulled on a lightweight jacket, stuffed some money in one pocket and started to leave, then turned back and slipped my pistol into the other. I noticed as I stepped onto the quay that a lot more people were going about their daily business again, so I didn't feel guilty ignoring Jenks's warning to stay on board.

Besides, I was packing, because a gal just cannot be too careful.

Stiff from hunching over my laptop in that ridiculous snoop session into the wee hours researching every aspect of Luc's life, I was pissed off at myself for engaging in such immature doings. What am I, anyhow, some kind of psychopath?

"Don't answer that, you might be called as witnesses," I said to Siegfried and Odette, those panhandling swans who'd paddled up looking for a handout.

An avid reader of mysteries, I imagined a scenario where the object of my murderous obsession was actually bumped off, and the police somehow tracked *me* down via my Internet searches into Jean Luc's website and Facebook page. The French prosecutor, declaring with a snippy, obviously anti-American sneer, "I put it to the jury,"—I guess they use juries?—"Hell hath no fury like a woman scorned. And this woman," (pointing an indignant, bony finger at me) "had twenty years, *TWENTY YEARS!* to plot her revenge." He used the French version, *revanche,* and followed it with a dramatic, *"J'accuse!"*

Rhonda walked up just in time to save me from an imaginary trudge to the guillotine. She reminded me we'd planned a foray into town anyway, for her to pick up a Wi-Fi hotspot like the one I'd rented so she'd have Internet on her boat. Up until now she'd relied on Internet cafés, but when I told her about the lack of those on the canal heading east towards Toulouse, we contacted

Hippocket Wi-Fi and had one sent overnight to a Castelnaudary pickup point.

As we ate a leisurely lunch at a café near the square, we both kept our cell phones on the table in case our men called, and I patted my gun every so often in anticipation of spotting a wild-eyed terrorist. Since neither called nor jumped out of the bushes, we drowned our disappointment with an extra carafe of excellent house wine.

After weaving a mite and giggling our way back to the quay, we stopped short when we saw a shiny, black. stretch limo at the curb and a fairly large group of people gathered near our boats. I picked up the pace, unrealistically hoping Jenks was back.

When we broke through the crowd though, I let out a loud whoop and told Rhonda, "Now we're gonna have some fun!"

Perched fetchingly on my deck, long limbs crossed to show lots of leg through a split in her pencil skirt, beret atop coiffed blonde hair, sat Jan. Wearing a tight fitting, low cut top in typical French stripes and a red cravat tied around her swan-like neck, she had her arm around Po Thang, who also wore French stripes, red cravat, and a beret with ear holes.

Thinking her someone famous, a little girl was asking Jan for her autograph.

My whoop caught Po Thang's attention and he lunged, almost yanking Jan butt-first onto the quay. He broke loose from her hold and charged us, but suddenly remembered his manners and stopped short of a full-on doggie tackle. I fell to my knees and burrowed my face in his neck fur—which smelled suspiciously of Chanel No. 5—and bawled like a baby while he whined and wiggled.

Jan, who'd regained her composure and tugged her skirt down—a disappointment to many of the men in the crowd, judging by their complaintive moans—yelled, "When you two get over that love fest, Hetta, we gotta get to figgerin' how to get a bigger boat." She waved her arms around, pointing to at least six large suitcases stacked all over the decks. "Just what the heck kinda cruise is this anyhow?"

As she stepped off the boat, aided by eager hands, I pushed Po Thang away and rushed to hug her. "How on earth? How did you…oh, hell, who cares? You can explain later. I've never been so glad to see two living beings in my entire life."

Po Thang had managed to insert himself between us, taking turns to woof at her, then me, frustrated at not being the center of attention. I was introducing Rhonda to Jan and swiping tears from my cheeks when my blurry peripheral vision picked up two blobs of white.

"Ohhhh, noooo," I hollered, lunging for Po Thang's collar but pulling back only a handful of red silk cravat. Successfully evading my second attempt to tackle him, he executed a perfect swan dive into the canal, landing not two feet from Siegfried and Odette. He paddled toward them to play. They hissed, stretched their necks, and attacked.

Po Thang, suddenly realizing that maybe not everything in the water is friendly, reversed and splashed towards us as fast as his dog paddle allowed, but the powerful Siegfried overtook him, launched his full weight onto Po Thang's head, and pushed him under. Balancing himself with his wings, it became obvious the big male fully intended to drown my dog.

Heart pounding, I was shedding my sweater and shoes, preparing to jump into the fray, when Jan reminded me I can't swim worth a damn in fresh water. Calling the canal's water "fresh" was a stretch, but, luckily, a whistle-blowing policeman arrived, causing Siegfried to swim away. Po Thang popped to the surface, whining and yipping pitifully, and headed for the quay faster than I'd ever seen him swim. The swans weren't really giving chase, just making a lot of threatening noise by hissing, honking, and flapping their huge wings.

My poor pup reached the quay's edge, where several by-standers helped us haul him out by his soggy fur. He was shaking, howling in fear, and had a couple of bleeding beak bites on one ear.

And he now smelled like *Canal* No. 5.

Chapter Fourteen

Jan broke out a couple of my best bottles of wine and offered glasses to those who helped rescue Po Thang from the canal, and those dastardly swans.

As I rinsed him down with a water hose and toweled him off, the swans retreated, so Po Thang's bluster was sufficiently recovered for him to scowl and growl at his foe, but he made no attempt to get even.

"I know how you feel, baby," I cooed. "They picked on you, the mean old bullies, and you just wanted to play. Just keep in mind, they're French, However, in their defense, you scared them." Little by little, his quivering subsided and he seemed to relax, but just in case he lost his little doggie mind and set out to avenge his dissed honor, I'd buckled him into his float jacket—thankfully, Jan remembered to bring it—and I had a firm grip on his leash. After the wine, and therefore our crowd, disappeared, we moved Po Thang into the boat's miniscule shower/toilet area, where I gave him a hot water shampoo to remove the canal stink.

While Po Thang napped in the warm late afternoon sun, Jan and I finally grabbed a glass of wine for ourselves and sat on deck with him. Clinking glasses with her, I asked, "Okay, now you can tell me how in the holy hell you two got here so fast?"

"For one thing, when you called last night we were already in the air, heading this way. I would've gotten here sooner, but we had to go shopping in Toulouse. We were whisked out of Mexico with barely the clothes on our backs."

"Aha. But what I really want to know is, how the heck you got to France, and why."

"Ya want the good news or the bad news?"

"Hit me with the bad."

"Okay, Jenks is on the way to Dubai, but he couldn't tell you on the phone or in an email. Security stuff."

"Well, crap. When's he coming back?"

"Dunno, but he and the Trob decided you needed a keeper, since you *are* here on a semi-official work permit and could do great harm to Baxter Brothers' reputation if left to your own designs. So, as luck would have it, they sent me!"

"That shows you how much they know. What's the good news?"

She slapped my arm. "Very funny. Anyhow, Jenks said we could get a bigger boat, what with the three of us on board this two-person tub, so that's what we gotta do, and fast, by the looks of it."

"Okay, so we upgrade. Then what?"

"Whatever we want, I guess." She surveyed the picturesque waterfront. "Looks pretty all right here, if you ask me. Maybe once we get the new boat we'll just come back. But Jenks says we gotta go to where the car is stored to get that boat."

"Argens. That's where the Fiat's stashed."

"How far away is it?"

I went inside and pulled out a spread sheet I'd made of the trip Jenks and I planned from Castelnaudary to Argens. Now that I knew the ropes, I'd plotted daily distances and number of locks we were comfortable with. I ran my finger down the list and threw numbers at Jan. She's good at adding in her head, so as soon as I gave her the last number she said, "That's only fifty miles. Piece of cake."

"There's a word the French get touchy about."

"Oh, yeah, the Marie Antoinette thing?"

"She never said it."

"Really? Anyhow, fifty miles isn't very far."

"Divide by five."

"Ten."

"That's ten hours actual running time, not accounting for waits at the locks. Guess how many locks."

"Uh, a bunch?"

"Forty-eight."

"That sounds like a lotta work."

"You have no idea. However, by my calculation, it is doable in two really exhausting days. *If* we don't have long waits while other boats clear the locks."

"So it looks like we're stuck with *this* boat for two more nights?"

"I guess we could ditch the boat altogether and go on a road trip, but then we'd need a bigger car. That Fiat 500 barely holds my two suitcases in the backseat."

"Nah, I want to do the canal."

"Good choice. If we leave early tomorrow, we'll get you a room in Carcassonne tomorrow night. That's only twenty-three miles and twenty-five locks away."

"Only?"

"Think of all the free exercise, Chica."

I sipped my wine, contemplated the situation, then broke into an overly dramatic imitation of Edith Piaf's "La Vie on Rose." Several passersby smiled and nodded approval. I raised my glass to Jan. "Here's to being stuck in the South of France with a ticket to ride, *mon ami*."

Jan raised hers in return. "*Vive la France*!"

Rhonda walked up to the boat as Jan and I were giggling about something and smiled. "You two are having way too much fun."

"Hey, come aboard. Want some wine?"

"*Mais oui*, although I had to take a quick nap to get over the lunch wine and all the excitement." She gave Po Thang a sympathetic pat, but he merely grunted in his sleep. "I had no idea swans could be so vicious."

Jan and I chorused, "They're *French*."

She laughed.

"They were, after all, only defending their territory. Po Thang has a habit of taking up with other species whether they want a new buddy or not. His last non-canine BFF was a dolphin, but she was friendly. He got quite an education in the unpredictability of the French today. Speaking of, have you heard from Rousel?"

She lost her smile. "Yes. Looks like he'll be away at least five more days. Thank goodness you three are here. I don't know what I'd do without you."

Jan and I exchanged a look. We were planning an early morning departure. "Wanna go on a boat ride?" I asked. I told her our plan to go as far as Carcassonne the next day and get Jan a hotel room, then on to Argens to pick up the bigger boat. She looked crestfallen.

"You can go with us, Rhonda. I'll spring for a room for you, as well. We can use the help with the lines."

"Oh, I would love to go with you, but I promised Rousel I'd stay here."

Jan cocked her head. "Why? He ain't here, *is* he?"

"Well, no, but he doesn't like me, er, not being where he tells me to be. He'll call to check."

I mentally checked another warning sign on my vast list of rat habits, and Jan's eyes widened. "Uh, hello? Cell phone? How the hell will he know *where* you are?"

"But what if he returns unexpectedly?"

Jan rolled her eyes and I knew she was going to say something rude, like, *How old are you, anyhow*? So I interrupted.

"I've got an idea. You take the boat ride with us tomorrow and you can drive our car back here for us the next day. You'll only be gone one night, and that way we'll have wheels right here in Castelnaudary if we want to use them."

Rhonda looked a little doubtful until I added, "You'll be back by late afternoon. Just park our car somewhere nearby and if by some chance Rousel's shown up, tell him you went for a walk. There is no way he'll be any wiser. When you get a chance, just give the Harbor Master the keys."

She eyed us. "You two are good at this."

Jan toasted her. "Oh, you have no idea!"

Chapter Fifteen

Back in the day, when Thomas Jefferson was the American ambassador to France, he'd visited the Canal du Midi and checked out *Les Ecluses St. Roch à Castelnaudary* because they were an engineering doozy for all time.

The total drop is over thirty feet, meaning we had to tie up, feed the lines out as we descended, untie, go into the next lock and do the whole thing over again, four times for this quadruple lot. At least down-locking is easier than up-locking, and we had two people on board to handle the lines, unlike when Jenks and I had to do it on our own.

I didn't tell Rhonda and Jan that I was more than a little concerned about handling the boat through those locks, but for me and Jan, this was not our first rodeo. We'd been boating long enough to handle almost anything and concluded it was just like docking *Raymond Johnson,* albeit without the aid of twin screws. Or reliable steering.

We'd walked over to the locks the day before our departure, joining the usual crowd of rubberneckers.

After watching others' really crappy boating skills, I was feeling more confident, figuring we sure as heck couldn't do much worse. One guy's crew tied his lines—tying up instead of just looping is a huge no-no—tightly to the bollards, so when the water dropped out from under him, his boat was left hanging by the lines, almost dumping his crew overboard until they figured out they had to let go. With a mighty splash that rocked all the other boats in the lock, the barge righted itself, no thanks to the inexperienced crew.

I used this snafu to emphasize to Jan and Rhonda that they never tie up to anything while in the locks, but instead to loop and hold so they could easily take in and let out lines around the bollards. I didn't mention to my own inexperienced crew that I noticed the lockkeeper here was much too busy herding boats to be the helpful, standing-by-the-side-of-the-lock *eclusiers* Jenks and I met along the canal; this guy had his hands full.

We had left the dock early so we'd be first in line when the locks opened. No boats, dogs, or swans were harmed during our departure, although Po Thang, from the safety of the highest deck, set up a half-hearted ruckus as we passed his feathered attackers.

By my estimate, if we were first-in/first-out of the locks, we had less chance of ramming someone.

When the gates opened at nine on the dot, we smartly cruised into the lock and Jan, who always has her own way of doing things, whirled a looped line over her head, let it fly with a, "Yee-Haw," and lassoed the first bollard from ten feet out.

"I gotcha, Hetta," she hollered as she reeled us forward, leaving just the right amount of slack, "put 'er in reverse."

I gave it full left rudder, goosed the throttle, and the aft cozied up to the dock so Rhonda could step off and loop her end.

We'd nailed it like we knew what we were doing, and Jan's rope trick garnered clapping and cheering from on-lookers. One declared, "*Coup d'èclat!*" A great feat.

"Dang, we're good," Jan bragged, as we watched other boats entering the lock bang into gates, and bounce off stone walls and each other, all the while yelling at feckless line-handlers (usually female) struggling to overcome the "captain's" (always male) lack of skill.

Our adoring public gathered by the boat and wanted to know how we came to be an all-American, all-female crew in France, then followed us from lock to lock. They videoed Jan's goat-roping skills and taunted disgruntled "captains" who shot us dirty looks. Some of the bicyclists followed us several miles to the next set of locks.

It seemed they weren't the only ones in pursuit. When Po Thang suddenly started raising all Billy hell, I was glad we'd secured him to the rails if he was going to act like a dog.

Jan stuck her head through the door to the steering station and asked, "Say, Hetta, can swans fly?"

"I dunno. Maybe. Why?"

"Cuz we have bogies on our tail."

I poked my head out the door and saw what looked like the swan thugs from Castelnaudary paddling behind us. We were doing a little over six kilometers an hour—four mph—and they were matching our speed. "Wow, look at 'em go. Who knew they could swim that fast?"

Rhonda was standing on deck next to me. "Not me. And look at those markings on that one's beak. That's Odette for sure."

"Quick, someone Google the speed of a swimming swan. I'll bet they can't do eight kilometers an hour." I edged the throttle forward to the max speed allowed on the canal. "Eat our wake, you bullies."

Not.

Nine hours later, when we pulled into Carcassonne for the night, they were still with us. When they fell behind, they scmi-flew to catch up. They didn't even have to go airborne, they just used their wings to walk on water. When we hit a lock, they waddle-walked to the other side.

And FYI, the buggers can swim up to five miles an hour in calm water.

We arrived at Carcassonne dog-tired after our unrelenting push to get through all twenty-five locks before the last one closed for the night. Luckily we found a tie up with amenities near the harbor master's office, and he recommended a hotel a few blocks away. Rhonda and Jan went to find a room while I took Po Thang for a walk.

Finding a nearby *boulangerie*, I scored a baguette for dinner and noticed they opened early the next morning, so we'd be able to buy fresh bread before leaving for Argens.

Back on the boat, I heated up soup, poured a glass of much-needed Merlot, and was eating when I heard a raucous squeal of metal on metal, the thunder of clack on track, and the growl of a locomotive. Multiple tracks ran way too close to the canal and I soon longed for those nights spent tied to a peaceful, grassy bank.

I dug out the earplugs.

At seven the next morning, Jan and Rhonda returned, much to the delight of Po Thang. Even the swans wagged their tails.

"Coffee's ready. You guys had breakfast? I have eggs for an omelet, and if you want fresh bread, there's a *boulangerie* right over there." I pointed. "Or, I can make French toast with last night's baguette."

"Ooh, French toast sounds wonderful. What can I do?" Rhonda asked.

"Get out the syrup, butter, and cut thin slices of bread."

"Will do." She looked around the galley. "Uh, where's the bread?"

"It's...gone. And no, I did not eat the whole thing last night," I said, before Jan accused me of gluttony.

Jan, Rhonda, and I glared at Po Thang, who assumed a hangdawg stance.

Jan took Po Thang with her to get another baguette and *pain au chocolat* for all of us, as we had to get going to be first in line at the locks and by now cooking breakfast was out. It was going to be another hard day on the canal, but at least by bedtime Jan and I would be settled into a much more spacious boat, and Rhonda could sleep in her own bunk back in Castelnaudary.

Once again, we were exhausted when we reached Argens, but we'd successfully covered twenty-eight miles and another twenty-three locks that day.

Rhonda was as tired as we were but so freaked out that Rousel might return unannounced that she was reluctant to stay the night.

"He's in Paris for cryin' out loud. You just talked to him," Jan said, her tone of voice clear she was losing patience with Rhonda's lovesick, bordering-on-panicky, behavior.

Rhonda, too concerned to pick up on Jan's chagrin, whined, "But what if he's doing something like I am? He said he was in Paris, but how would I really know? What if he's decided to surprise me and shows up at the boat?"

"Call him back and ask for a selfie with the Eiffel Tower in the background?" I suggested. Rhonda was trying my patience as well.

Rhonda looked sheepish. "Well, he *could* be planning a surprise."

"Oh, I think you're in for a surprise, all right," Jan muttered.

I gave her a throat-cut sign to cool her jets. "Look, Rhonda, if you're so concerned, go ahead and take the car tonight. You'll be back in Castelnaudary in less than an hour."

"Oh, thank you. Yes, I think I will. I won't be much fun if I stay here and fret, anyway."

Jan mumbled something under her breath that I read as, *Who said you were* ever *any fun?* Or some such.

I gave Rhonda the keys to the Fiat, then walked her to the office to let them know I was springing my car from the storage lot. Po Thang trotted along behind us, as we now pretty much trusted him not to jump into the canal after his swans or anything else. My two suitcases took up the entire backseat of the tiny car, so she threw her knapsack into the trunk, and we stuffed what we could of Jan's smaller bags where we could.

The Cinquecento is fairly simple to operate, but I gave Rhonda a quick overview of where everything was, like the headlight switch in case she got caught in traffic and arrived after dark. She had little trouble mastering the quick clutch because, luckily, her mom's old car had a stick shift, and she was soon on her way.

When Po Thang and I returned to our new tri-cabin boat, Jan had stored the things we dumped from the suitcases that would fit into the car, set us up with coffee makings, wine, and toiletries, and made the beds to get us through until morning.

"Thanks, Auntie Jan."

"I cannot tell you how happy I am that that pathetic creature left before I was forced to put her out of her misery."

"Oh, come on, Jan, a little empathy here. We've dragged her way out of her comfort level. She's in love, probably for the first time in her life, and desperate not to do anything to mess it up. Trust me, I've been there."

"Ha, you sure got over the habit of *not* messing up. Yes, I know you fell ass over teakettle, whatever that means, for a couple of heels, but lemme ask you this; if one of them ever told you you couldn't do something, like drink alcohol, what would you have done?"

"I'd'a gotten drunk and told them to go you-know-what themselves."

"See? Therein lies the difference."

"Yabbut, I know the warning signs now on how not to fall for them in the first place. Saw a check list somewhere. I even went to the website and downloaded it, lest I ever fall victim to abuse again."

"Abuse? You? You gotta be kidding me."

"That's what I thought, but then I took a test they offered online, and oddly enough, the two rats who dumped me never ticked a single box, but I remember that list. This Rousel has already waved the red flag with two of them. Lemme bring it up and you can see for yourself."

I'd bookmarked the page and read the warning signs aloud as she opened a bottle of wine for us. She handed me a glass. "Yep, two big ones already. Forbids her to drink, and wants her where he wants her when he wants her there."

"I guess the good news is, she's defied both edicts, but only because he's gone, and she's fallen in with a bad crowd."

We clinked glasses, toasting ourselves. "She does need to grow a pair. By the way, the insurance on that rental only covers me and Jenks as the drivers, so I swear, if she wrecks it because she falls asleep at the wheel I'm gonna say she stole it."

"How very empathetic of you."

I shot her the finger. "Want to get the rest of our stuff transferred from *Villepinte* before I collapse in a heap?"

"Nah, I got us what we need for now. You said there's a good restaurant right next door, so let's go find it and finish hauling stuff over here in the morning. And speaking of morning, are we going back at the same pace that got us here? That's gonna be a bear with only two of us on board."

"Why should we? We got nuthin' but time. We'll leave sometime tomorrow and break this return voyage up into three days or even more. That sound okay?"

"Absotively. Let us go out in search of fine cuisine, even finer wine, and lots of both. I'm sick of sandwiches."

The quayside café at Argens served up the promised great food, wine and dessert, and dogs were welcome. At least French dogs. I'm not sure how they felt about the likes of Po Thang's eye-begging everyone in the place. I tied him to my chair lest he hoover plates from unsuspecting diners, who would probably chalk up his lack of manners to being American.

"Ya know, Hetta," Jan said when we were happily entrenched back in our new digs and enjoying a final glass of wine before crashing, "that Rhonda? She was telling me her story while we were underway. I'm dead sure she's destined to get taken for a ride. If not Rousel, then someone else, but my money's on Rousel."

I nodded. "Tell me about it. She's spent her entire adult life taking care of Mom, then mom dies, she inherits a bunch of money, and now she's in the South of France with a guy she hardly knows, but who is already controlling her."

"Sounds like you in Paris a long time ago. Without the dead mom and a bunch of cash."

I laughed. "But I was young and stupid and had little to lose. She, on the other hand, does."

"Yeah, maybe we should do her a favor and steal her money before someone else does."

Our new boat, even though only a few feet longer, boasted two master cabins with our own showers and an aft cockpit with seating for two. No bow thruster, but, as I learned during our shakedown the next morning with an instructor, much easier to handle.

Now that Jan and I were self-proclaimed canal cruising experts, our reverse trip to Castelnaudary was much more relaxed. We broke it up into a three-nighter, and Jan's unorthodox locking techniques made life easier on both of us. *Sauzens,* as our boat was named, actually went where I aimed it and as long as I was even close to my target, Jan pulled me in like a rodeo pro. Once again, she attracted admirers in the *eclusiers* and gawkers alike. The fact that we had two swans dogging our dawg added to our élan.

I called Rhonda each night, letting her know of our progress. She was down in the dumps; Rousel, true to his word, had failed to pop out of a cake to surprise her, so she was stuck in Castelnaudry by herself and was eagerly awaiting our return.

She was standing on the quay when we arrived, motioning us into an empty space two boats down and behind her this time.

Taking a line from Jan, Rhonda was practically jumping up and down with glee. I thought all this joy was for our return, but then she announced, swallowing air in her excitement, gasping between sentences, "Guess what? Rousel is coming back later tonight! We're gonna cruise the canal to as far as we can toward Toulouse, then," and here I was afraid she'd pass out from oxygen deprivation, "we're taking the train to Paris!"

"Calm down, girl," Jan drawled, "before you bust a gut."

"I can't. You haven't heard the best part. He's flying *home* with me! He already bought our tickets!" Her cheeks were bright red and those blue eyes popped. I could imagine her as a child, before her crappy life with Mom stole her youth.

"Gee, that's...amazing," was all I managed to say. I was in no way going to steal her moment by saying something like, "Rousel's probably a gigolo who will break your heart and steal your money."

I'm an incurable romantic that way.

She took a deep breath. "Sorry, it's just that I never *dreamed* someone like him…something like *this*, would ever happen to me." She stepped on deck and hugged Po Thang who was doing his tail-bashing welcome of an old friend.

I heard Jan hiss, "Dream, my rear. More like a nightmare," under her breath.

We secured the boat, checked in with the Harbor Master, hooked up to power and water, then settled on deck for a glass of wine. I offered Rhonda one, but she held her palm out in a stop sign. "I'd love one, but Rousel will be here in a few hours and he'll smell alcohol on me."

Jan, standing behind her, did the mock finger down the throat *gag me* thing, then asked, "So this dreamboat of yours wants you *where* he wants you, *when* he wants you, and doesn't *let* you drink?" My best friend has never been one for subtlety.

Rhonda, oblivious to the scorn in Jan's tone, gushed, "Isn't having someone care for you so much just wonderful?"

"Oh, for cryin'—"

I cut Jan off before *she* busted a gut. "Yes, Rhonda, I'm sure it is. Take a load off—" I patted the deck next to me, which Po Thang decided was meant for him. Shoving my dog out of the way, I repeated my invite for Rhonda to sit. "Okay, tell us details. This is quite a dramatic twist for such a new relationship. He's going home with you? Wow, that's some move. Maybe he has business in the States and he worked you into his schedule?"

"Oh, no. He arranged it as a surprise. Well, I should have known something was up when he left, because he took my plane tickets, credit card and passport. He said it was to get me a refund so I could stay longer, but he really just wanted to make arrangements for us to travel together."

Jan's eyebrows threatened to climb into her hairline. "Whoa, you gave someone you hardly know your passport *and* credit card?"

I was thinking the same thing. Maybe Rousel just wanted to make sure she didn't go anywhere until he got back. I wondered if she'd checked her credit card balance recently.

Rhonda frowned. "Yeah, I guess that's not too smart, huh? Handing over my passport like that?"

Jan opened her mouth, but for once was so incredulous she was at a loss for words.

Not me, of course. "Um, no, it's really not. Never let your passport out of your sight. That's my hard and fast rule."

"Okay, lesson learned."

Jan had recovered enough to ask, "What exactly does Rousel do for a living? I know you said he's part of a family business, but what kind of bidness?"

"I'm not sure. Something with import and export."

Jan rolled her eyes. The import/export business is a well known euphemism for drug smuggling in most of the world. I pinched my lips in our *let it go* signal, but she can be a mite on the stubborn side. "Hey, Hetta, wasn't that French dude who broke your heart all those years back in the so-called import bidness?"

"Thanks for the memory. That was eons ago."

"Bad memory, I'd say. You came home from Europe in a body bag over that jerk. He freakin' broke your little heart and you mooned for years."

"Did not."

"Did too. Anyhow, he was an alleged importer, right?"

"No," I said. I could see where Jan was going with this, trying to give Rhonda a warning based on my own stupidity, but, for some reason I felt like arguing with her. "FYI, Jean Luc is an architect and took over his father's firm a few years back. The most prestigious in France, as a matter of fact." *Crap, why am I defending that rat, anyhow?*

Jan squinted one eye. "Ah, the infamous DooRah suddenly has a name. Jean Luc, is it? And you say that, after treating you like a piece of ca-ca, he went on to better things? You know this *how*?"

Uh-oh. Nailed for a cyber-stalker.

Chapter Sixteen

After dinner, Rhonda left to await her prince charmless, and Jan zeroed in on me.

"You got some 'splainin' to do, Chica. Like how you know what happened to this Jean Luc after all these years. You told me he just disappeared and you never heard from him or about him again. One might be inclined to ask you how you came to have this new info. Oh, wait, I taught you everything you know about running people to ground, and it sounds like you've done so, but why in Heaven's name would you do this to yourself? Have you gone round the bend?"

"I was lonely after Jenks took off and curiosity got to me. Okay, and a few memories. First off, Jenks and I stayed at the George V, the scene of the crime so to speak, and then we went to Gruissan."

"Which is where?"

"Just southwest of here, on the Mediterranean. Didn't have the Internet back when Jean Luc disappeared, and I had no way of knowing why he never came back to Paris. And you're right, I was devastated. I was such a damned idiot I followed him to where he said he was going,

Gruissan, but again, once there I still had no way of tracking him down."

"He didn't *want* to get tracked down, you bimbo."

I downed my wine and poured another glass to stem the tears of stupid threatening my eyes. Jan reached over and patted my hand. "Sorry. You were so young, and I'm just so pissed with this SOB who hurt you like that."

"I was a bonehead."

"So, getting back to what you've been up to on that computer, now you're still a bonehead, just an older one? Just kidding."

I took a deep breath. "I never really told you the details about Paris, only that I'd fallen hard for someone who dumped me and broke my heart."

"You whined ad nauseam, but I thought you'd let it go long ago. You probably told me his real name, but we haven't talked about him in ages."

I nodded. "Jean Luc d'Ormesson. I named him DooRah with good reason."

"Sounds appropriate."

"Well, I was sort of surfing the net and found him."

She tilted her head and drawled, with a good deal of irony lacing her words, "Yeah, right. You were *casually* searching the net and up he popped?"

"Smarty pants."

"So, pray tell, why on earth were you looking him up now, after all these years?"

"I told you, I was bored and lonely and being back in France resurrected memories."

"I'll give you that. But what reasonable purpose can be gained by checking up on this guy *now*? Why?"

"Because I could. Remember, DooRah simply disappeared from my life and I pined for months, seriously hurt and brokenhearted, even fearing he was dead. As it turns out he got married in a huge society bash *one week* after he walked out of my life."

Her mouth fell open. "The bastard."

"My thoughts exactly. The entire month he lived with me, he said he was attending classes, or working at his father's office every day, and all that time he was planning his wedding and getting fitted for a morning coat."

"A morning coat?" she said with mock indignity. "That does it, let's kill him."

This made me laugh at myself. "It has crossed my mind."

"I'm in. I'll get more wine, and then I want a look at this world-class dirtbag."

While Jan fetched the wine, I brought up the folder on my laptop entitled: Jean Luc DooRah. Jan chided me for even having such a folder, but jumped into my sordid past with great glee. Reading over the file, looking at downloaded photos and newspaper articles, she whistled. "You're right, Hetta, the dude was, and by the way, still is, a looker. Hells bells, I'd'a jumped his bones, too. Says here the wife's some kind of debutante…oh, jeez, and a *model* for Christian Dior? Now that was some kinda serious competition."

"Thank you for your undying support, Miz Jan. I wasn't *that* ugly!"

"That's not what I meant."

"I know, but it does sting, even now. But I'm madder than sad."

"I hope to shout you are. Says here she was off on a shoot for the time he was boinking you. You were his pre-marriage fling. His bachelor party. His—"

I pointed my finger at her, our signal for that's enough.

She stopped talking, but then an evil grin followed. "Ya know, I think this guy needs some kinda comeuppance. He *used* you."

"I doubt he even remembers me."

"Well then, maybe we need to change that. Wanna track him down and de-ball him? We got nothin' else to do."

Of course we didn't.

Who else but Jan and I would use an all-expenses paid trip to the South of France to zero in on a couple of guys we perceived as rats?

No one, that's who.

The phone rang at ten that night and I hoped it was Jenks, but I'd been warned he might not be able to call. What was he doing that was so secretive? Had to be something to do with the Paris attacks. I sooo wanted to talk to him, but it was not to be. Caller ID said, René.

"*Bonsoir,* René. So nice to hear from you. I was going to call you tomorrow, as our plans have changed. Jenks and I still want to visit you before we leave France, but it might be later than we thought."

"Yes, I see you 'ave many new friends."

"What? Are you here in Castelnaudary?"

"No, you were (he pronounced it "ware") on the local television news this evening. You, the lovely blonde cowgirl, a very 'andsome dog, and another woman. I think we saw 'er on the beach 'ere with that *Beur*. And, of course, two swans following."

"We were on TV? Why?"

Jan, who had been on her laptop stalking Jean Luc in depth, looked up, all ears. She whispered, "René? Who's René?"

"Tell you later," I mouthed.

René was saying, "At the end of the news each day they show videos taken by local people, and an all-female crew with a bollard-roping Texan and a swan entourage on our canal they found interesting. Where is your *Monsieur* Jenks?"

"Uh, he had to go to Lille on business."

"Ah, the Paris thing. He mentioned he was in security. Those bastards need to be eliminated. Will you be in Castelnaudary tomorrow? I would love to meet…."

"Jan. And Po Thang, he's my dog."

"Yes. Charles and I would like to take you all to lunch, if you are available."

"We'd love it!"

I hung up and smiled at Jan. "We have a luncheon date tomorrow."

"With whom, I might ask?"

"René and Charles."

"Jeez, Hetta, Jenks leaves for a few days and men start coming out of the woodwork."

René arrived at ten sharp in his shiny, vintage limo. André was decked out in full chauffeur's livery.

Charles bounded from the car and headed straight for me, knowing full well what a sucker I am for handing out treats and ear scratches. Po Thang, corralled inside the cabin in anticipation of his unruly doggie ways, didn't like me disloyally petting another dog one little bit. His fury bordered on apoplexy as he fogged up the galley windows with hot breath and slobber.

"*Allô!*" René called to us, then chided his poodle. "Charles! Do not be rude. Cannot you see the American dog is *jaloux*? Well, of course he is jealous...not everyone can be French, *n'est-ce pas?*"

Charles did an about-face, trotted back to René, and sat politely at his side. He totally ignored the hissing, wing-flapping swans who'd sidled over to check out the commotion.

Jan, a huge grin on her face, stepped off the boat. "Oh, Hetta, I can always trust you to deliver a surprise." She shook René's hand, said, "So nice to meet you both," and leaned down to give Charles a hug.

This bit of added betrayal sent Po Thang into further fits of barking and howling. "Looks to me as though your Charles could teach Po Thang a thing or two about the rules of etiquette. That dog of Hetta's almost got us kicked out of a couple of cafés already."

René kissed Jan's hand, causing her to blush. "What do you say, Charles? Do you think an old dog can teach a young dog new tricks? Come, you must meet this unhappy *chien*."

My unhappy *chien* was attempting to eat a window in order to escape. "Uh, René, do you think that's a good idea?"

René gave me a Gallic shrug. "We shall see, shall we not?" He bent down, talked into Charles's ear, walked him to the boat, pushed him inside the slider and slammed it before Po Thang could charge.

I held my breath. Po Thang, to my knowledge, had never attacked another dog, but if there is one thing I've learned about dogs it's that what you think they won't do, they will. I fully expected a mêlée to ensue, but things went quiet. Ominously quiet. After what seemed like an eternity, Charles barked, "*Wouf, wouf,*"—French for "Woof, Woof,"— René opened the door and the two dogs trotted out with Charles in the lead and Po Thang meekly following. He didn't even give the swans a glance.

"Very good, Charles. You may sit now."

Both dogs sat.

Jan and I shared slack-jawed looks.

"What in holy hell went down in there?" she asked.

"My Charles? He is *une vieille âme*—an old soul. Perhaps like that gentleman, *César, l'homme qui parlait aux chiens*? Except Charles must have whispered in dog language. Now that the dogs have settled, shall we go for our lunch?"

"Ya think Charles could do anything with those swans? Or Hetta, for that matter?"

"Hey! I—" my nasty rebuttal was lost as I realized we had company. "Oh, hey there, Rhonda." I turned and stuck my hand out to her companion. "And you must be Rousel."

For a moment the good-looking Frenchman looked as though perhaps my fingernails were fangs, then he recovered and gave me a limp shake. Up close, I was convinced for sure his hair was not naturally blonde. He was probably thinking the same about my enhanced red tresses.

I made introductions and although they were not overtly rude, both Charles and René seemed less than delighted by Rousel. I didn't know a poodle could sneer.

Po Thang, picking up on the vibe and nowhere nearly so genteel as René and Charles, let loose with a low growl, but remained seated. I reached down and tapped Po Thang's head in warning. He raised his eyes, whined, and leaned against me. "Sorry, he's cranky from

131

jet lag. And getting beat up on by," I nodded my head at Odette and Siegfried, "those guys."

Rousel shrugged and said, in French-accented but grammatically correct English, "I was unaware of their potentially violent nature."

"Kinda like Hetta," Jan quipped.

Rousel looked puzzled, and Jan added, "Never mind. A failed attempt at wit."

"Ah, a jest." Rousel was doing his best to keep his eyes off of Jan's cleavage but was losing the battle, so he cut his eyes to the woman cleaving to his arm. He patted her shoulder. "Rhonda tells me you and the dog flew here from Mexico. Perhaps being in a crate for such a long flight in a cargo hold has left him unhappy."

Jan lowered her sunglasses, fixed her big blue peepers on Rousel and said, "Oh, please. We do not fly commercial."

René's wide grin let us know he approved of Jan's smart remark, and as soon as the couple were out of hearing range, let go with a perfect Maurice Chevalier, "*Hon, hon, hon*," laugh. Actually, I've never heard anyone except Chevalier, in movies, laugh like that, so I figured René was having some fun with us.

Jan shrugged. "I dunno, something about that Rousel just ain't right. Rubs me the wrong way."

"Looked to me like he'd like to do just that," I said.

"Yeah, there's that. Plus some stuff Rhonda told us. René, it looks to me like you and Charles don't care much for him either."

"Charles is very opinionated."

I smiled. *There's the pot calling the kettle black.*

"So's Hetta."

"Hey, I'm not the one who just judged Rousel. Aren't you just a tad quick to pull the judgment trigger yourself?"

"Justified. He comes off as a slime ball."

"You just met him." *Why was I defending this dude?*

"Ladies, please, let us go have lunch."

That we could both agree on.

In my opinion.

André, after being introduced to Jan, opened the back door on the elegant motorcar and Jan slid across the soft leather seat, all grins. "Wow! What is this? Some kind of Seville?"

André chuckled. "No, *mademoiselle*, this is a 1966 Austin Princess. Almost in original condition. Or it was, until ten years ago when a certain puppy ate the backseats."

Charles dropped his head and whined. René petted him fondly. "In defense of our Charles, it was a very fine leather, so he already exhibited a taste for the finer things in life."

I ran my hand along the elegant paint job and gleaming chrome. "It is, without a doubt, the most beautiful car I've ever seen."

"That is what my wife thought when we bought it new, in England."

"I wondered why the steering wheel was on the wrong side."

André nodded, but said, "The British would, of course, take exception."

René settled onto a rear-facing fold-down jump seat across from Jan and me. "*S'il vous plaît*, André, you must convey us to the best *déjeune* in all of the South of France."

"I thought *déjeune* meant breakfast," Jan said.

"Ah, *non*. Breakfast is *le petit déjeuner.*"

Jan said, "Since I missed breakfast this morning, I don't care what you call it, just don't call me late to the table."

André ushered Po Thang and Charles into the front with him, and Po Thang shot me his eye-roll beggy look over the seatback, but Charles nudged him with his aristocratic nose, so my dog circled and curled for a nap.

I was going to have to figure out how to kidnap that poodle.

"So, lovely ladies," René whispered, "I suggest you buckle in. We added safety belts years ago, as that maniac up front spent his good years on the race circuit."

"I heard that," André threw back over his shoulder.

René pushed a button and a privacy window glass slid shut just as André stomped the gas.

"Wow, this thing has some power," Jan said. She has a thing for horsepower after dating a guy who raced muscle cars. He'd taught her a thing or two, which comes in handy once in a while. For instance, that time we stole a drug dealer's truck. Don't ask.

While André drove as though warming up for the first lap of the upcoming Twenty-Four Hours at Lemans, we held on and tried distracting ourselves from impending death by discussing the Paris attacks, what it meant for France, and René's town in particular.

"I do not think," René told us, "Gruissan or anywhere in my area of France is a target. We locals all know each other, and the tourists? Well, they *look* like tourists, not terrorists. We have adopted your American *if you see something say something* mode. And, we are armed."

I caressed the Taurus in my pocket. "I thought you weren't allowed to have guns."

"The government, much to their dismay, has little control over us. Many of us have survived a war or two and have no intention of being sitting ducks again. The new generation? Perhaps another story but they are learning. After all, they are the targets of these Beurs in their cafes and nightclubs."

There it was again, that butter thing, but this time I asked, "I heard you call Rhonda's boyfriend a butter. What does that mean?"

He broke out in a deep belly laugh that brought on tears and a coughing fit.

Alarmed, André slid the privacy window open and both dogs stuck their heads through it and whined.

René waved them away with the back of his hand. "I'm fine," he gasped. "For God's sake, keep your eyes on the road so I can remain so!"

Opening a burled mahogany velvet-lined cabinet, René grabbed a bottle of Perrier from the mini-fridge, downed it, and motioned for us to help ourselves. I latched onto a mini-split of Champagne and Jan opted for a beer.

Little hiccups of laughter still escaped his lips as René tried to regain control.

"Okay, what's so funny? What did I miss?" Jan asked.

René sucked a breath. "What Hetta said. I called that guy back there a *Beur*, and she wanted to know why I called him a butter."

Now it was André's turn to howl, which set Charles to howling, which set Po Thang off. Just for fun, Jan and I joined in even though we didn't know why.

A passing trucker, spotting all the gaiety and me drinking champagne direct from the bottle, wrapped his nose into a clenched fist and screwed it back and forth, the French gesture for saying you're drunk. Of course this made all of us laugh even harder. After we settled down, I asked, "No really, what *did* I say that was so funny?"

"Not butter, *Beur*. I am certain this Rousel is one. An Arab. Or more likely, the child of Algerian parents, but born in France. I am old and my time in Algeria during the *Guerre d'Algérie* was very unpleasant. Charles' namesake," Charles perked up his ears, "President de Gaulle, gave them their freedom. Fine with me. But then a million of them, plus Europeans who lived in Algeria called *pied noirs*, or black foots, returned to France. We were in no way prepared for this onslaught. They stayed, and now look what we have. So, call me a racist—he pronounced it rahceest—if you wish, but I did not care for them in their own country and certainly do not like them here in my homeland."

Jan and I exchanged a look and shrugged. I'd spent my childhood around his generation and had gotten an earful of his type of thinking, so I knew if I didn't change the subject we were in for a one-sided rant. I sure as hell didn't intend to mention I'd read that before the French pulled out of Algeria, they confiscated the guns of loyal Algerians, leaving them behind to die at the hands of rebels. The revolutionaries murdered about fifty-thousand defenseless people. The lucky ones were the very people he didn't want in France.

"Gosh, Rousel doesn't look like an Arab," Jan said. I jabbed her with my elbow to shut her up, so she quickly changed the direction of the conversation. "So, René, Hetta tells me you know just about everyone in Gruissan?"

"Everyone who counts. We old timers are not fond of the *nouveau riche*."

André glanced in the rearview mirror and brayed. "I might remind you, René, you *are* the *nouveau riche*."

"Not so. I am *old* money because I married it. And my wife's family stole it, fair and square. "

The men enjoyed another chuckle based on a long relationship not at all typical of an employer/employee status.

"So, André," Jan asked, "you raced cars?"

"Yes, when I was much younger. René was my mechanic for the matches, as he had learned much about engines from our fathers' fishing fleet."

"And now you're his chauffeur?"

"Only because he insists," René explained. "I have told my cousin many times we can hire someone, but he wants to kill us personally. He is very stubborn that way."

The men's camaraderie, banter, and warm laughter made me smile. I could only hope that when Jan and I reached their age we'd still have that kind of friendship.

Unless *I* got us killed.

We screeched into René's garage a scant forty-five minutes after leaving Castelnaudary.

"And so, here we are," René declared. "And amazingly alive."

It was no surprise to me we'd headed for René's house at Gruissan. As he'd told me before, why go out to eat when he had Celeste to cook for him?

René gave Jan the tour of his fabulous home, André took the dogs for a walk, and I sneaked into the kitchen to talk with Celeste, who surprised me by asking for my recipe for biscuits and gravy.

"*Monsieur* is very fond of your biscuit—she pronounce it biskwee—with sauce."

I wrote down my grandmother's recipe for biscuits with sausage gravy, making notes of the substitute ingredients I'd had to use. I told her if she could get her hands on some buttermilk, they would be better, then I spent ten minutes trying to explain why on earth anyone would *want* buttermilk.

Getting back to making our lunch, she rebuffed my offer to help and shooed me out to the library, where one of Renés fabulous bottles of wine awaited.

All of us sat at the enormous round table that I'd learned started life in the great hall of a castle. Charles and Po Thang had their own chairs and place settings, which set me to worrying.

While we conversed in Frenchlish so Jan could follow, I kept a wary eye on Po Thang. I had a mental picture of him taking a run across the polished table top, snatching up and scarfing down any and all edibles and maybe a candle or two, while sending priceless crystal and china flying with a sweep of his tail of doom. The only thing left standing would be a heavy cut-glass fruit bowl that probably outweighed him. Charles must have read my mind, for he pawed down Po Thang's slightly elevated leg before he could gain traction.

The pooches, well, at least one of them, waited patiently while Celeste dished oversized rimmed soup bowls full of specially prepared dog food before we humans served ourselves family style. Po Thang sniffed and stretched his nose a bit toward a platter piled high with braised lamb chops surrounded by tiny roasted potatoes, onions, and baby carrots, but I gave him the stink eye and he sat back.

After a cheese course, followed by *soufflé au chocolat et au Grand Marnier*, I moaned and rubbed my stuffed gut. "Okay, René, that's it. I am stealing your dog, your chef, and your home."

Jan nodded agreement. "And the car."

René shrugged. "So be it. You have already stolen my heart, as I love seeing women actually eat. The French women, Celeste here the exception, claim to love their food, but then barely take a bite. You two can really eat."

I was sure that was meant as a compliment, but Jan howled with laughter. "You have no idea. Between Hetta and her dog, one can barely keep the larder full."

René smiled. "It is good. A woman who enjoys food? I am surprised you remain unmarried, Hetta."

"That's cuz she keeps picking men who are betrothed to others."

"No, I do not."

"How about Jean Luc d'Ormesson?"

All sounds of clinking cups and silver stopped as mouths around the table dropped open. René recovered first. "Jean Luc? He is one of my best friends. Much too old for you, Hetta. And himself married," he chided.

André piped up. "Perhaps she means Jean Luc, the younger? He is near to Hetta's age and is not married. At least, not at the moment."

"Really?" Jan grinned like a Cheshire cat. "Gee, Hetta, maybe we should look him up so we can kill him for old time's sake, and all."

Chapter Seventeen

When Jan suggested the possibility of offing one of their countrymen, and a friend of theirs to boot, our hosts exchanged puzzled looks across the dining table.

"Jan's just kidding," I said. "We Texans josh about things like this, but we rarely go about doing in people. Almost never. Besides, Jean Luc is ancient history. I once thought I was in love with him, but it was many years ago. And then he married someone else." I didn't want to get into how shabbily I'd let myself be treated by one of their own. It was downright embarrassing.

"And so now you have *Monsieur* Jenkins, who seems like a very fine fellow." He lifted his brandy snifter. "To Jenks."

I returned the toast with enthusiasm. Other than my father, Jenks is far and away the best man I've ever known, and certainly the best one I've dated. So why on earth was I even checking up on that rat, Jean Luc?

René begged off on the return trip to Castelnaudry, so André and Charles delivered us back to the boat. When we arrived just before dark, I found a note on the door from Rhonda.

"What's it say?" Jan wanted to know.

"They're leaving tomorrow morning and she hopes to see us before they go."

We walked to their boat, but it was dark. "Guess they went to dinner. Let's sit out and enjoy this weather while we can, cause it won't last. When it blows, it gets downright chilly."

Even without a breeze we needed a sweater. We had a glass of red, decided we were still full from lunch and skipped dinner. As we were getting ready to go back in for the night and play cards, I spotted Rhonda and Rousel returning to their boat and waved.

"Hey, you two," Rhonda trilled, earning a dark look from her hunk, who had reluctantly followed her when she picked up the pace to see us. "How was your lunch? You guys really know how to live, what with limos, chauffeurs, and the like. I want to be you."

Rousel, trying to catch up with Rhonda, evidently wasn't warming to *that i*dea. He was struggling to look pleasant and interested, and failing badly at both. Po Thang, staring intently at the man, snarled softly when he put his hand on Rhonda's shoulder, trying to stop her forward movement.

Strike three on the possible abuser's list: putting on of hands in a controlling manner. Rhonda slipped away and continued toward the boat. Which is, of course, why I insisted they come aboard; I knew it would piss him off.

"Grill him like a French McDonald's Grand Royal Cheese," I whispered to Jan, letting her know we were going into our good-guy/bad-guy routine.

After Rousel turned down the wine offered to both of them, then coffee offered to both of them, he reluctantly sat down. Rhonda scooted next to her prize and clamped onto his arm like a limpet. She didn't seem to notice she'd practically become a ventriloquist's dummy with her dreamboat doing the talking for her.

"So," I chirped, using every chance I had to annoy Rousel, "how long do you think it'll take you two to cruise up the canal before you catch a train to Paris?"

Rhonda found her voice before Rousel could usurp it. "We're gonna take our time. Maybe a week? Then to Paris, and then fly home. Right Rousel?"

Rousel just nodded, but I could tell he didn't like Rhonda sharing their plans.

"How romantic," Jan cooed, joining in on the roast. "You just met and, bingo! You clicked. What were your plans before you met Rhonda, Rousel? I mean, this is like, life-changing."

She said it so innocently I don't think Rousel smelled a rat yet, but he squirmed a bit. "I was on a short vacation before going back to work at my father's firm. But now that has suddenly changed." He gave Rhonda's shoulder a squeeze.

My turn. "And how very fortunate you met again in Gruissan, after seeing each other in Cannes."

Rousel glowered, and rather than deny the encounter at Cannes, clammed up.

Jan zeroed in on the man, who was visibly unhappy with us. "And even more fortuitous, you can just change horses, so to speak, in the middle of the race and take off for the United States."

Rousel looked confused at Jan's turn of phrase. Rhonda giggled and told him, "It means being able to act upon an impulse." He nodded, but I could tell he still didn't get it.

"I guess the flexibility of working in the family business has its perks. What exactly *do* you do?" I asked.

He sighed, probably happier to get the conversation onto safer ground. "We import food stuffs from the Middle East and distribute them to grocery stores throughout France."

Never one to let a clue like this lie fallow, Jan blurted. "Hey, with all the Muslims here in France, that has to be a good business to be in. Are you a Muslim?"

Even I was surprised by her bluntness, bordering on rudeness. I mean, I am rarely PC, but these days one needs to tread a little lightly on ethnic and religious territory.

"One is not *a* Muslim, one *is* Muslim," Rousel said, his eyes flashing angrily.

Rhonda blinked rapidly and looked at Rousel, who smiled. Not a very genuine smile, I have to add. "My parents are Muslim. My generation is not very much into religion."

Jan nodded her head. "Kinda like Hetta and me. We're what are called backsliding Baptists in Texas."

Rousel relaxed a mite, but I could tell he didn't like being put on the spot like that. Maybe more than a little of his parents' religion was embedded in him than he realized, at least where women were concerned, what with his control freak ways.

Maybe it was time to lighten up? Not! "Your family lives in Paris, right? So I guess you're looking forward to introducing Rhonda to them while you're there. How exciting for both of you."

Rousel looked decidedly uncomfortable and didn't answer.

Ball to Jan. "And, Rhonda, what will you do when you two get back to your hometown? I know you cannot wait for your friends to meet your handsome Frenchman."

"Well, gosh, I guess I haven't thought much about it, other than selling the house. I'd already planned on that, but now things are happening so fast...."

Her answer let me know she hadn't asked Rousel about their future, probably out of fear of being pushy. Strike four: avoiding certain topics out of fear of angering your partner.

Jan has no problem with pushy. "Yeah, Rousel, what's the plan here? We nosey broads want to know. Will you come back to France together? How long can you stay in the States? Do you need a visa, or what?"

"We French only have to produce a valid passport." I could just picture René hearing that "we French" thing and hawking up spit. He continued his explanation. "We must produce a return ticket to prove intent, and can stay ninety days, just as you were allowed when you arrived."

Hmmm. I didn't have a return ticket, so did Jan? I was still steamed that I spent three days getting to France on a cargo plane while she and my dog were whisked over in a corporate jet. For the first time I wondered how and when we'd all get back to Mexico.

"Which airline are you flying?"

Rhonda looked at Rousel. "You exchanged my return ticket for the new ones. Hope it didn't cost you a bundle to switch to Air France."

"It was not a problem." He looked at his watch. "We must be going, I wish to leave early."

"Not too early, or you'll have to wait for the locks to open."

"That is so. Well, good evening." He stood to leave, pulling his extra appendage to her feet.

"Maybe we'll see you in the morning before we leave," Rhonda said. "If not, you have my phone number and email address. Please let me know what you two are up to."

"Oh, trust me, we'll keep in touch," Jan said, and surprised me by giving her, and then Rousel a hug. Maybe it's just that French thing, but I didn't like him ogling Jan with poor Rhonda by his side. Even though he'd been making crawdad eyes at her, Jan's embrace obviously embarrassed him, so I loved her taking him by surprise. Po Thang, not liking his Auntie Jan that close to someone he didn't care for, growled softly. I agreed.

The minute they were gone, Jan declared, "Gigolo for sure. I bet he doesn't even *have* a job. Family firm, my rear."

"I know. I hate this. He's gonna clean out her bank account and dump her like a hot baguette."

"But what can we do? She's a grown woman, naively and madly smitten with a libertine. She's not going to listen to anything we have to say. And we don't have one iota of evidence, besides our well-honed instincts." She reached over and patted my hand. "*Your* instincts, especially. You're practically the Queen of catastrophic dumpees."

I wanted to protest, but she was right. Seemed like once a decade I got dumped, first by Jean Luc, then again about ten years ago by Hudson in Tokyo. Both were devastating events I wouldn't wish on anyone. At least that rat Hudson was seriously out of my life after "surfacing" face down in my hot tub in Oakland.

And no, I didn't do it.

But if I could've, I probably would've.

What with time on my hands in France, I might just have to even the score with that first rat to gnaw his way into my heart, Jean Luc d'Ormesson, a.k.a. DooRah.

My murderous thoughts were interrupted by a ding on the computer and a carefully worded email from Jenks telling me and Jan to enjoy France, but to stay south. No word when he'd return.

Jan looked up from her own screen. "Jenks?"

"Yep, No real news, but I can tell he's worried about something happening again."

"Hope not. Meanwhile, we have a boat, car, money, and we're in the South of France. Whatcha wanna do, Chica?"

"I've been thinking—"

"Oh, hell. That's never good."

"I think you'll like what I'm thinking this time."

"Only if it doesn't entail getting' me shot, kidnapped, thrown in jail, or ending up in an emergency room."

"How about a mystery cruise aboard the luxury ship, *Sauzens*, on the beautiful Canal du Midi toward Toulouse?"

"Ooooh, I love it. How did I know you were gonna say that?"

"Did you bring the bugs?"

"Is there a Stetson in Texas?"

"Good. We have to find out just who this Rousel is. Hell, we don't even know his last name."

Jan reached into a pocket, raised her arm in a victory pump, and waggled a slim wallet. "As my grandma used to say, let's tip over the outhouse and see what stinks."

Chapter Eighteen

Once upon a time Po Thang was a stray, which is how he got his name.

He was stranded on the side of a lonely, lava-based road on the Baja, and it took us days to get him, but in the meantime, I'd throw food from the car on my way to work. Our quest to rescue the poor thing, as we called him, led to bags of food labeled Po Thang, and the rest is history.

When he went from being a free-range animal to a pet, he didn't quite grasp that concept and had recidivist tendencies to stray once again. Enter one of my best friends, Doctor of Veterinary Medicine, Craig Washington, who had perfected a chip for tracking livestock that went off the reservation. He sent me one for my errant pooch.

Now, with this clever device, I can track Po Thang via GPS for up to five miles.

Jan and I have some recidivist tendencies ourselves when it comes to spying on people. We have amassed a nice array of bugs and tracking devices for planting on people, cars, and perhaps on a boat at the Canal du Midi?

And what world-class snooper wouldn't have a critter cam on her dog? Where his collar goes, so goes the cam.

To sum it up, Jan and I are equipped to delve into other peoples' bidness like nobody's bidness.

Later that evening, after Jan lifted Rousel's wallet, I took Po Thang for a walk right past Rhonda's boat, and tossed Rousel's wallet on their deck to look as though it had fallen from his jacket. I made sure it was unseen from the quay, just in case there was someone as disreputable as Jan and me about.

The next morning we watched as Rousel stepped outside, spotted his wallet, picked it up, and patted his back pocket in surprise before slipping the billfold he hadn't known was missing back where it belonged.

A few minutes later, he and Rhonda busied themselves in the business of clearing the decks, unplugging the electrical cord and water hose, and then Rousel went to the Harbor Master's office to check out.

The minute he disappeared through the office door, I rushed to their boat with a bon voyage gift, a box of candy Jan hid from me and therefore was still intact. Once inside, I distracted Rhonda while Jan planted a bug under a cabinet where it couldn't be seen. It could be activated in short spurts if we needed it, and the battery would last a good ten days. Not that they could really go anywhere we couldn't easily find them by biking along the canal, but I didn't want to accidentally catch up with them until we wanted to.

I considered planting Po Thang's critter cam on their boat as well, but that would be much too invasive, *n'est-ce pas*?

Rousel returned and was less than pleased to find us on his boat, but being the good neighbors we are, we helped them with their lines, shoved them off, waved gaily as they motored away, then went back to *Sauzens* and tested the GPS trackers. Trackers, plural? Yep, the tiny bug embedded in the soft leather in Rousel's wallet worked just fine, thank you.

Before turning in the previous evening, we'd scanned everything in our target's wallet and were dismayed to find Rhonda's credit card still in his possession. The last time we'd discussed this lousy practice with her, she said she'd get it back.

"Two credit cards, one belonging to Rhonda. What a dork she is," Jan grumbled. "So, we have his driver's license, a train ticket stub and whoa," she counted out some bills, "Five thousand Euros? Rhonda better check that card's balance for a heavy cash advance."

She handed me the license. "Rousel Badiz al Bin Jasseron, born 1981, in Paris. So he's five years younger than Rhonda. Well, at least he's given her his real first name. And quite frankly Rousel Jasseron sounds plenty French to me."

"I'd bet René would take exception to the 'Badiz al Bin' part. Is there a home address?"

"Nope. I read somewhere only the police can read that info with some kind of decoder."

"Well, phooey." She took the license back from me. "What are all these letters, you figure?"

"No idea. Probably personal info that's encrypted into the card so people like us can't figure it out."

"The cads. Well, we have his name, so that's better than nothing. Load him up."

I did, but his name garnered almost zero on Google. Then I adjusted my search to include Jasseron Paris Groceries, and up popped: *Marché Badiz al Bin Jasseron.*

Coincidence? You be the judge. Were we wrong about this guy? Was he legit?

I put those questions to Jan, who shook her head. "Doesn't matter if he turns out to be President of France. He's bad news for Rhonda. Forge on."

Jan, never one to let evidence get in the way of a good hunt, doesn't let go easily.

That's one reason we get along so well.

We really had no agenda, other than maybe saving Rhonda from herself by somehow getting her to wash that weasely Rousel le Roué right out of her badly-styled hair. I would like to say we were on this mission strictly in good conscience, but Jan and I are a mite short on what most folks consider a normal moral sense of right and wrong, and generally err to the side of good old vigilante justice.

The first lock Rousel and Rhonda had to clear was a little over four and a half kilometers away, and we wanted them to pass through that one well before we arrived.

We took the car for a major grocery run at a super store, since we'd be cruising a part of the canal Jenks and I had already covered, and I knew stores were few and hard to get to on foot.

After loading up with enough provisions to start our own store—just in case our quarry spent an entire week underway—we decided to double check our tracking device's accuracy. Of course, it's not like Rhonda and Rousel's boat could disappear on the canal like a ship at sea, but we wanted to know *exactly* where they were.

Driving to the next set of locks, we parked out of sight and spotted them waiting to pass through along with two other vessels.

I checked the GPS against a chart. "Perfecto. We're golden and good to go."

"What are we gonna do with the car?" Jan asked.

"What do you think? Leave it at Castelnaudary or leapfrog it to somewhere ahead?"

"Since they don't seem to be in a big hurry, we have time. You've been on this part of the Canal. Is there a place where you can drop the car and take the train back?"

"When we get back to Castelnaudary I'll Google the train schedules. Maybe I can do it today."

My BFF, Google, told me I could drive to the port of Negra, where Jenks and I picked up the first boat, put the car in their storage lot, catch a train in a nearby village, and be back by Happy Hour.

"Okay, while you stash all the goodies, I'll drop the car at Negra and catch the train back. We can leave tomorrow morning and still keep within striking distance of their boat.

"Sounds like a plan. But, Hetta, you hate public transportation."

"Yes. It's so public, but when in France and all that."

"Po Thang and I'll do the laundry while you're gone. I saw a washer and dryer at the harbor master's office."

"Great. You need any help with the machines before I leave?"

"Oh please, just because I don't speak French doesn't mean I can't load a danged washing machine and dryer."

"Hookay, just remember I asked."

On the way to drop off the car, I looked for *Trebes* as I drove the country lanes near the canal. I spotted her staked to the bank near a lock and she seemed settled in for the rest of the day and night. Hopping onto the autoroute, I quickly reached an exit near Negra, and got there ahead of my own schedule, with plenty of time to catch a train back to Castelnaudary.

Much to my surprise, I actually caught someone in the office at the marina, arranged to store the car, and they called a taxi for me. Things were going way too smoothly, which made me highly suspicious, but I was back at the boat without a hitch. I had to remember to buy a lottery ticket.

Jan and Po Thang were sitting out on deck when I returned. Po Thang was keenly watching his swans, who were keenly watching him. They seemed to be having some kind of ESP conversation involving little yips, long-necked head shakes, wing lifts, and a hiss or two.

Just as I approached the boat, Po Thang sprang to all fours and began furiously barking, but not at me. Jan, who'd stood to greet me, whirled to see what Po Thang was so upset about, and yelled, "Hetta, there's a rat in the water the size of Houston. Come look at this thang!"

Po Thang, literally at the end of his rope, was going crackers.

I rushed onboard and peered over the side. "Holy crap, what *is* that?'

All the commotion had snagged the attention of a passerby who spat, "Coypu."

According to the Internet, the Coypu (Myocastor couypus, to you nerds) this two-foot long, orange-toothed critter who had Po Thang in such a snit, is a large, semi-aquatic vegan rodent that has origins in South America.

They were hunted almost to extinction for their fur at one time, which, judging by the disdain of the woman who identified him for us, was fine with her.

We asked why people didn't like them and it turns out they not only beg for treats on the canal, they also burrow better than Roto-Rooter, demolish gardens, eat tires off cars, and use wooden homes and fences for teething.

In other words, a rat is a rat no matter what you call it.

And speaking of, René called to tell me he'd learned that should I be interested, Luc DooRah was in Gruissan visiting family for the next two weeks.

"Oh, goody. DooRah is in our trap. We gonna bait it up and do something bad to him?" Jan asked, rubbing her hands gleefully.

"We are not. We are going to do something far more noble for as long as it takes, namely stalking someone far more deserving, Rousel le Roué."

"Dang. So many rats, so little time."

We went inside, where I was greeted with damp laundry draped over every imaginable space throughout the boat.

"What happened?" I asked.

"I dunno. I ran the dryer at least six times, then it just quit working."

"How very French. Its thirty-five hour work week must have been up."

Our clothes were not much drier by morning, thanks to a light fog that moved in overnight. The boat smelled like laundry detergent. I rigged a line on the aft, ran out to a local store for some clothespins and, before we left, we hung what we could to dry in the breeze while we were underway. It would take several batches. We looked like Romas, the gypsies as some called them back in the day, who plied French waterways in barge communities. Well, before they deported them back to Romania.

Jan gave our moving clothes dryer a critical look. "Wouldn't get away with this Beverly Hillbillies decor at Marina de la Paz, I'd bet."

"Not likely. Oh, well, so much for looking chic while cruising *le* Canal. Let's get this show on the road."

Dodging wet laundry, we untied the shore lines and left for our self-assigned rescue mission of a fair damsel who didn't know she was in distress yet.

Call us a couple of meddling broads with too much time and money on our hands, but...well, I guess that sums it up.

Chapter Nineteen

Just before we left the dock at Castelnaudary, I checked on *Trébes'* coordinates with the tracker. They hadn't moved, but as we waited to enter the first dock of the day, a beep let me know they were underway again.

"Off they go. We've gotta keep close tabs on that boat, because we don't want to run up on them, but once in a while we'll have to get a visual. You'll have to use the bicycle to ride ahead and see what's up with them."

"Me? Why me? I haven't ridden a bike in a million years, Hetta. You do it."

"No way. I'd probably kill myself. Okay, if we need to take a look ahead, I'll walk it. That I can do."

After we cleared the first locks, Jan gave in and rode the bike ahead to take a gander at *Trébes*. Yes, we knew the boat was only a kilometer and a half ahead, but had no way to be sure Rhonda was. With everything we knew to date, we were honestly afraid he might settle for whatever he'd already pilfered from her accounts and throw her overboard. Quite a stretch for even my overworked imagination, but we were now so mistrustful of Rousel, we wanted an occasional visual health and welfare on our friend.

Po Thang was not happy behind left with me on the boat while Auntie Jan took off on her bike, but our quarry was too close and if he followed Jan, he might run ahead and give us away. From the sketchy schedule Rhonda gave me, and my calculation of time and distance, I figured they wouldn't be in a big hurry to get to Toulouse. *If* Rousel had told her the truth about their plans.

We planned to surprise them in the flesh with our unwelcome presence soon, but not so soon he freaked out and took off.

Jan came back a little winded. "Did they move? I rode to the next set of locks at Pont du Rocie but didn't see them. We're okay to clear those locks today, but I guess we'd better hunker down right after that for the night."

I checked the tracker and sure enough, they'd moved a few kilometers, but were no longer underway. Since there were no locks near them, we figured they were tied up for the night. "Okay, let's roll, and then I'll walk ahead after we tie up. I hope to heck they don't decide to walk or bike back our way. We're way too easy to spot. We're the ones with all the laundry. Oh, and swan groupies." I pointed to the other side of the canal.

"Crap, when did they show up?"

"Right after you left. Po Thang actually wagged his tail when he saw them. I think they've achieved detente."

"Yeah, as long as he doesn't try to swim with them."

"I think he's learned his lesson there."

After we cleared the last lock of the day, we tied to the bank and settled in for Happy Hour. I felt a tee shirt on our improvised line. "Dry. How about that."

We spent time folding and stowing our clothes, and then I dismantled the line before one of us clotheslined ourselves. And once, before Jan got her bollard-lassoing mojo back, she'd snagged the clothesline, almost dumping half our wardrobe into the drink and around our spinning propeller.

Po Thang whined. "What do you think, Auntie Jan? Safe to let the critter loose on the path?"

"I think so, but let's put on his cam and GPS tracker, just in case."

We took out folding chairs and stationed ourselves in the path to block him from taking off in the direction of Rhonda and Rousel. He ran a bit then doubled back, sniffing all the way. A couple of friendly backpackers went by, so he followed them. When the path disappeared around a bend, I whistled and he trotted back with a huge and shaggy critter in tow that could've been a dog. Or a miniature musk ox. He finally barked, so we decided he was part of the canine family.

With the beautiful countryside all around us, large trees shading the canal, and Po Thang and his new buddy's antics for entertainment, I sighed with contentment. "You know, Jan, Po Thang's turning out to be a great dog."

"Yep, until he's not so great."

We shared a laugh and clinked glasses.

I fetched us another wine and settled back into my chair. "You know, it has occurred to me maybe we're getting a little too focused on this Rhonda thing instead of enjoying this trip for ourselves."

"Ya think? I'm sure of it. Screw walking ahead tonight to see if the queen of passivity has gotten herself offed. Let's eat a big old steak and play cards."

"Deal."

The big animal finally trotted off, probably returning to a nearby farm or zoo, leaving Po Thang to stare at his dust and whine. I warned him not to follow, so he set up a game of chase with Odette and Siegfried. Fast as they are, swans are no match for a flat-out retriever, so he slowed his pace to keep them interested.

Jan videoed the dog-and-bird game for a few minutes, then put down her phone. "By the way, while I was biking, I spotted a boulangerie ahead that'll be open tomorrow morning. Should'a bought something for dinner, I guess. I notice we're out. Again, I might add."

"What? We bought a baguette this morning."

She shrugged. "Okay, Hetta, fess up. Did you eat the whole thing while I was gone?"

"No, I did *not*."

We both glared at Po Thang, who turned and looked behind him.

Jan and I both recalled what I'd said just minutes before, and repeated, in unison, "Until he's not so great!"

The next morning I printed out a blank monthly calendar and we began planning our next two weeks, figuring by then surely Jenks would show up.

I wrote in the day Rhonda said they were leaving for Paris and worked backward. "So, they gotta turn in the boat, get to Toulouse, and catch a plane or a train."

"Why can't they take the boat all the way to Toulouse?"

"For the same reason we can't take this one. The rental company doesn't allow it, and since they control the lock at Negra, that's that."

"So, they can only go as far as where you left the car?"

"Yep. So, how long do you think, given this time frame, before we make an appearance?"

Jan studied the calendar. "Two days, before we surprise them with our fulgurous gloriousness."

I gave her the look that sentence deserved. "You're playing with the thesaurus again, aren't you?"

"Yep. If Rhonda gave us the right date they're going to Paris, they'll probably turn in the boat here," she tapped a square on the calendar, "and go to Toulouse. However, there are no guarantees on that. They *could* drop the boat day after tomorrow and be in the wind," she snapped her fingers, "just like that."

The snap woke Po Thang from his first nap of the day, but when he realized it wasn't meant for him, he grumped and went back to snoring after his morning canal path swan chase.

Those swans were turning out to be great dog walkers.

We stopped for a fresh baguette and *pain au chocolat* at the boulangerie Jan spotted while on her bike ride the day before. After breakfast, our GPS detected *Trebés* in place where they'd stopped the night before, so despite our wine-inspired declaration to let Rhonda stew in her own folly soup, clearer minds prevailed.

I reluctantly agreed it was my turn to go ahead for a peek at *Trebés*. Despite saying I'd rather walk, I wasn't going to let Jan get one up on me. However, it ain't true what they say, you *do* forget how to ride a bike.

"Jan, turn that damned camera off," I yelled. Taking my eyes off the path for that second was a bad idea.

Rolling out of control toward the canal bank I barely saved myself and the bike from a good dunking. Throwing my weight to the side, I tipped the bike over and ended up under it. The wheels were half-in-half-out of the water, and I was face down in muddy grass.

The swans honked in derision, Jan guffawed and continued to video my humiliation to share with hundreds on Facebook, and Po Thang raced over to jump me, probably thinking this new game was much more fun than tormenting swans.

Jan finally stuffed her phone in her pocket, grabbed a bottle of water and shooed Po Thang away. She pulled me to my feet and poured Evian over my muddy face. "You okay?"

"Nothing damaged but my dignity."

"You have dignity? Where have you kept it hidden all these years?"

"Very funny. That's it. I'm walking."

"Up to you, but you know what they say?"

I pushed the bike at her. "What do *they* say?"

"You know you're getting old when you quit taking left turns. It means—"

Grabbing the handlebars, I cut her off. "I know what it means." I pointed at her and growled, "I'll be back," in my best Schwarzenegger.

The only thing kind I can say about the bike that came with the boat is it was a basic girl model without gears, and the seat was low enough so I didn't have to stick my butt in the air. After twenty wobbly minutes, I got the hang of it and enjoyed the ride. Not that it was like I was ten again, racing the wind without fear; every time I saw bikers or walkers coming, I stopped and rolled my ride to the side of the path and pretended to watch those fascinating ducks or boats on the canal.

When I found myself on a surprisingly smooth patch of dirt, I picked up speed, almost forgetting my mission in the joy of conquest. Then I turned a curve and almost fell again in my haste to stop. Rhonda was walking toward me. She looked startled, then waved and chirped, "Hetta!"

Pushing the bike slowly toward her, I tried to come up with a fast story, but decided the truth would just have to do.

I hate it when that happens.

When I returned to *Sauzens*, Jan was waiting impatiently. "Where the hell have you been? I was getting worried, thought you were dead in a ditch."

"You are not going to believe it. I was talking with Rhonda."

"Really? You went to the boat?"

I told her how we met on the path.

"So what did you tell her."

"The truth."

"Just in case I have to testify one day, what exactly would that be?"

"We decided to take the boat to Negra."

"That's it? Gee, I wonder if that truth thang could work more often?"

After a moment of silence we both said, "Nah."

A fist bump later, we settled down for an iced tea. "Did you pump her for info?"

"Of course. You think you're playing with kids here? We had a nice long chat."

"Dish. Tell all."

"Well, for starters, she was dying to talk to someone. Evidently, her phone has *mysteriously* gone on the blink so she couldn't call us or her friends back home, and go figure, her pocket Wi-Fi hotspot somehow got knocked overboard."

"How very convenient. And that happened how?"

"She went for a walk, and they lost the signal while she was gone. Rousel took it outside to see if it would work better and danged if it didn't slip off the deck and into the canal when a work barge went by and threw a wake," I said dryly.

"Good grief. I know Rhonda's about as sharp as a marble when it comes to common sense, but she's well-educated and not stupid. How can she be so dumb in the face of all this glaring evidence that that man is isolating her? Lemme guess, she can't use Rousel's phone either."

"You nailed it. He says it is only for company use."

"Oooh, *reeks* of rat."

"No shite, Sherlock."

"I'm surprised he lets her take walks by herself."

"Why shouldn't he? Her French is crappy, he has her credit card and passport, and he doesn't know we're on his ass like buzzards on guts."

"Is she going to tell him she saw you? And where we are?"

"No way. She's afraid he'll think she planned to meet up with us." I stuck out my lower lip and whined, "It might hurt his widdow feelings."

"This is worse than I thought. He's got her...Svengalied. Surely the sex can't be *that* good."

"No, it isn't."

Jan's eyes widened. "He's no good in bed, to boot?"

"*Au contraire*, y'all. He ain't *in* her bed. I saved the best for last. No. Sex."

"He's cut her off?"

"Never happened. They have what he calls a *pure* love."

"Pure BS, if you ask me. I'll bet he's a *gay* gigolo stringing her along to get to that dough. That does it! Saddle up, Trouper Coffey, the cavalry is goin' in."

Jan chewed on a mouthful of omelet and chased it down with coffee as we were enjoying a second breakfast for lunch. "So, I guess the big questions of the day are, how does one go about saving someone who doesn't want to be saved, and why are we doing it?"

"Cuz we are stoopid? Deep questions for so early in the day."

"I have another one."

"What?"

"Why am I drinking coffee from a friggin' bowl?"

"Because we are embracing the true French experience."

"It's stupider than Rhonda. *S'il vous plaît passer le pain et le beurre*."

"Very good. However, we French do not butter our bread."

"And we Texans do not ask for anything politely twice," she warned.

I reached for the breadboard. It was empty.

Jan and I scowled at Po Thang. He stuck out his tongue.

I broke out laughing. "That's new."

"I taught him that on the plane. Only took half a jar of peanut butter."

"You are a very bad influence, Aunt Jan."

"I can see that. Okay, I'm gonna wire that little bread-stealing turd-dropper right now."

"I'll get the critter cam. I was going to put it on him anyhow. We are, after all, sending Agent Thang on recon this morning, as Rhonda and I arranged."

Chapter Twenty

Rhonda and I had agreed to meet on the path again the next morning. She didn't even question that we knew where she would be, she just wanted to have a few minutes of chit chat. She was in a foreign country with a man who was keeping her off balance and isolated. Finding out we were nearby was reassuring for her, even if she refused to pick up on what we were trying to tell her.

Jan and I talked about this before I left for my rendezvous. "Men, no matter where in the world they are, don't have a clue about women's relationships, do they? The pompous patootie thinks he has Rhonda under his spell, which is somewhat right, but has no idea he can't completely control her need to talk with friends. Well, short of tying her up on the boat."

"Don't forget, he also thinks he's ditched us, his only threats. I cannot wait to see his reaction when he learns otherwise. Are we gonna tell Rhonda about the camera?"

"I don't think so. She is too emotionally fragile and might spill the beans."

Jan tightened the vest and critter cam on Po Thang, we tested it, and I left for my rendezvous about a quarter mile away, around a bend. I had sneaked down earlier to make sure they were still parked and saw Rousel on deck with a cup of coffee. He didn't look like he was ready to pull up stakes yet, but just in case, I pocketed the tracker.

I kept Po Thang on a leash until I saw Rhonda coming our way, then let him go. He bounded toward her and circled happily, tail going crazy in his joy. Rhonda, although she'd been expecting him, seemed overwhelmed with happiness herself. When I caught up to them, she was hugging him tightly. "I had to stall Rousel this morning, because he wanted to leave early, but I told him I really wanted a walk before we left."

"Well done. Didn't have to go to plan B."

She laughed. "My goodness, all those years I was fossilizing in singledom, I thought I wanted someone to love, but I had no idea having a boyfriend could make life so complicated. Are they all this difficult?"

I wanted to say, "*Honey, you're still single, and no, you have landed yourself a world-class control freak,*" but I actually said, "Some of them can be. He seems to want you all for himself." *Major understatement there.*

"You don't think he'll, like, be too upset when you guys turn up, will he?" Her fear of annoying *le bâtard* was so tangible I wasn't sure whether I wanted to slap *her* or *him*. Or maybe her dead mother, who set her up to be subservient.

Rhonda, with her sweet nature, and unreasonable need to please a man she was in love with, was her own worst enemy right now. Luckily Rousel was unaware he'd acquired his own new worst enemy. Two, in fact. Three if you count the dog.

"I promise, if he's really that pissed off, we'll slow down and stay out of sight, but we can still meet and chat, like today. Okay?"

She beamed.

I activated the critter cam, gave Rhonda a handful of dog treats and a five-minute start down the path, and encouraged Po Thang to follow her.

Running as fast as I can, which isn't very, I wheezed onto *Sauzens* to find Jan already monitoring the critter cam on her computer.

At first Po Thang stood still, slightly confused by which way to go, turning to look back at me, then back at Rhonda. But then his little puppy brain must have registered, *bifteck haché!* and he loped off after Rhonda and the bag of mini-hamburger patties in her jacket pocket.

"How many does she have left?" Jan asked as Po Thang loped down the path. Twice he stopped and sniffed a tree, but the call of ground and grilled filet mignon took over, and off he went again.

"Think she'll save us some for dinner?" I joked.

"Not if Po Thang has anything to do with it. Oh, look, there's the boat. This should be good."

Po Thang had stopped again and was looking back where he came from. We held our breath, hoping his homing instincts didn't overcome his nose. His head swiveled back and we saw Rhonda sitting next to Rousel, then she stood, said something like "Oh, look, isn't that Po Thang?" and went to meet him.

With her back to Rousel, she squatted down, dumped the rest of the hamburger on the grass, and stuffed the empty bag in her pocket. So much for leftovers.

A pair of shoes appeared in the camera and Po Thang looked up into Rousel's glowering face. For a moment I was afraid he'd kick my dog, but Po Thang scooted back and Rhonda stepped in to pet him.

This was our cue. We had rigged Jan with a mic and she took off on the run.

I knew Rousel would be much happier to see Miz Jan in her ever so short and tight running shorts than me *or* my dog. Besides, Jan actually runs.

"Well, that went, uh, not so well," Jan said when she returned to our boat.

"Yeah, I saw and heard. And *au contraire*, I thought it went *quite* well. I had a hopeful moment there when it looked like Rousel was gonna have a coronary. And I don't think it was only over those shorts of yours."

"True, that. I guess we do have to go to Plan B, after all. We'll stay behind them, well out of sight. It's all too clear he doesn't relish our precious company."

"Yep. So be it. We will lag behind but keep an eye on Rhonda."

"However, he can't do a danged thing about us when we pass through locks at the same time. That way we have eyes on him at least part of the day. Then we'll leave the love-nesters on their own for the night. If we don't show up to borrow a cup of sugar every night, he should be all right."

Jan nodded, then frowned. "Here we go again, obsessing about that creep instead of enjoying the trip for ourselves. What's wrong with us?"

"I like to think we have a strong sense of loyalty to our fellow woman."

"Or an even stronger dislike of rats?"

"There's that." I tapped the calendar on the dining table. "Only three more days, anyhow. Once they turn in the boat, Rhonda's on her own. We'll have to take any and every opportunity to somehow make her see what a horrible situation she's gotten herself into."

"No phone, no credit card, no passport, no Internet, and she steadfastly refuses to put two and two together. She's..." I took two spoons and began a drum beat on the table before leaping to my feet and grabbing a ketchup bottle for a mic. Jan joined me and air- strummed a guitar as we both sang and danced to the lyrics of "Addicted to Love" by Robert Palmer, our 1985 favorite.

Thinking this dancing and singing thing great fun, Po Thang howled along. When we finally collapsed to the settee, I put my arm around him and said, "We're gonna have to face it, Furface. Just like the song says, Rhonda's lights are on, but there's no one home. She's addicted to love."

Like a cocklebur under his saddle, we aggravated Rousel just enough to make us happy, only catching up with them in time to clear a lock or two, then letting them get ahead and out of sight. Once a day, however, we let Po Thang go to meet Rhonda, always out of Rousel's view. He had to realize she was seeing us during her daily walks, because even though Rhonda didn't say so, we got the definite feeling we were making life difficult for her.

She hardly ever smiled anymore and exuded tension, so I finally whispered, as we both squatted to pet Po Thang while waiting for a lock to open, "Rhonda, if you want us to leave you alone, we will. You seem so unhappy."

Tears sprang into her eyes. "Oh, no. Having you two around is good. *I'm* the problem. I just always say the dumbest things to Rousel. He's so nice to me, and then I blurt out dumb stuff."

"What kind of dumb stuff?"

"Well, last night I mentioned how I wanted to call Rhea, my friend he met who went back home, and he got his feelings hurt."

"Why?"

"He said if he wasn't enough to keep me happy, then maybe we'd just better cancel our plans together. Then he wouldn't speak to me for the rest of the night."

I took a deep breath, and took a chance I felt necessary. "Rhonda, surely you must realize this is a form of abuse, right?"

"Don't be silly. He's just sensitive, that's all," she protested, but then shifted her eyes away from mine.

Did I get through, just a little bit? Not wishing to overstress my point, I raised a shoulder. "I'm sure that's it. Anyway, once you get to Paris things should lighten up. When do you meet the family?"

Jan and I had penned and practiced a list of probing questions, like the family thing, to throw into conversations with Rhonda that might snag her attention and shake her up a bit. This one got a reaction, all right.

"I have to go now," she said, standing abruptly.

I stood as well, and Po Thang scooted behind me as Rousel stormed toward us.

"Rhonda," Rousel barked, "you need to get back on the boat, right now. They'll be opening the gates any minute."

Po Thang barked back, and I cooed, "Oh, and a fine morning to you, too, Rousel."

He glared at Po Thang and me and with an abrupt jerk of his head, grabbed Rhonda's arm roughly and marched her meekness away.

Jan, who had miraculously watched the whole thing without decking Rousel, shook her head and huffed in disgust.

Back on the boat, I told Jan we really had to back off, lest Rhonda, in her fear of losing Rousel, refused to talk with us anymore. Matter of fact, we got up early the next day and by-passed them, honking and waving as we cruised by and out of sight.

We made it to Negra that day, got the car, hightailed it to the nearest Super U, and checked on Rhonda's boat on the way. They were waiting a couple of locks back, which meant they could catch up with us later in the day.

However, on the way back we saw them staked up a few miles back, probably for the night. We double-checked the GPS reading and continued on to our boat.

After our run into town, we settled in for a sandwich. I'd picked up cold cuts and a fresh baguette from the Super U. And a good thing, for last night's baguette, even though we'd hidden it in the oven, had gone missing.

"I'm gonna eat this sandwich and then we're going to watch our entertainment of the day. I turned on the critter cam when we left and *some*one furry and larcenous is gonna get busted," Jan said, pointing at our number one suspect.

Po Thang pulled his head-on-the-paws-I'm-so-precious-you'll-forgive-me-anything move and left it there until we started clearing the lunch dishes. Unable to resist, he dove in and snagged a small piece of pâté from a plate before I could wrap it for the fridge.

"That, my thieving friend, might be your last supper. I'm giving you one final chance to come clean before we roll the evidence. Where's the bread?"

He turned his head.

"Okay, then. Auntie Jan, let the incriminating video roll."

The camera boggled as Po Thang jumped up on the settee and watched us walk away earlier that day. He sat very still until the car rolled out of sight, then all we saw was settee fabric as he lay down as if for a nap. This lasted a good ten minutes and we were getting bored when the camera jumped and, once again, we could see out the window

"Holy crap, would you look at that?"

We were eye to eye with Odette, easily recognizable by the markings on her beak. "Hetta, she's on the boat!"

"So I see. Let's see what happens."

The swan waddled around the boat, Po Thang following and jumping up at each window to watch her. She pecked on the glass, and my dog shook his head. Morse code between a dog and a swan?

It seemed so, for Po Thang padded over to the oven, pawed the door down, took the baguette and then jumped back up onto the settee. Pushing a sliding window with his head as far as the stop allowed, he dropped the baguette on the deck. Odette picked it up and tossed it overboard to Siegfried before semi-flying back into the water herself.

Chapter Twenty-one

When Jan and I finally quit howling after watching Po Thang feed our daily bread to the swans, I posted the video on Facebook. "If I hadn't seen it myself, I wouldn't have believed it. No wonder the freakin' swans are following us."

"This might go viral, you know."

"I'm already getting lots of hits."

We'd spent the afternoon finalizing our last-ditch shot to save Rhonda. The line in the sand was drawn. We were failing badly in our quest to make her see the light and our patience, which had been tried beyond endurance, had flat run out. As Jan said, "Sometimes you just can't fix stupid."

"Agreed. Enough is enough. We'll sit here until they leave for Toulouse, then it's out of our hands."

"I guess we could offer to drive them to the train station, or even Toulouse?"

"Let's see what happens. If our latest idea fails, there is really no reason to stay here at all. We're throwing the ball squarely in Rhonda's court."

The Trob called as we were making canapés for Happy Hour, tiny open-faced *crème fraîche* and black radish sandwiches. We were now keeping the bread in the ship's safe. Po Thang did not have the combination.

"Hey, Trob. How's things?"

"Okay, everyone's a little on edge, but we all got a laugh from your Facebook post today. That dog is really smart."

"Too smart for his own good, I'd say. But hey, never a dull moment, right? I just want to thank you for making this trip possible. Of course, I'd much rather have Jenks here than Jan, but you take what you can get."

Jan threw a radish at me, but Po Thang caught it in mid-air. He bit down, looked startled, and spit it out.

"I guess getting a call from Jenks any time soon is out of the question?" I asked the Trob.

"Sorry. He sends his love."

"Guess that'll have to suffice for now. Give him my love back."

"I will. He'd like to know your schedule for the next week or so."

Did this mean Jenks might miraculously materialize? "Luckily, we just worked one out. I'll email it to you tonight."

"That's good. Bye."

As always, Wontrobski is a man of few words.

After dinner—we'd splurged on Lobster—I sent our schedule to the Trob, read tons of comments on our Facebook post out loud to Jan, and checked the GPS for *Trebés*, which still hadn't moved. My guess is Rousel was well aware we couldn't go any farther on the canal and was hanging back.

Jan unearthed an old flip cell phone she'd thrown into her bag when she left Mexico, just in case her smart phone wouldn't work in France. She'd spent the evening clearing all but a few numbers from the phone the night before, and we'd had a SIM card added on our trip to town. She activated it and called my cell number as a test, then added her number and René's to the contacts list.

René called to make a lunch date, and we told him we'd be more than ready for a diversion in two days, once we bid *adieu* to our friend, Rhonda. Of course we didn't tell him our concerns over Rousel's intentions yet, saving it for great gossip over lunch. By then either the couple would be gone, or Rhonda would have had an epiphany and dumped him.

"Yeah, right. Wanna make some odds on that one?" Jan asked after we discussed it.

"Nope. Okay, Chica, once Rhonda's off, let's go back to Castelnaudary and then head for the Med. This area," I pointed to a map of the Canal, past Argens, "is all virgin territory for us."

"Speaking of virgins, ya think Rhonda is?"

"I have no idea and didn't think it polite to ask."

"You? Polite?" Jan scoffed.

I ignored that. "And you want to know this, why?"

"Just wondering. I've been researching Rousel's control techniques, and oddly enough they mimic those used by pedophiles. Befriend, tell them they are loved, shower with affection, but no sex. Yet. Also a favorite with human trafficking recruiters."

"Oh, come on. I detest Rousel and I'm convinced he's a gigolo, but Rhonda is hardly white slavery material."

"That's for sure. They like 'em young. The whole thing just bugs me and I'm trying to put a name on it, I guess. Just what is the bastard up to?"

"Jan, that's brilliant."

"Huh?'

"I know we agreed that planting a bug on their boat was way too intrusive, but now that we know they don't do the nasty, I think we should have a listen. Wanna take a walk tomorrow morning? Po Thang needs a good run."

We timed it so *Trebés* was in a lock and offered to take lines from Rhonda, who gladly handed them over, even though Rousel was not a happy camper.

"Gosh," Rhonda gushed, "I thought I'd never see you two again. We'll be in Negra tonight. Will you still be there?"

"Yes, we sure will."

This also didn't set well at all with Rousel, but he bit his lip. I knew poor Rhonda would get an earful later.

"So, Jan what are the chances of rigging a lasso and snagging Rousel around his chic, turtleneck-clad throat?" I snarled quietly.

"Oh, no. That would be so wrong."

"Yeah, I guess so. Too many witnesses."

"Really, Hetta," she huffed, "who cares about witnesses? That turtleneck is obviously an Armani."

When we finally assisted *Trebés* into the last lock Jan broke all yachting protocol and stepped, uninvited on deck. Waving her water bottle she, said, "Hope you don't mind if I get a refill before they close the gates? We're gonna walk back to Negra, and I'm empty."

Rousel, who had come out on deck once they were secured to the bollards, turned to follow Jan inside, but was knocked aside and blocked by Po Thang, whose growl backed the man up.

"Oh, so sorry, Rousel," I said, not sounding very sorry. "How very rude to growl at you on your own boat. Po Thang, you get your furry butt back on this quay."

Po Thang obeyed, much to my surprise, and sat between me and Jan, who had her water and was back by my side. Despite my reprimand, he didn't look all that contrite. Maybe the dog cookie I slipped him as a reward had something to do with it.

Once *Trebés* cleared the dock, Jan and I took off on the path toward Negra. Rhonda waved as they cruised by. She'd offered us a ride, but we demurred, figuring we'd more than worn out any welcome we might have had with Rousel.

"Get it planted?" I asked in a low voice, just in case my voice carried.

"Yep. Under the table, far enough in, but not too far to catch a knee."

"They'll be settled in when we get there, so I'll activate the system. We can watch the boat and if they leave, I'll turn it off to save batteries. Or I can just reset it to voice activation, but that burns power and sometimes all you get is someone's music playing. We'll just have to wing it."

Jan rubbed her hands together in pure joy.

That girl is such a snoop.

How very unfortunate for Rousel that there was only one empty spot on the quay, right behind us. Gee, wonder how that happened?

I boiled shrimp for a Louie for dinner, and while they chilled, we poured a glass of wine, activated the bug and waited. And waited.

"Crap! What happened?"

"I don't know. It was working this morning. We'll have to give it a test. Go knock on the hull. Ask to borrow a cup of sugar."

"That's lame, Hetta. Take Po Thang out and throw his ball for him. He'll bark."

He'd heard "ball" and was already yipping and circling. I threw his tennis ball six or seven times, right next to *Trebés*. After a few minutes, Rhonda stuck her head out. "Jeez, Hetta, I was trying to catch a nap here."

"Ooops, sorry. Come on Po Thang, let's quit disturbing the peace." I waved at Rhonda and went back to my our boat. "They were asleep."

"I heard. Well done, you two," Jan said, giving me a high-five and Po Thang a paw-five. "Shhhh."

I grabbed my earphones just in time to hear Rousel say, "I cannot wait for us to get away from those Americans. They are so loud."

"They're just being friendly. Why don't you like them?"

"I do not think they like *me*."

Jan and I bobbed our heads. I mouthed, "Ya think?"

"I like you," Rhoda said, sounding shy.

"And I you. You are everything a man wants in a woman. Not a...I do not know the word in English...*salope*. "

"Jan, I do believe that man just called us sluts."

"How does he know that?"

"Shhhh. Gotta listen."

"Oh, Rousel, you say the sweetest things."

"I mean each one. You have nothing in common, save your nationality, with those two."

Jan whispered, "He's got that right."

I made a zip-it sign as Rhonda said, "They seem to enjoy life. I've never really done that."

"You will. That is my promise. I think perhaps we should leave in the morning, get away from those annoying women and that bad-tempered dog. Why don't you pack tonight?"

"Can I at least say goodbye?"

"I think it best if you do not."

"If you say so, my love."

"Gag me!" I spat, pulling the earbuds free.

"Wanted to, many a time."

"Very funny. Okay, so now we know. I have to get to her for at least a few minutes before they leave, even if you have to hogtie that SOB."

"Atta girl."

Chapter Twenty-two

We were up before dawn, ready to move. Since they were behind us, they had to pass our boat to get to the office and check out. I tied Po Thang outside to sound the alarm in case our bug crapped out.

Jan and I took turns listening into their boring business of packing, eating breakfast, and then Rousel calling for a cab.

"He must have somehow checked out yesterday. The office doesn't open until nine. Good thing we bugged 'em or they might have slipped away."

Around eight, Po Thang set up a ruckus as a cab pulled into the parking lot and honked. Rousel and Rhonda, loaded with bags, left their boat and headed our way.

Luckily, Rousel led the way, leaving Rhonda to walk a few steps behind, another thing that pissed me off. Jan reached out and unhooked Po Thang, then stepped off the boat with him. I went to our aft cockpit, and as they passed, intercepted Rhonda and gave her a big old goodbye hug.

"Oh, you're leaving already? Here, let me help you with your bags."

I heard Jan engaging Rousel, throwing out a barrage of questions as a distraction.

"Rhonda, listen to me," I whispered. "Take this phone and do *not* tell Rousel you have it. Do this for us and for yourself, just in case something doesn't go right and you need to talk. Jan and I are the only people in the entire world who know where you are and what you plan to do." I refrained from adding, *And who you're with.*

She started to protest, but then nodded and tucked the phone into her pocket. "Can't hurt, I guess."

"Exactly. Please, let us know where you are, when you can. We wish you only the best of luck."

Tears filled her eyes, she put down her bags and returned my hug. Po Thang, spotting this bit of dogless frippery, ran to us and got his own good-bye hug.

Jan followed Po Thang and then we let Rhonda go, keeping our distance from the obviously annoyed Rousel. When Rhonda caught up with him, he roughly grabbed her arm and she reacted by jerking it away.

Shocked at her resistance, he let her go and stormed to the taxi.

When she hesitated to follow, I held my breath, thinking for a couple of hopeful seconds that Rousel's pugnacious behavior might have rattled her cage and shaken loose a modicum of common sense. Evidently Jan was on the same page, because when Rhonda trotted to catch up and jumped into the taxi, she hissed, "I thought we had her for a minute there, but as granny used to say, I reckon there just ain't no fixin' a bad case of the dumbs."

As soon as they were out of sight, I boarded their boat through an unlocked slider and retrieved our bug before the cleaning crew showed up to prepare the boat for the next renters.

A low fog layer made for a dreary day, matching our sentiments. Even Po Thang seemed down in the mouth.

"Well, that's that. We gave it a good go," Jan said.

"True. The ball, or phone in this case, is in her court. At least we know she can call if she gets cold feet. I told her we'd come get her." I sighed. "I need a bowl of strong coffee."

"I need a mug."

"Barbarian."

I called René to see if we could do the lunch thing a day early and then spent the rest of the morning trying to reverse the damage resulting from days of personal neglect. We'd barely taken time to slap on sunscreen and run a brush through our hair, so there was major work to be done.

"It ain't Elizabeth Arden, but we have all their stuff," Jan said as she applied what looked like red mashed potatoes on my head. "While you're marinating I'll get out the manicure kit."

After three hours of overhauling, we had sugar-shined faces, perfect makeup jobs, bouncy tresses, and had donned pressed slacks and real shoes. Po Thang, watching these goings on, got nervous. His humans were up to something and he didn't like it one little bit.

He, too, got a hot shower and a blow dry, much to his chagrin at the time, but when I added his cravat, he perked up. Whatever was happening, he knew he was included.

Charles bounded up on deck at noon and he and Po Thang took off running up the path, yipping greetings and running in circles. The swans followed, probably hoping their bread winner would find more to share. They weren't counting on the boat having a safe.

We went out to greet René and André, inviting them in for a glass of iced tea before we took off for lunch. They politely sipped their drinks, but I could tell they were not thrilled with this American way of ruining perfectly good tea.

Lunch was at a nearby vineyard/winery/restaurant and it was obvious by his hearty greeting that our host knew René well. Fat and juicy scallops steamed in white wine, more white wine to wash them down, the best *frits* I've ever tasted, especially when dipped in a to-die-for béarnaise sauce. Turns out the owners were Belgian, so we had something in common: we both agreed the Belgians were better cooks than the French, which of course, set off a hearty discourse.

During lunch Jan and I shared our worries over Rhonda, and all agreed her amour had all the makings of a first class roué. "But, hey," I said, throwing up my hands, "she's a grown woman, albeit a naive one."

André nodded. "Yes, American women are no match for a determined Frenchman." After he said it, he got flustered and added, "Sorry, *mademoiselle* Coffey, I was not thinking."

I waved away his concern. "Ancient history. You're right. We aren't. I sure learned *that* lesson the hard way."

René cleared his throat. "Jean Luc would like to see you."

Jan's mouth dropped open, as did mine. "Say what?" we both drawled.

"Jean Luc—"

"I heard you, René. I'm just in shock. Why on earth would I ever want to see that man again? The, the...nerve!" I slugged down half a glass of wine.

"Oh, I dunno, Hetta," Jan said with an evil grin, "seems to me like he *deserves* seeing you again."

I glared at her. "What the hell does that mean?"

"Just that I think if he met the grownup Hetta—and I use that term in the loosest possible way—he'd see what he's missed all these years."

The past twenty years of my tumultuous life flashed through my mind like a surreal version of *Absolutely Fabulous* and I guffawed. Evidently having the same thoughts, Jan joined in.

After letting us have our moment of levity, René said, "And, I must add that Jean Luc has his finger on the pulse of Paris. The least he can do to make amends for his scurrilous past is to help us learn who this Rousel fellow really is."

"Help *us*?"

"Of course. It will give two old men like me and André great pleasure to mount our chargers and, like the knights of old, come to the aid of a damsel in distress. Right, *mon amie?*"

"To a Crusade!" André toasted.

Back on the boat after saying our goodbyes, Jan and I were jacked that we had a team to help us find out who, or what, Rousel was. Our gloomy morning of helplessly watching a friend we felt was in peril walk away suddenly didn't look quite so hopeless.

René was delighted when I produced our photos of Rousel's driver's license and credit card, as well as a business card we found in the wallet. "Send me the photos in an email. And I might add, if I ever need a friend I would hope to 'ave two like you ladies. You 'ave gone well out of your way to help a stranger. Not many would go to such lengths."

"Awww, hell, we just don't have anything else to do," Jan said.

I shook my head. "True enough, but it's time we turn in our Superwoman costumes and start our vacation instead of chasing someone else all over the Canal. We'll head the boat back your way, René, but slowly."

"I am sure you will be very much in demand as you travel. I forgot to tell you that the Facebook video of your bread thief and his swan friends was on television last night. Then they showed the prior video of the roping. I should think you are celebrities by now."

Jan fluffed her hair and vamped. "Our public awaits."

René laughed and left.

"Won't be the first time we went viral," Jan said.

"At least this time we aren't being accused of being involved in anything shady."

"Oh, I'm quite sure someone will come up with something. I long for the good old days when not everyone had a camera. Your dog even has one."

"It's the age of technology and the Internet. Everyone's a star," I said, then had a jolting thought. "Oh, dear. I hope Rousel doesn't see Rhonda on the tube. He doesn't know she deceived him and went with us to Argens."

"I hadn't thought of that. Oh, well, it is what it is. And speaking of what is, what are you going to do about Jean Luc?"

"Nothing."

"Good. For once I agree with you. He's a jerk."

"That, of course. But the truth is, I'd feel, I dunno, *disloyal* to Jenks, meeting up with an old boyfriend during a trip Jenks arranged for me. It just wouldn't be right."

"Dang, you suddenly got scruples? Where's the fun in that?"

At least twice a day I left messages and sent texts to the phone I'd slipped to Rhonda, but she never responded. I also called her own cell phone, in hopes she had it working again, but no luck there, either.

We left Negra and took our time getting back to Castelnaudary, where we decided to stay a few days. I tried wiping my worries over Rhonda out of my thoughts, but not very successfully. I could have kicked myself for not getting her schoolteacher friend's last name and contact number.

Meanwhile, I reluctantly agreed with René we should use Jean Luc's extensive connections in Paris to get information on Rousel le Roué, so long as I did not have to talk with, see, or anything else with Jean Luc.

"Ya know, Hetta, there's something downright upright about one rat ratting out another rat."

"I shall refrain from calling the grammar police on that one. Besides, he hasn't gotten anything on Rousel as yet."

"Betcha he will. In the meantime, we can spend a little time learning more about Rhonda and her friends. Where was it she said she taught school?"

"Ummm, somewhere in the Midwest?"

She mimicked making a phone call. "Hello? It this the Midwest? I'm looking for a teacher named Rhonda."

I laughed. "Okay, let's put our heads together and see if we can come up with one brain."

We both turned on our computers, and Po Thang sighed and curled up for a nap. He knows when we're on those dastardly machines we are no fun at all.

I reached over and gave him an ear rub. "I think we'll make a play date with Charles soon." At Charles's name, he opened an eye, thumped his tail and sighed again.

"Yeah, I know, pup, things have been way too quiet in your world for a few days. Well, except for people stopping by to get your autograph."

It was true. Almost daily someone recognized us from our videos and asked for a paw print. I'd purchased a basic, non-toxic finger painting set in town and kept it and a roll of paper towels handy. After a few disastrous attempts requiring a major cleanup, we had it down.

"Okay, Chica, let's get to it. But where to start?"

"Last night I had a three o'clock epiphany. Rhonda said something about a Facebook page for traveling teachers. "

We both went to work, putting in key words, like Teachers, and going back through posts during the past months. Jan suddenly yelled, "Bingo!"

"Which site?"

"Teachers Who Travel. Here's her friend, Rhea, posting a photo of herself and Rhonda in Cannes."

"Okay, going there," I found the site, clicked Rhea's photo, which took me to her personal Facebook page. Rhonda was listed as a friend, and one more click led me to *her* page. "I'll dog Rhonda, and you go back to the Teacher's That Travel site for more postings, okay?"

Jan looked up. "Who."

"What?"

"Teachers *Who* Travel. Grammatically correct, and these *are* teachers, ya know."

"Since when did you...oh, never mind. I'm on Rhonda's, and oddly enough I can see her entire timeline. You would think she'd be more careful and restrict her postings to friends she'd vetted. I certainly do."

"*She* probably has nothing to hide."

"Har, har. But, really, she needs to be more careful."

"Are you kidding me? She's shacked up with a *guy* she hasn't vetted."

"Not in the true sense, but point taken."

I hit the ABOUT button on Rhonda's site. "Fifth grade teacher in the Jefferson, Missouri, school system. Got her degree in Education from Lincoln University. Of course she did. God forbid she should escape her mother's needy clutches. And, of course, she still lives there. Now, let's Google her."

Within seconds we were reading Rhonda's mother's obituary, and what with Mom having lived in the same place for-*ever*, we got the home address. Just for fun, I put the address into Zillow to see what it was worth and was surprised to find it on the market already. "Jan, I'm sending you a link on email. You gotta see this."

She fiddled with her keyboard. "Just under two hundred thou. No great shakes there."

"Look at the date it went on the market."

Jan grabbed our timeline calendar we'd made up when stalking *Trebés* to Negra. I'd made notes of things Rhonda told me along the way, and Jan stabbed a day. "The day *after* she lost use of her phone and Wi-Fi."

"This is getting worse and worse. If I can get a message through to her friend, Rhea, maybe she can clear this up. She'll know when Rhonda makes it back home, because she's keeping an eye on the house for her."

I sent Rhea a private message, explained who I was and the situation with Rhonda, not mentioning our suspicions Rousel was a gigolo. I only said we hadn't heard from her friend since she left the boat a few days before and that Rhonda had told us her phone wasn't working properly.

"That sounds reasonable. No scary enough to set off a 9-1-1 call, but still alerts her so she knows what's happening in case Rhoda hasn't clued her in. Add our phone numbers and email addresses, as well."

"Done. What say we go to Cannes?"

"Where did that come from? We gonna go there and look for a dastardly ring of gigolos preying on teachers?"

"Actually, that's not such a bad idea, but that wasn't what I had in mind. I just think we should do something...extravagant."

"I'm in. Let's pack up some cool beach duds, and...ooops, what are we going to do with you-know-who?" She tilted her head at Po Thang. "Can he go with us?"

"Too much trouble. Nope, I think I'll take René up on his offer and dump the dawg in Gruissan for a visit."

The dog in question stuck out his tongue. How does he know when we're talking about him?

Chapter Twenty-three

After Jan and I decided to take off for Cannes and dump Po Thang on René, I called him. He said Charles would be delighted with his company, as would the rest of the household. I wondered if when we returned, they would still be so delighted. My beach-and-boat dog wasn't exactly accustomed to upscale living.

"We're going to have to fetch the car from Negra tomorrow, then we'll come to Gruissan the next day, drop off your guest, and go on to Cannes for a short stay. Any suggestions on a hotel?"

"We always stay at a friend's guesthouse. I'm sure this time of the year there are no other guests, so I would be happy to enquire, if you would like to use it. I think you would really enjoy it."

"Oh, I don't know, René. That's a wonderful offer, but I'd feel uneasy staying with someone I don't know."

"The main house is not occupied this time of year. Let me make a call, and, I assure you, you will not regret taking me up on the offer."

"Well, okay, go ahead and find out, but let me talk to Jan about it. Anyway, I'll call you tomorrow after I've picked up our car at Negra. *Á bientôt*."

"What do you want to talk with me about?" Jan asked.

"René has use of a guest house in Cannes and says we can stay there. Knowing him, it might be really nice, but it seems almost like we're taking advantage of his generosity."

"Yabbut, I think he enjoys his ability to help us out. Besides, there's that gift horse thing, and all."

"Okay, then. I'll call him—"

Jan's phone rang. "Oh, hi, René, were your ears burning?"

I looked upward for heavenly intervention. This witticism of hers was going to cost me at least a ten minute translation.

"Uh, look I'll let Hetta handle that when we finish talking." She listened for a couple of minutes and nodded her head. "I like it and we accept."

René must have asked a question for she shook her head. "No, I don't need to discuss it with Hetta. We accept," she repeated. "Yes, thank you. We'll see you in the morning. Here's Hetta to explain that ear-burning thing." She handed me the phone.

I mouthed, "I'll get you for this," then was delighted to learn the French also use a similar term when discussing someone who is not present. I didn't bother to ask what he and Jan had conspired on that didn't need my approval, for once deciding to give over control.

When I hung up, Jan waited for me to grill her and when I didn't, she demanded, "Well?"

"Well, what?"

"Don't you want to know what René and I agreed on?"

"Nope. Surprise me."

"Fine, go pack those beach duds. He'll pick us up early tomorrow morning."

"Fine. What's for dinner?"

"What do you want?"

"Anything you want. I'm going to take Po Thang for a walk."

The "W" word brought Po Thang, leash in mouth. As we left the boat, I turned to wave and saw Jan frowning, hands on hips.

Once in a while it's just soooo much fun to confound your friends.

Dinner was poached salmon with a lemon, butter and parsley sauce. Jan had outdone herself so I decided to play nice.

"Oh, man, that salmon was to die for. Okay, now tell me is René picking us up in the morning?"

"I thought you'd never ask. You haven't been into the Valium again, have you?"

I hadn't told her I'd smuggled my favorite drug and a gun into France. "Of course not."

"Then how did you manage to go," she looked at her oversized watch, "an entire two hours without asking what I'd agreed to without consulting you?"

"Maturity," I said airily. "I've decided to mature."

"Ack."

"Just kidding. Okay, dish."

"He, or rather, André, is driving us to Cannes. They'll stay in the main house tomorrow night, then haul the pooches back to Gruissan. We get the pool house."

"Cool. We're gonna be doing the French Riviera in style."

"Hetta, we do everything in style."

"Well, our own style, that's for sure."

We fell into silence, each of us probably thinking about some of our less than stylish moments. At least I was.

When René, André, and Charles arrived the next morning, we loaded up and headed for Cannes. I had not been there in years but doubted much had changed. Boy, was I wrong.

Before we went to our digs, André gave us a driving tour of the town. While the basic shoreline was how I remembered it, there were a few new hotels. I was surprised by so many mega-yachts med-tied in the marina. The last time I was in the town, there were a few hotels near the beach—none of which I could afford—but now mega-yachts, luxury hotels, restaurants, and designer stores had taken over. Spoiled by the pristine and unpopulated beaches in the Sea of Cortez, I couldn't imagine sitting under one of the jillion umbrellas obliterating a view of the sand.

"Gee, it's just like in the movies," Jan said in awe. "I can't even imagine what it's like during the film festival."

René grunted. "It is ruin-ed. It was a small fishing village when my friend bought his villa here. It is a good thing he purchased in Le Suquet, or his view would be block-ed by now. Of course, he has updated the house over the years, thank God, so we no longer 'ave to use an outdoor toilet facility."

Yes, thank you, God. "I remember Old Town," I said. "I loved it. I wish I could remember where I stayed, but it's probably gone by now, judging by what's happened on the waterfront."

"*Non*, Le Suquet, it does not change. Oh, there are many more chic shops, but the basic buildings, they remain the same."

My heart sank. I've stayed in decaying villas over the years and the enchantment wears off fast. They are charming to look at, but in practicality, moldy, and damp. Especially here on the coast. Had I packed my sweats?

We left the *Plage du Casino/Cannes la Croisette*—the popular crescent beach area—and turned onto a cobblestone street, yet another visually endearing feature that quickly wears down the spine and kidneys, even in an Austin Princess. Five bumpy minutes later, André stopped before a set of giant ornate gates, spoke into a speaker box, and the heavy gates swung slowly open. Entering a tree-lined drive, we pulled under the portico of a three-story stone mansion. And yep, it was covered in ivy and looked a little moldy. Call me unromantic, but in my book, ivy equals spiders. I am such a romantic.

A young, willowy, elegantly dressed woman met us, shared air kisses with both the men, and shook hands with us. She introduced herself as the *gestionnaire de propriétés*, which I guessed was property manager, said she hoped we would be satisfied with the pool house for a few days, gave us her card, jumped into a Porsche, and exited through those grandiose gates.

"Jeez, Hetta, how do we get jobs as property managers over here?" Jan asked.

René shook his head. "Do not be misled. They give themselves job titles for tax purposes. She is a relative, the daughter of one of the owner's cousins."

I looked at her card and quipped, "Nice work, Nicole, if you can get it."

I insisted on taking René and André to dinner at a restaurant of their choice. Quite naturally, they picked a dog-friendly place on the touristy Le Croissette beach walk where we could eat outdoors while admiring designer *everything*, mega-yachts, and fancy dogs.

"Paris Hilton, eat your heart out," Jan said, as a woman walked by with a fluffy white chicken stuffed in her designer bag. "I could sit here for days, just watching the parade."

"Me too. Matter of fact, let's walk back here for breakfast tomorrow morning. Thanks, René for introducing us to your Cannes. Our pool room," I put finger quotation marks around *pool room*, "is wonderful. Meeting you on the beach in Gruissan was the best thing that could have happened."

"It is my pleasure. Making new friends like you, Jan, and Po Thang has given these two old men something to look forward to. We will miss you when you return to Mexico."

"You can visit us."

"We might do so. It is easy at my age to settle in and spend my days with Charles. Not that he is bad company, but our household can use a little young blood."

"Calling us young just earned you major Brownie points," Jan said.

Oh, hell. Now I have to explain Brownies?

Our cabana, as they called it, was actually a two bedroom cottage off a spectacular infinity pool. What with the pool's water melding with sky and ocean in the distance, the impression was one of being on the beach, rather than smack dab in the middle of Old Town. Whoever designed the pool was a genius. Also, much to my relief, everything was upgraded inside the cottage walls, while the outside retained an old-world look. René told us the house was over a hundred years old, so whoever owned it must have hired a pro to do the upgrades. Not a spider in sight, nor any mold.

We helped the men load up the Austin the next morning, kissed both them and the two dogs goodbye and went back to our pool house to plan our day.

Jan checked for any replies from Rhonda and declared, "No luck. But after our tour of Cannes, something struck a note, *et voila!* Look familiar?"

I walked behind her and squinted at the screen where I saw a field of umbrellas on a beach. "Sure does."

"Now, check this out." She brought up a selfie of Rhea and Rhonda under one of those umbrellas, and I yelled, "That's Rousel!"

"Jeez, Hetta, my ear."

I lowered my voice. "Sorry. Rhonda said she and Rhea first saw Rousel and a friend in Cannes and here they are, in living color." In the selfie, the two women were in the forefront, but behind them, two men, one of them Rousel, were clearly captured. And, although Rhonda told me the men totally ignored her and her friend, that was clearly not the case when the women's backs were turned. I *know* snooping when I see it, and said so.

"Yep, you've got a PhD in snoopery. I wonder where *exactly* this was taken."

"Let's go find out. We got nothing but time and the day is beautiful. Let us go on a fact-finding mission."

Returning to where we had dinner the night before, we bought a map from a street vendor, found a table, and ordered coffee. Jan had loaded the selfie of Rhonda and Rhea into her iPhone so we could compare backgrounds around us.

I pointed to an outcropping down the beach. "See that? I visited it years ago, but it's worth a revisit. That was before all this," I swooped my arm toward the huge marina, "was even here. It was called the artist's castle or something like that."

Jan looked at our map. "Château de la Napoule?"

"Yeah, that's it. Anyhow, if we walk in that direction, we should be able to find where Rhonda and Rhea were sitting when they spotted Rousel and friend."

"And we are doing this, why? Never mind, why *not*?"

It didn't take long to zero in on the spot, even the very table where Rhea snapped the selfie. Just for fun I took a selfie of me and Jan, with the now unoccupied table from which Rousel le Roué and his friend were eavesdropping. I thought it would be fun to give it to Rhonda someday if we were dead wrong and she and her dreamboat got married or something.

After the waiter took our orders—since it was mid-morning we decided it was okay to have champagne—we dug out our map again and planned a day of playing tourists.

My phone rang and, miracle of miracles, it was Jenks. I told him we were goofing off on the Riviera and staying at a chateau with a pool house.

"I'm glad you're having a good time, but I would rather you didn't hang out in tourist areas right now," he said.

"We're only here for two days, then we'll take the train to Negra and pick up the car."

"Hetta, please, no trains or planes. If you have to rent another car, I'll cover it."

"Jenks, you're worrying me. What's up?"

"We aren't sure, but you need to be on the alert. Stay away from crowded areas."

The beach was filling up, as was the café. Matter of fact, the table next to us was now occupied. I grabbed my champagne and took a gulp.

Jan, who was watching me intently, did likewise.

"Okay, Jenks, I read you, loud and clear. We'll head back to Castelnaudry soon and keep a low profile here. Dang, and here we were, planning to dance on the tabletops tonight."

He sighed. "Sorry, Red. I don't want to throw a wet blanket on your fun, but do it somewhere safe, okay? Gotta go. Love you."

"Wait a minute, where are you?" I asked, but he was gone.

"What?" Jan asked.

"I'll tell you later. We should go."

"Don't have to tell me twice."

While she packed up her laptop, I signaled the waiter for our check.

"Hetta," Jan whispered. "Act like you're taking a selfie and reverse it so you get the table next to us, okay?"

"Why?"

"Just friggin' do it. I'm gonna move next to you so it looks more natural."

The check arrived just as I snapped off two selfies, I threw too much money on his tray, and we left. A block away, I asked, "What was all that about?"

"You'll see. Slow down and let's window shop along the boulevard."

"Jenks said to get out of here, or anywhere else people gather."

"We will, but first we gotta check out those photos you just took."

I pulled out my phone. "I look like crap in the first one. Gotta delete this one for sure. Why do you always look so danged good?"

"Send me the second one, right now."

"Jeez. Okay, sent."

Jan's phone dinged and she pulled up the photo and zoomed in with her thumb and finger. "Look familiar?"

"Holy crap. That's Rousel's friend."

"And don't look now, but he's following us."

"Way creepy." I caressed the Taurus in my shoulder bag. "Why and how did he hone in on us?"

"I've got a theory on that. Let's just move slowly and keep an eye on him."

"Tell me your theory. I've already got one of my own."

"The waiter. He called this guy and said he had a couple of hot prospects for him."

"That's what I think. Great minds and all. What say we lead this jerk on a merry goose chase?"

After fifteen minutes of meandering, we found another café and ordered lunch. Our tail took up residence at a table behind us. Jan winked and said loudly, "Isn't being in France romantic? Let's toast that bastard I divorced. May he remain forever broke and homeless."

I jumped right in, following her lead. "By the time you get through with him, you'll even have the yacht." I nodded toward the marina, chockablock with megayachts.

"But I'll still be on my own. I hope you change your mind and hang around a little longer to keep me company. Money's no object," Jan whined.

"I really have to get back to Dallas, honey, but I do feel bad about leaving you here *all* alone." I suddenly swiveled in my chair and said, "Say, you look French. Where would you go if you were a woman alone on the Riviera looking for a good time?"

Startled at my loud question, our tail blanched and looked around as if seeking a hole to scurry into. Jan and I didn't give him a break, just stared and waited for his answer. I repeated the question in French. A couple of women sitting nearby hid smiles behind napkins.

The man, model gorgeous, recovered and smiled. "I would make friends with me, of course."

"Charming. You got a name?" Jan was pouring on the Texas thang.

"Étienne."

"Well, dang, I think I have a pair of your shoes. Or is it a handbag? You live around here?"

"Uh, yes, but I am not the designer."

"Well, that's okay. Come on over here and have a drink, Cutie Pie. I don't speak French, but looks like you know English. Lemme get a photo for the girls back home." She pulled out her phone and snapped him before he could react.

Jan's full frontal onslaught made him squirm. He was used to being the predator, not the prey, and the last thing he was looking for was an aggressive female. That's not how gigolos work. He threw money on his table and skedaddled.

The women at the next table laughed and raised their wine glasses to us.

"You know him?" Jan asked.

"That one? He works the waterfront. We see him often, looking for women to...what is the word?"

"Fleece."

They didn't understand, so I said, "Take money from."

This cracked them up. "Yes, that is it."

"Have you seen him with another man?"

One of the women nodded. "Yes. But the other has not been here for some time. He must have found someone to fleez."

Jan pulled out her laptop and showed them the photo of the men Rhonda's friend posted on Facebook. Tapping Rousel's face on the screen, she asked, "Is this him?"

The women peered at the photo and agreed they were looking at the two men we were talking about. "You are the police?" one of them asked.

"No. But we are concerned for a friend. She saw this man here in Cannes, then actually met him in Gruissan. We think he followed her there."

"That is how they work. They do not seek French women but prey on foreigners. "*Mais*..." she looked embarrassed.

"But what?" I asked.

"You must forgive me, but if your friend is near your age, that would be...unusual."

"Why is that?"

"We noticed he, the blonde, seemed to prefer very much the...young ones."

"As in younger and maybe stupider?"

They nodded, so I asked, "But why would a gigolo, if that is what he is, go after someone, uh, less seasoned, but who probably has no money?"

They shrugged. "We do not know. That one," she sniffed in the direction of the man we scared off, "he is a local who simply picks up free meals and gifts for his company. As a gigolo, he is not very good at it. The other, the one your friend is involved with, he is new to Cannes and I think," she sneered, "Algerian."

Boy, were we ever getting an education in French bias; evidently it's more desirable to be a French gigolo than an Algerian in France.

"Really? With that blonde hair?" Jan asked, fishing for more info.

"You are blonde, *Chérie*, that man's skin is quite dark."

"Dang, I just thought he had a tan."

We finished our lunch, said so long to the ladies, and doubled back to the beach. Our admirer was at the café where we first saw him, striking up a conversation with an older lady with a poodle in her lap. Obviously he was not pining for our sweet selves. Love can be so fleeting, and fickle.

Back at our pool house, we discussed our next move.

"So, Jenks says we should leave Cannes, but not by train or plane. How we gonna get back to Castelnaudary? Or Negra to pick up our car?"

We were sitting by the pool, watching the sunset, and lights blinking on in town.

"Not sure. Let's stay here for at least another night. We'll figure something out. These terrorists are starting to really piss me off."

"Hetta, you have the most amazing knack for the understatement."

I had to laugh at what I just said. "You know what I mean. I'm starting to take it personally."

"Don't do it. That's what they want."

"Yeah, I guess. So, what do we do about Rousel now that we *know* he's a gigolo?"

"We absolutely have to reach Rhonda. Anything back from Rhea yet?"

"Nope. It's chilly out here, so we might as well go back in and dig some more. I'll call René and see if they've got anything on Rousel yet."

"Don't tell him we're not gonna take a train or plane. He'll insist on coming to get us."

After calling Nicole, the elegant property manager, and telling her we'd probably be leaving in two days, I touched base with René.

"Hetta! Po Thang was just about to call you! He has news."

"Ha. Put him on, then."

After Po Thang went through his entire vocabulary of woofs and whines, René told me his news: Rousel le Roué actually did work for his family business.

I hung up the phone, thoroughly confused.

"So," Jan said after I told her this turn of events, "Rousel is *not* a gigolo?"

"Sounds more like he's a playboy, if what those women said today is true. He stalks young women for fun and games, while his friend zeroes in on older gals for profit."

"Now that pisses me off. I'm not even forty," Jan huffed. "Unlike you."

"Thanks for that pleasant reminder. The question is why did Rousel go after Rhonda?"

Jan shrugged. "Maybe he wants American citizenship? Seems like he'd get a much better reception back home. It's hard not to pick up on the disdain René and that woman today have for French-Algerians, second generation or not."

"Still, something stinks like a Parisian *pissoir* in July here."

"Try that phone you gave Rhonda again. Leave a message that'll make her call. Tell her I'm dying or something."

"Which won't be a stretch if you age-shame me again."

"Sorry. I feel so helpless. Does Jean Luc know where Rousel is right now?"

"René didn't say."

"Okay, Hetta, the time has come to swallow your pride. Get Jean Luc's phone number and call him."

"No way, Jose. I ain't doing it. Besides, what happened to us just emasculating him?"

"I do believe one would have to be in close proximity to the victim to do that, huh? Can't exactly remove someone's nuts by remote control."

"Dang."

"Miz Hetta, we gotta find Rhonda, and right now. And for that, we're gonna need Jean Luc's help, simple as that."

I sighed. "I guess you're right. She said they were flying out day after tomorrow, so maybe DooRah's contacts in Paris can check for them on passenger lists. Seems like Jean Luc is indeed connected."

"Ain't no way are the airlines giving out that kind of info, even if we knew which airline they, or rather, *Rousel*, booked them on."

I sat up straight. "Air France! Rhonda said Air France"

"Then, get on the horn, *now*."

After downing ten milligrams of courage from my secret stash, I dialed the number René gave me for Jean Luc DooRah. My heart thudded with each ring, until I was forwarded to voicemail.

I hate modern technology.

Chapter Twenty-four

I listened, heart still a-thump, as Jean Luc's sexy voice asked me to leave a message.

Hanging up without doing so, I glared at the phone. "If this damned thing wasn't so expensive I'd throw it in the pool right now."

"Calm down. He'll see your number and probably call back. After all, *he's* the one who wants to see *you*, remember?"

"Maybe I should send Jenks an email and tell him what we're doing, and why. I'm taking a nasty guilt trip here."

"Oh, for cryin' out loud, it ain't like you're jumping in the sack with Jean Luc. We're just trying to protect a friend here, not rekindle an old affair. Get real."

"I still feel bad. Jenks is so good to me, and here, once again, I've embroiled myself in another freakin' mess."

"Uh, please allow me to rephrase that. As in, you've embroiled *us* in another freakin' mess."

"Sorry."

"Sorry? Hell, I love it. We're in France and on the trail of some bad guy who deserves to get his comeuppance. If we hadn't been here, goodness knows what would have happened to Rhonda."

"Goodness only knows what *still* might. We're spinning our wheels."

"Let's sleep on it. We can't do anything more tonight."

"You're right," I yawned, "and I'm beat."

"Want a glass of wine?"

"Nah, I'd better—"

"I knew it! You've taken a Valium, haven't you? That is the only reason on God's green earth you won't drink."

Dang.

Beat or not, even my drug of choice didn't put me to sleep.

I read for a time, then got up and did more Internet searches, including another look at the Teachers Who Travel site to see *exactly* when Rhea had posted that clandestine reverse-selfie of Rousel and his gigolo friend. It was before she left Europe.

Hmmm. Wouldn't you think she'd have loaded up the site with tons of photos after she returned to the US? We all post pics of ourselves after vacations in glorious spots, so why hadn't she?

Next, I Googled Rhonda's name, putting in keywords, addresses, even names from her mother's obituary, anything that might give me *someone* to contact. Anyone at all.

By three, I figured the Valium had cleared out of my liver and a wee dram of white might help me sleep. I took a heavy throw from the foot of my bed, stuck a pillow under my arm, and went outside to a lounge chair by the pool. It was cool, but I was in my sweats and heavy socks and there was no wind. Settling in, I tucked the blankie around me and immediately regretted not bringing the bottle with me. Snug as a bug, I gazed down at the well-lit marina and all those yachts, and I suffered a wave of homesickness for my own boat.

My eyes grew heavy and were on the verge of closing when a blink caught my peripheral vision. Turning my head, I spotted an upstairs light on in the main house that hadn't been lit earlier. I was trying to ignore it when it went off, and a couple of minutes later, another came on.

No one was supposed to be there, because the property manager told me so just a few hours before. Not wanting to disturb Nicole with a false alarm at this hour, I reluctantly uncurled from my cozy nest and went back inside. Slipping on a jacket and sneakers, I stuffed my old friend, Taury, in one pocket, and a mini-flashlight and my phone in the other.

Sneaking down a path leading to the front of the house, I peeked around a corner but didn't see a car in the drive, and the solid garage doors didn't have windows. Rats.

As I stood there looking up and trying to decide my next move, a shadow passed by a curtained window. I was backing up, out of sight of that window, intent on getting out of hearing range and calling the property manager *tout de suit,* when I collided with Jan.

"Ouch. What in the hell are you doing out here?" she asked.

"Shhh. Someone's in the main house skulking around. I was going to call Nicole when I got back to our house. I was afraid whoever is in there would hear me if I called from out here."

As we rushed back to the pool area, Jan whispered, "Did you actually *see* anyone?"

"No, just a light came on, and a shadow. Like someone is sneaking around up there, going from room to room."

"Kinda like you are down here?" she hissed.

"We're *supposed* to be here. You don't think that gigolo dude followed us home today, do you?"

"Why would he?"

"Maybe he moonlights as a cat burglar?" I speculated. "I guess we'd better call Nicole."

"Or, we can just go find out who's here, and why."

"How are we gonna get inside?"

"For once we don't have to break and enter. Follow *moi*." She spun and took off for the back of the main house and led me to a large heavy door with a smaller one built into it. "Here we have it, the service entrance."

"Aha! How'd you know about this?"

"René showed me. And gave me the combo." She hit numbers on a lighted keypad, opened the door and waved me inside. "Age before beauty."

Refraining from bopping her one for impertinence, I stepped into a very dark entryway, thankful when a dim motion light flicked on.

"Creepy, just like in the movies. Where's it go?"

"Basement, and a surprise."

About ten feet down the hall, another door, this one built of heavy, ancient-looking wood, screaked open with enough noise to wake the dead when Jan tugged on the handle. "Jeez, they could use some WD-40. I'll just betcha this was an original entryway," I whispered.

"I think you're right." She flipped a switch and those crappy energy-saving lights I hate barely illuminated yet another corridor leading to a narrow staircase.

I started forward, but Jan held me back. "Hold on, you gotta see something." She flashed her beam onto yet another door along the corridor. This was metal and looked like it belonged in a mediaeval prison. She ran her hand over the frame and came back with a key the size of my cell phone.

She swung the key in front of my face and her teeth gleamed in the dim light.

"Oh, joy, I've never been in a crypt," I quipped.

"Oh, ye of little faith." She unlocked the door, and pushed it. Once again, the screeching of metal against metal resounded off stone walls, making me cringe.

Jan went through the door and turned on a light, this one bright.

"Holy crap. I think I've died and gone to Heaven. Why didn't you tell me about this?"

"Are you kidding? *You* and a wine cellar like *this*? I was saving you from yourself."

"If we lived here we'd never leave the house."

"Maybe we should just grab a bottle and go back to the pool and mind our own bidness for a change?"

I thought about that. "Tempting as that sounds, we either need to see who's here or call Nicole."

"Fooey. Okay then, from now on, you lead, I'll follow."

"Why do *I* have to lead?"

"Because you have the gun?"

"How do you know I have a gun?"

"Because, Hetta, you always do. Besides, I found it in your purse, right next to the Valium."

"Snoop."

"You've taught me everything I know. We need a rope."

"Stand by."

I returned to the pool area, untied the line from a life ring hanging on a wall, grabbed one of the flashlights placed around the house in case of a power failure, and returned to find Jan opening a dusty bottle of wine.

"Jan! I'm shocked. What on earth is wrong with you? That's a sweet white!"

She blew dust from the label. "Crap. Oh, well, any port in a storm." She turned it up and took a glug. "Wow, not bad. Try it"

After a sizable gulp, I smacked my lips. "Very good, but requires chocolate. I'd love to stay and drink, but we have an intruder to intrude upon."

The theme from the *Pink Panther* came to mind as we skulked through a huge professional-style kitchen suitable to an upscale restaurant, and into another kitchen, this one decked out for domestic use. In the owner's kitchen, a large round table with a seating capacity for at least twelve evoked a homey feeling, whereas the next room, obviously the main dining area, was downright grandiose. It was evident the family did some large-scale entertaining, but also a lot of their own cooking.

A thirty-foot table that probably started life in a monastery was lined with ornate silver candelabras larger than my rental car, and was flanked by leaded glass sideboards, a soaring rock fireplace I could've walked into, and hand-carved *boiserie*, those wooden panels the French love so much. Accusatory ancestral eyes followed our progress from *grand-luxe* gold picture frames. "Okay, this is a lot creepy," Jan whispered, quickly shining her light away from the paintings.

"Probably pretty over the top with the lights on. Okay, let's find the main staircase. I'm a little turned around right now, but I'm sure if we go left at the top floor, we'll find the room where I saw the last light come on."

From the second dining room we entered an enormous foyer we'd been in before when René stayed there. I'd marveled at the opulence at the time, and decided immediately that Po Thang, lest he do something doggy, would be staying in the pool house with us that night.

Jan shined the flashlight on the staircase that Po Thang, new to stairs on this scale, had raced up and down a few times before being called to task by Charles. *Évidemment*, French dogs do not roughhouse in the manse.

"Here we go, Chica. Last chance to chicken out and call Nicole." I sort of hoped Jan would vote for chickening out.

"Nah, we got this. Take off your shoes."

We tiptoed in stocking feet up the wide, and thankfully, solid wooden stairs; there was no carpet, or even a runner, to muffle our steps. Years of use left indentations in the wood, and Po Thang had probably added scratches that were sure to be buffed out soon by a dedicated staff. If we were to be welcome in most homes in France, he was going to have to get some manners. Or socks.

At the top landing, I tapped Jan on the shoulder and pointed to faint light leaking from under what I surmised was a bedroom door. All was quiet except for my shallow panting. "Jeez, Hetta, you sound like Po Thang. Take a deep breath."

I gulped and tried practicing breathing in a method my yoga instructor called Pranayama.

We waited, hugging the wall on either side of the door and listening. "Music," Jan whispered.

"Somehow I can't quite picture a second-story guy hanging out in a bedroom listening to Edith Piaf," I whispered back.

"Maybe it's where the safe is. What should we do?"

"Knock?"

"What if he's armed?"

"*We're* armed."

"Oh, yeah. Okay, you open the door. I'll draw a bead on him."

Jan looped her rope into a lariat, held it in her right hand, and turned the huge brass knob with her left. The door creaked open, banged against the wall, and Jan ran inside. She was supposed to leave me a clean line of sight but forgot that part.

"*Merde!*" someone yelled.

"Got 'im. Get in here fast, turn on the lights, and keep a sharp eye on him while I wrap this up, so to speak."

I found a light switch and saw Jan was in the middle of a huge Louis XV-style bed, astride a man she'd evidently flipped over. She was binding his crossed wrists behind him. Her knees were digging into her victim's bare calves, pretty much rendering him helpless. That Jan really knows her ropin' and ridin'.

Jumping off the bed, she threw her arms in the air as though she'd just beat a competitor's time at a 4-H Club Fourth of July rodeo. I could, for just a moment, picture her back in Texas in a dusty corral, vying for a blue ribbon.

"So, who we got here?"

"Dunno, but he sure smells good for a thief."

The man was yelling into a feather pillow and squirming against his restraints but like I said, Jan knows her stuff.

"Turn him over before he suffocates."

Jan grabbed one end of the rope and rolled the guy over easily. He evidently had a mouthful of pillow, because it rolled with him. Unfortunately, the sheet didn't. "Ooops," she said as she threw the duvet over the naked man.

She wasn't fast enough for me not to get an eyeful.

There are some things a gal just never forgets.

"Oh, hell, Jan. That's Jean Luc DooRah."

Chapter Twenty-five

"Ya don't say," Jan drawled when I identified the man we just attacked and hog-tied as Jean Luc DooRah. "Funny that after all these years you'd recognize him with his head and nuthin' else covered." She reached over and pulled the pillow off the victim's face. "Hey, there, Jean Luc. I've heard *way* too much about you, you low-down dirty skunk."

Jean Luc spit out a couple of feathers and sputtered a string of curses and threats, then stopped when he saw me standing at the foot of the bed, my laser beam painting a red dot between his eyes. He tried to throw his arms up, then realized his hands were tied behind his back. "Hetta! Don't shoot! Please. I'm sorry. I never meant to hurt you. Give me a chance to explain."

I did lower the gun, but a little on the slow side. Jean Luc's eyes traced the beam as it moved down his body and rested, for just a few heartbeats on his manly parts, before I put the pistol away.

Jean Luc smiled and said in that knicker-melting accent of his, "*Alors, ma petite vachère*, is that a pistol in your pocket, or are you just glad to see me?"

First light bathed Cannes as Jan, Jean Luc, and I sipped strong coffee from bowls. We sat inside a glassed area off the pool as a cold front moved in with the dawn.

Evidently recovered from the indignity of being trussed and menaced by a couple of women, Jean Luc donned sweats—Pierre Balmain, of course—and had joined us at the pool house. We sort of apologized for roughing him up, but he shrugged it off, pulling a face before saying, "Oh, I quite enjoyed it."

Just to let him know I hadn't forgotten his lying ways, I filled my cheek with air and pushed in with my finger, making a "Ppffff," sound, the classic French gesture for, *I don't believe a word you say*.

He laughed. "I've missed you, *ma petite vachère*."

"Can it, Jean Luc. That false charm of yours doesn't work any longer. And I am not your little cowgirl anymore, so quit calling me that."

"Yeah. Besides, Hetta ain't the cowgirl in this rodeo," Jan chimed in.

"*Évidemment*, Jan. You are quite accomplished with that rope. I watched René's video of you and the bollards on the canal. *Bravo*."

Jan wasn't ready to accept compliments from the enemy. "Let's get down to business here. We know René gave you the information we have on this Rousel dude, so have you learned any more about him?"

He shrugged. "He is who he says he is."

"He is? Then maybe we are overreacting here?"

Jean Luc shook his head. "Not necessarily. He seems legitimate on the surface. No troubles with the authorities, but that does not mean he will not take advantage of your friend."

Unable to edit my mouth, I grumbled, "Says the world-class expert on taking advantage of women."

"Would you kids like to be alone?" Jan asked.

"No!" I yelled at the same time as Jean Luc said, "Yes!"

"We have a tie. I have a great idea. Let's just shelve your past crap until we deal with today's crap? How's that sound?"

I nodded, as did Jean Luc.

"Okay then, let's get back to the subject at hand. We've gone above and beyond for Rhonda, but I say that after tomorrow, when she gets on that plane, we wash our hands of the whole danged mess. Agreed?"

We did.

"Jean Luc, do you know anyone with enough pull in Paris to check if Rhonda and Rousel have reservations on an Air France flight tomorrow? Who knows if he even bought those tickets?"

"I just might. Give me her full name and address in the United States, and I will contact a friend in Paris. After breakfast, I suggest we go into town for *le petit déjeune*, and then I will make my calls. We French cannot work on an empty stomach, you know. And, being attacked by wild Texans in my own home has given me quite the appetite."

"This is *your* house?" I blurted.

In his best Inspector Clouseau English, he said, "But of curse."

I stomped back into the pool house, a little dazed to learn we were staying in the rat's nest. Or, as he made clear, *one* of his nests. As I paced in our living room, I threw up my hands and told Jan, "We gotta get out of here. Right now. I mean it."

"Why? You skeered you'll fall under his spell again?"

"Not at all," I huffed. "He's hardly irresistible."

"Oh, please. This guy could charm the skin off a rattlesnake."

"Not me. Never again. My skin is perfectly safe."

"And now you bite."

I grinned. "True."

"Then why do you want to run away? One more day and we'll be done with the Rhonda affair and set off on new horizons, but we need Jean Luc's resources in Paris today. And I'm starving and he's buying."

We piled into a Land Rover—which the family must have deemed appropriate for braving the cobblestones of Cannes—parked along with two other cars in his large garage, and Jean Luc took us down the hill to the imposing and historic Carlton Intercontinental Hotel. Pulling up in front, he was greeted by name as he turned his car over to a valet. We entered the century-old Belle Époque lobby and Jean Luc was repeatedly fawned over as we made our way to the breakfast area.

"It is unfortunate you are here off-season," he told us. "Outdoor dining during warm weather is a wonderful location to watch the rich and famous. I once saw Grace Kelly."

"I'm surprised you didn't know her, what with your wife's social ties," I sniped.

"Why, Hetta. You have been checking up on me? I am delighted."

I opened my mouth to let him have it, but Jan intervened. "Hetta, put a plug in it. You two can duke it out later, but right now I want a large cheese omelet without a side of lip. From either of you."

Jean Luc looked a little smug, but Jan stabbed a finger at him. "Oh, and by the way, you rat, I ain't through with you. However, we have to work together right now, so I will try to keep Hetta from emasculating you. I want in on that part later."

"Somezing to look forward to," Jean Luc said drolly.

In my anger over the years, I had forgotten what a great sense of ironic humor he has and how well he delivers it. *Ye gads and little fishes, did I just think a kind thought about a man I've wanted to murder for twenty years?*

"Champagne. We need champagne," I told a hovering, snooty-looking waiter, who turned to Jean Luc for affirmation.

Sensing possible trouble on the horizon, Jean Luc said, "I shall let mademoiselle choose our Champagne today, as unfortunately she is without her personal sommelier."

The waiter did a half bow, I chose a champagne, he complimented my choice and I replied, "*Merci, garçon.*" He slinked away, properly put in place.

"Bravo, Hetta," Jean Luc whispered. "You have not forgotten some things I taught you."

I think I blushed. *Oh, I have not forgotten many things you taught me.*

Jan giggled. "Were you two always this funny together? I can see why..." I kicked her under the table, "never mind."

Jean Luc wisely chose to ignore Jan's question. "René tells me you are leaving tomorrow. What time is your train?"

I didn't think it necessary to mention Jenks's warning about trains and planes. "We have to pick up my car at Negra, on the Canal du Midi. We'll rent a car."

"Nonsense, I shall drive you. And tonight, perhaps you will join me for dinner?"

"Sure," Jan said, before I had a chance to say something like, *No. Way. In. Hell!*

"Wonderful, I am having a few friends in this evening, so come over around eight?"

"And me without a thing to wear," I said.

Jan and I were sorting and packing for our trip to Negra and back to the boat the next afternoon. Jean Luc said we'd head out mid-morning because he had a meeting earlier. This would still leave Jan and me plenty of time to get back to Castelnaudary before dark.

"This is the Riviera. Everyone seems to be decked out in beachy stuff." She held up a gauzy dress she bought the day before. By my estimates, it cost around a hundred dollars an ounce. "How about this? Cool, huh?"

"Cool being the operative word. I'm freakin' freezing. I hope it'll be warmer in Castlenaudry, but if not, the heater on the boat works well. Maybe this wind won't get that far inland."

Jan threw the filmy frock into a suitcase and pulled out a lightweight sweater and slacks. I plucked a navy boyfriend blazer, striped turtleneck, and white denim pants from the closet. I had no intention of freezing my butt off at a dinner I didn't want to attend in the first place.

When we entered Jean Luc's kitchen, the warmth of a crackling wood fire and candlelight galore greeted us. The table was set for twelve, and on the hearth sat at least a dozen bottles of red wine already uncorked and breathing. A sideboard held an array of bottles: Pastis, Dubonnet, Perrier, and ice buckets with bottles of Campari Soda and Champagne, alongside plates of fancy hors d'oeuvres.

Memories of Jean Luc standing at the head of a makeshift table in my tiny Left Bank apartment made my knees go weak. It was a weekend ritual, when we invited friends for an evening of food and fun. At least for the five weekends we spent together.

"Gee, I guess I didn't get the memo," Jan drawled, taking in the fact that, under his apron, Jean Luc was dressed in a blue blazer, striped turtleneck, and white jeans.

What the hell kind of sick psycho crap led me to dress exactly the same? Oh, yeah, now I remember, that's what we used to do.

Jean Luc DooRah gave me a once over. "*Tres chic*," he teased.

"One of us has to change clothes, right now. This is seriously sick."

"Oh, lighten up. I think it's kinda cute," Jan said, grabbing her phone and snapping a wide-angle selfie of the three of us.

Jean Luc poured a bottle of Campari Soda over ice, put in a twist of lemon, and handed it to me. *Crap, after all this time he remembers what I used to drink?* "I will, as you wish, change my clothes. I did not even realize I was..."

I took a sip of the bitter drink, recalling how much I used to love it. "No, it's okay. Neither did I. I'm just...." *I'm just what? Confused?*

"Jan, might I have a moment alone with Hetta?"

"I'll go hang out by the front door and greet your other guests as they arrive." She hoofed it out of the kitchen before I could object.

"Please?" DooRah gestured to a chair and scooted one to face me.

My face burned and my heart ping-ponging between my chest and stomach, with the odd trip much further south. If I was ever going to get a case of the vapors, it was probably at that moment.

"Hetta, I do not have the words to tell you how very sorry I am for what I did to you. I have no defense, only regrets. Deep regrets."

"So do I. I regret ever meeting you," I mumbled, staring into my drink. Tears threatened, damn it!

"I, too."

Anger blazed, bringing me to my feet. I whirled to leave, but he caught my arm. "I did not mean I am sorry I met you, but that it is devastating I couldn't...I should have fought to...." He sighed and wiped his eyes. "I was a coward of the worst kind. I didn't even have the courage to share my agony with you. Because of my selfishness, we both wasted years wishing things could have been different."

"*You* did. Not me. I forgot you within a week and went on with my life. Which, by the way, has been fabulous."

He smiled at that bit of bravado. "Then I am happy for you. I was miserable for years, always on the verge of trying to find you."

"You *knew* where to find me, which is a hell of a lot more than I can say about you. You just vanished and, I might add, never let any information slip that might lead me to you. Not," I lied, "that I wanted to look after I realized how calculating you were. Oh, at first I worried you were dead in a ditch. Later, I hoped it was true."

"I was not in a ditch, but part of me was dead. The part you created."

"What *I* created? What the hell does that mean?"

He was interrupted before he could answer by a group of people rushing into the kitchen, complaining about the sudden onslaught of winter while shedding coats. Multiple cheek kisses were exchanged as they headed for the *apéritif* spread.

Jan moved to my side and gave my hand a squeeze. "Sorry, but you needed to face him one-on-one. I see he survived, but you look like you could use another Campari or two. Are you all right?"

I nodded, and then smiled. "Yes, I am. I just realized he's spent the past twenty years hating himself, so I guess I don't need to do it for him."

"Ha! Atta girl. Let us mingle with the beautiful people of the French Riviera."

Jean Luc clapped his hands and shouted, "*Á table!*"

"Soup's on," I told Jan. "Find your place card."

"Good, I'm starving."

"Pace yourself, Chica. Trust me on this one."

Chapter Twenty-six

When I told Jan she'd better take it slow on each of Jean Luc's courses, I spoke from experience.

Le Entrée: Crème de champignons: Not to be confused with the American use of the word; in French this means the appetizer, not to be confused with the *hors d'oeuvres* and *aperitifs* course, which is not technically a course. Confused yet?

Jean Luc stood at the head of the table, with Jan and me seated on either side. I was significantly placed to his right, raising an eyebrow or two from his other guests.

As he had all those years ago, he flourished a plump white *champignon de Paris,* recounted their historical significance—they were found in catacombs when excavation began for the Paris Metro—and garnered an expected titter by adding, "Well, not *this* mushroom of course."

He then expertly sliced scallions, chopped parsley and chives and scooped the mixture into a large glass bowl. Picking up a shallow bistro-style soup bowl, he hand-placed what he called his "salad" in the middle, then ladled a steaming scoop of *crème* of mushroom soup over it and topped it with a dollop of *crème fraiche*. He handed me the first bowl, which I automatically passed down the table.

This familiar ritual set my cheeks, and a few other places, on fire.

A champagne sorbet, served to cleanse the palate, did little to put out the burn, so I tried dousing it with a slug of crisp white wine. One does not drink red wine with *le entrée*.

Le Plat Principal/Plat de Resistance: The main course: *Moules*.

Jean Luc, by serving mussels as the main course, bypassed the fish course, which probably broke several French laws.

In this case, he rolled out a mobile restaurant-style, gas-fired, stainless steel cooking cart that probably cost more than my pickup. Lighting the burner under a huge pot, he brought the contents to a simmer, then removed the cover and waved it, sending us an aromatic whiff of white wine, shallots, garlic, rosemary, thyme, parsley, with just a hint of the sea. He declared it, "*Parfait,*" then dumped ten pounds of shiny black mussels into his perfect broth, covered the pot, and in five minutes began serving up our bowls with plump and perfectly cooked mussels. On top of each bowl, he placed an empty shell to be used to pull out the meat.

Once all the bowls were passed out, he melted a good quarter pound of butter in the broth, and then poured the savory sauce into pitchers for us to add to our mussels.

As I tore off a piece of baguette, sopped up the buttery, savory broth, and stuffed it into in my mouth, I moaned with pleasure. I had not had a meal like this since

I left Europe, and I'd forgotten how fabulous it was to share such a feast with good company, great wine, and—

Warm breath caressed my ear as Jean Luc leaned over and whispered, "Was that moan for me, *mon petite chou*?"

I didn't bother lowering my voice and growled loudly, "*Non, mon petit rat*, it is for the food. And I am not your little cabbage or your anything else."

Jean Luc laughed heartily, and after a slight hesitation from the other guests to see his reaction, everyone joined in. And when he added, "She *is* Texan, you know," they raised their glasses to me.

"So," Jan asked, "is being Texan a ticket to ride, so to speak?"

"*Absolument!* We French are *enchanté* with Texas and," he nodded toward me, "some special Texans."

"And *some* Texans are totally *not* enchanted by you, Jean Luc."

"I think someone protesteth a bit too much," Jan drawled quietly.

"I think someone needs to eat her mussels and mind her own bidness."

Le Fromage, Le Dessert, Le Café et Le Digestif :

A huge board of local cheese and fruit, a fruit torte, strong coffee served with dark chocolates and, as if that were not enough, brandy.

The dinner lasted until two, ending with that Napoleon brandy which was probably left over from the little dictator's personal liquor cabinet.

My phone rang at five.

I almost let it go and cuddled back down under the duvet, then thought it might be Jenks, and answered.

"Hetta?"

"Huh?"

"Hetta, it's Rhonda."

That sat me up. "Rhonda! We've been worried about you. Why didn't you call before?"

"Well, you know, I didn't have a chance, really. Rousel has been by my side all the time and I didn't want him to think I was...disloyal by taking the phone you gave me."

"*Your* phone's still out of order? Where are you?"

"In an apartment his family owns in Paris. He had to leave early for a last minute family problem, so I got a chance to call you."

"So, you're all right?" As I asked, I had to fight to keep little spikes of temper from raising my voice. Here we'd jumped through all kinds of hoops, and she'd been blithely going on about her love affaire?

"Oh, yes. We leave tonight, you know. Rousel's cousin is taking us to the airport."

As annoyed as I was, I couldn't help mining more information. "Air France, right?"

"I'm pretty sure."

"You're *pretty* sure?" I grabbed a bottle of water by the bed and tried to will my blood pressure out of the ozone layer.

"Rousel has the tickets and all that stuff."

"All what stuff?"

"You know, passports and tickets. He'll be back in enough time to make our flight. They want us at least four hours early now that the country is on high alert."

"Well, I'm glad you called." *Actually I wanted to strangle her.* "And please, let us know when you get home, okay?"

"Sure. I'll text you as soon as we arrive in the States. My phone should work there. Speaking of, what do you want me to do with this phone of yours?"

"I'll let you know where to mail it. Right now we don't even know how long we'll be here in France."

"Where are you now?"

"Cannes."

"Oh, that's where I first saw Rousel."

"I know. Rhea posted a photo on the Teachers Who Travel Facebook page. Rousel and his friend are in the background."

Rhonda giggled. "Oh, I remember that. The men were so handsome and we wanted to get a picture without them knowing. I'll look at it as soon as I get Internet again."

"Okay. I guess you'd better save time on that phone I gave you. Maybe text me if you get a chance before you take off tonight."

With my worries about Rhonda partially assuaged, I slept soundly until nine when Jan rousted me out.

"Rise and shine, Sunshine. We gotta go on a road trip. Luc just knocked and said he'd be ready to roll in thirty minutes."

"Jeez, I just went to sleep."

"You got seven hours."

"No, I didn't. Rhonda called."

"About time. Where the hell is she?"

"Paris. She and Rousel are leaving tonight for the States."

"About time, again. I'm just a *lit*-tle tired of her crap running our lives. Bon Voyage, and good riddance is what I say."

"Yeah, I guess."

"You *guess*? Don't tell me you're still fretting over her."

"No. Well, maybe a little."

Jan blew her bangs off her forehead. "And why?"

"Rousel stashed her in an apartment and took off for a meeting this morning."

"So?"

"He has their tickets and passports."

"So?"

"So, what if he disappears? She has no tickets, no passport, nada."

"Hetta, will you *ever* get over Jean Juc disappearing on you?"

"I'm projecting here, huh?"

"Ya think? You get outta bed while make *café au lait*. Mine in a cup."

"Savage."

Chapter Twenty-seven

The six-hour trip from Cannes to Negra took Jean Luc under five in the fancy car he selected from his garage. With minimum road noise and the famous soft Citroën ride, it was like traveling on a cloud. I nodded off a few times in the backseat.

Jan sat in front with Jean Luc, and I was just a little annoyed that she seemed drawn, like flies to a warm turd, to his charismatic personality and heart-melting French accent. Okay, so I admit DooRah is hard not to be mesmerized by, but then, so is a cobra. In spite of all his bewitching charms, I well knew his true colors. He was, unlike Jenks, who would be back soon, thank goodness, a rat capable of epic treachery.

The night before, DooRah made it very clear he wanted to pick up where we left off twenty years before, and I have to admit I was flattered that this handsome, rich, and charming Frenchman still wanted me. He was divorced, his kids were doing their own thing, and he wanted someone to spend time with. Me.

I noticed his friends at the dinner, all in our approximate age group, taking great interest in his obvious, and embarrassing, attention to me. They were mostly family friends and cousins, none of whom I'd met back in Paris, of course. From their chit-chat I gathered they spent their time bopping to the chic spots to meet with others of their ilk.

They found Jan and me *très amusant*, but I was wise to the ways of these dilettantes who pick up people like us like the would stray puppies, thinking us amusing and interesting until we pee on their Aubusson Rugs. It was a reminder that, *charmant* or not, Jean Luc d'Ormesson was one of their aristocratic clubby breed.

We were almost to Negra when my phone dinged. "Hey, I have a text from Rhonda."

"Please tell me she's boarding a flight out of our lives," Jan groaned.

"Not exactly."

"Jeez Louise, now what?"

"I'll read it to you. **'So Excited. At Air France passenger terminal at Orly waiting for R. He was delayed so his cousin dropped me and luggage and went to park the car. More later if I can.'** "

"Text her back and ask what she means by 'if I can'?"

I did. There was a delay, but then she texted, **Cousin might tell R about phone**.

When I read this aloud, Jean Luc shook his head. "Some family."

I refrained from mentioning that *his* family had pushed *him* into a marriage he didn't want, or so he says now.

I texted back: **From Ladies room**, and got a thumbs-up.

"What time is her flight?"

"Not sure, but tonight."

"So Jean Luc, now that we know she's leaving on Air France tonight from Orly, can your friend at least confirm there is a reservation in her name?"

"Let me try. Normally that kind of information is hard to get unless you are on the police force or in the military, and then only if they think something is wrong."

He made a call, despite all kinds of signs along the road warning of a forty euro fine if caught on the phone while driving. It took a few minutes, then he greeted someone named Claude and told him the situation. After waiting a minute, he asked me, "Are you certain she said Orly Airport? "

"Yep, that's what she said. Why?"

"Because my friend Claude says there are no Air France flights to the United States from Orly tonight, only from Charles de Gaulle airport. Perhaps they have another destination?"

"I guess it's possible. What a mess. Anyhow, can he at least check her name and destination so if we never hear from her again we'll know where she went?"

He asked, and then hung up. "He says he will, but it is highly irregular."

"I can't help but wonder what Rousel's game is here? She let him make all the arrangements and hold the tickets. Betcha a euro he shows up with some bull crap story to keep her here in France, because he can't let the Bank of Rhonda get away until he cleans her out."

Jean Luc looked at me in the rearview mirror. "You are such a *cynique*, Hetta. Do you not think that just maybe this man is in love with her?"

"How would I know? My romantic experience with Frenchmen has been limited to total libertines."

Jan blew her bangs up. "Settle down, you two. If she's at the Air France terminal, that means the cousin who took her there knows that's where she's meeting Rousel. Problem over. *Adios*, Rhonda."

We all agreed that bidding Rhonda *adieu* and wishing her good effing luck was the way to go at this point.

Jean Luc exited the autoroute, followed a narrow road down to the Canal du Midi, turned right where Jan told him and crossed the bridge at the lock. We parked next to the office.

"I'll spring my car and be right back. You guys stay warm."

A brisk breeze blowing down the canal set up a wind chill factor far below the actual temperature, and gathering dark clouds didn't help. I rushed into the office to find the staff huddled around a propane stove, probably counting the minutes until closing time and hoping no more boats showed up at the lock.

They greeted me like an old friend. I don't think they'd had too many people who had not only upgraded their vessel, but had an open-ended rental. If Jenks didn't wrap things up soon, we might as well *buy* the damned thing.

I joined them by the stove and warmed my hands. "I came for my car. The boat is in Castelnaudary."

"Yes, we know. The Harbor Masters and *eclusiers* give us a daily report on the location of our boats."

I had noticed the lock keepers writing down the names of boats in their locks but didn't know they reported in every day. Now I also knew how our reputations preceded us up and down the Canal.

"I'll bet everyone stays put until tomorrow. It's getting ugly out there."

"Yes." He looked at his watch and smiled. "One boat passed through an hour ago, but they were going to tie up for the night very soon. As will your friends. They left early enough to pass a few locks before they closed, as they were anxious to do so before the weather worsens. I am sure you will see them in Castelnaudary soon."

"My friends?"

"Yes, on the vessel *Trebés*."

I think my mouth dropped open. Why would Rhonda tell me she was in at the airport when she was here? What they hell was going on? "Uh, you saw my friend, the *American* woman here today?"

They all shook their heads.

"But you saw the man?"

They all nodded.

"I thought he turned the boat in last week when they left."

"*Mais non, mademoiselle*, they only left for a few days but retained the boat. It is somewhat unusual, but then you...." I think he wanted to say *you and your friends seem to have more money than good sense*, but let it slide. "Well, now they returned and are on their way. You only missed them by two hours."

One of the other men said something, but I couldn't hear him, so the other one added, "Ah, he says he is sure the woman was not on the boat today, as he helped the man with his lines when he left."

Unable to stop myself, I said, "That son-of-a-bitch. Can you tell me where the boat is, like right now?"

Looks were exchanged, then the manager shrugged and picked up the phone. Within minutes I knew *Trebés* was docked at Port-Lauragais for the night. Jenks and I had spent one night there. It was the only real marina we found in this part of the Canal. The Harbor Master was actually an American.

They gave me a slip of paper with the numbers for the combination lock on the storage area gate, and I left. Getting back into Jean Luc's car, I slammed the door harder than necessary and yelled, "AAAARrrrgggg!"

"What now?" Jan asked.

"You are not going to believe this, but Rousel came back here today and took off in *Trebés*."

Jean Luc frowned. "He went to Trebés? But why would he go there?"

"No, he didn't go *to* Trebés, he went *in Trebés*. That's the name of the boat they rented."

"What? How? Why?" Jan rattled off.

"You forgot Who, When and Where."

Jean Luc cocked his head, waiting for an explanation, so I told him, "Journalism class. A story, to be whole, should contain the following: Who, What, Where, When, Why and How."

"So," he nodded, "we know who, what and when and how. The question would be, why, yes?"

"*Exactement*. Stand by, I'm texting Rhonda." I'd still not mastered the thumb texting thing, so I tapped out: **What's the latest?**

I got a return message quickly. **Nothing. Cousin never returned. Worried about Rousel.**

Jan and Jean Luc both shook their heads when I read the text to them. Jan suggested a text and I sent it. **Can you see if maybe your ticket is at the counter?**

Good idea, getting in line.

Long line?

Yes.
Let us know.
K.

"So much for the Rhonda problem being solved. What should we do now?" Jan asked.

Jean Luc pursed his lips. "Even should there be a ticket waiting for her, you say she has no passport. She cannot board."

"Jean Luc, while we wait to hear back from her, would you mind following us to Port Lauragais? I wouldn't mind having a little *tête-à-tête* with Rousel le Roué."

"Ah, so he is a roué and I am a rat. Very amusing, your way of classifying men."

Had he overheard me referring to him as DooRah? "Only when they deserve it. Oh, never mind. Can you follow us? I'd just feel better with backup."

"Better yet, leave your vehicle here. I shall drive you. It is not far. What will we do when we get there?"

"I want to be absolutely certain that's him on *Trebés.* When I am, I'll tell Rhonda so she can…hell, what *will* she do?"

Jean Luc started the car. "I will have her picked up at the airport and she can stay in one of the family apartments in Paris until we can return her passport to her."

"Ya think we can talk Rousel into handing over her passport and credit card?"

Jean Luc nodded. "Oh yes, he will. I can assure you of that. Perhaps this is my chance to make some amends for my past bad actions?"

"Don't count on it," I muttered.

He sighed a very Gallic sigh and put the pedal to the metal.

Chapter Twenty-eight

Several local inhabitants shook angry fists at us as Jean Luc skillfully threaded his luxury automobile through tiny villages at well over the speed limit of fifty kilometers an hour. On the narrow two lane roads, some of them cobblestone with no sidewalks, we could have reached out and touched the old buildings. Twenty minutes and a couple of close-calls with a sheep or two later, we pulled into Port-Lauragais, which is basically a marina with a restaurant and a few shops.

Trebés rested at a side-tie, but was completely buttoned down, with all doors and windows shut and curtains pulled.

"There she be," I told Jean Luc as he parked behind another car just in case Rousel was outside the boat. Not that Rousel would have an inkling we were inside the Citroën, even if he saw it, but better to err on the side of safety.

"But is he in the boat? That is the question."

"Yep, he sure is," Jan said, showing Jean Luc a blinking light on her tracker device. "Well, at least his wallet is cuz I've got him, see."

"You have somehow located his wallet?"

"Yep, got it on my GPS locator."

An astonished Jean Luc asked, "Who *are* you women?"

Unable to resist, I warned, "If we tell you, we'll have to kill you." I checked my watch. "We've got a little over an hour and a half until it gets dark. Anybody have any ideas on how to roust the roué out?"

"Knock on the boat? See if anyone opens the door?" Jan suggested.

I thought about that. "Seems reasonable, but I doubt he would open up for me or you. We are hardly his favorite people."

"I will go," Jean Luc volunteered. "He does not know me and I look innocent enough, *n'est-ce pas*?"

"Looks can be deceiving."

"Hetta Coffey, you just lighten up on Jean Luc for now, okay? You two can duke it out later, but right now we need to nail the *other* rat bastard."

Jean Luc barked a laugh. "I am certain I have been doubly insulted, but I am willing to take my just desserts. However, let us deal with that," he pointed to the boat, "rat bastard first. Agreed, Hetta?"

"Okay, peace. For now."

"You two stay in the car. I shall approach the boat. But first, I will speak with the people on that one." He pointed to a boat behind Rousel's. The wind had died, and even though it was quite chilly, several bundled-up partiers on a good-sized barge sat out on deck having drinks. "Perhaps they have seen him."

We watched as Jean Luc casually walked around the quay, looking at boats, greeting other walkers, and finally approaching the Happy Hour crowd.

Rolling down the window, we heard him greet them in French. They answered in kind. Jackpot! They were French and, from their hearty reception of Jean Luc, delighted with their handsome countryman's friendly approach. Within minutes, he was onboard with a glass of wine in hand.

"Who says the French aren't friendly?" Jan said. "Dang I could use a glass right now myself."

"Later. We can't take a chance on Rousel spotting us. Let's see what Jean Luc learns from his new BFFs."

The minutes passed, Jean Luc finished his wine, politely refused another, waved goodbye to the partiers, and returned to the car.

"You could'a brought us a drink, ya know?" Jan teased. "So, what's the deal?"

"They saw him once, but not since he tied up and went inside the boat."

"And he was alone?"

With a slight nod, Jean Luc said, "They think so, as they saw no one else."

"So, now what?"

"*Aller vois*. Or as you say in English, pay him a visit."

"And what are you gonna say *if* he opens the door? 'Hey, Rousel, it seems we have much in common, what with you also being a world class rat and all, so I thought I'd stop by?' "

"Hetta, put a sock in it. How about Jean Luc says he's looking for *us*?"

"Oh, what a grand idea, what with Rousel being so enamored with us."

"Smarty pants. Hear me out. Jean Luc can say he lives in Castelnaudary and met us *and* Rhonda there. So, when he saw the boat sitting here, he thought maybe Rhonda might still be on board."

Jean Luc waved his arms, "Hey! He, of whom you are speaking, is sitting right here. But it sounds like it will work."

I gave Jan a we're-not-worthy two-handed bow. "It's genius. This way you can mine him for info on Rhonda, as well. Dang, and us without a bug to our name."

"Bug?" Jean Luc asked.

"Listening device," Jan explained. "We usually have several, but they're on our boat. The only reason we have the GPS tracker for Rousel's wallet is it was in the bag with our other trackers. We always take 'em whenever we travel with Hetta's dog. He's chipped."

Jean Luc cocked an eyebrow. "Interesting. I wish to hear more of your espionage talents later."

"Ooh, I've got another idea," I said. "Once you're face-to-face with Rousel, I'll call your cell phone and you can act like you're not taking the call, but hit the TALK button and We'll hear everything. Uh, if we call you while your phone is engaged, do you get some kind of signal?"

"Yes. It will not ring however."

"How about a vibration?"

"I thought you'd never ask."

I glared at him. "What I mean is, can you set the phone to vibrate for an incoming call while the line is open?"

"Yes, it is possible."

"Okay, troops, phones at the ready."

Jean Luc, a sardonic smirk on his lips—which, by the way, I was doing my best not to acknowledge existed—raised his phone and saluted with it.

"This will work. So now, all I have to do is get him to answer the door?"

"Yep, you tackle him and we'll move in as backup. You got any rope in this car?" I was warming to the idea of giving the bum a rush. "Once we've got him, we'll make him give us back Rhonda's credit card, passport, tickets, *et voila*! Our work here is done!"

Jean Luc shook his head. "We are not in Texas. In France he will have us arrested for assault. We must first try diplomacy."

"Yeah, that'll work," I scoffed. "Okay then, we try it your way first. But," I handed him a paper baguette bag, "take this with you."

He looked inside and his eyes went wide when he saw my .380. "I shall refrain from asking where this came from. For now. Do you think this Rousel is dangerous?"

"Who knows? Anyhow, it's chambered and I've wiped off all fingerprints, so don't touch it. Well, unless you have to."

"You expect me to hold him at gunpoint."

"Nope, I have other plans."

We discussed the next few critical minutes, and what had to be done.

"Okay, then. From now on we'll have to play it as it lays. You are the key, Jean Luc. He has no reason to suspect you're up to anything, so go do your thing."

Jean Luc slowly slid out of the car, then stuck his head back inside and said, "Why is it I think this might be the most idiotic thing I've ever done besides the abandonment of Hetta?" and slammed the door.

"Whoa," Jan whispered, "that was about the best apology I've ever heard."

I was still so stunned I just nodded. What the hell was going on here, and what was I going to do about it?

Light was fading fast as Jean Luc sauntered up to *Trebés* and rapped on the hull.

Jan and I waited, me with my fingers crossed, Jan humming "The Battle Hymn of the Republic" quietly. Jean Luc knocked again, much harder, this time on the wooden door.

"Maybe Rousel's asleep? The way I figure it, that *roué's* had a very long day. If he left Paris early, like Rhonda said, and we're pretty sure he did, then he's been traveling all day long on either planes, trains, his own car, and maybe a taxi or two. Why he did it is anyone's guess."

"Because he's a *bâtard!*"

"Your French vocabulary is expanding daily, *Chérie*."

"*Parfait!*"

"Perfect, yes."

"No, I meant *perfect*. The door just slid open on *Trebés*."

I hit Jean Luc's name on my phone. "Calling. You watch. Okay, ringing. Shhhh."

Jan whispered, "He's taking his phone from his pocket."

As we watched he turned away from Rousel, hit the TALK key as planned, swung back to face Rousel as he stuffed the phone in his front pocket, and we heard him say, in French, "It was unimportant. I will call them back later. As I was saying, I am sorry to disturb you, *monsieur*. I live in Castelnaudary and met some Americans there last week. One of them was from this boat and I wondered if you knew how to get in touch with the ladies on *Sauzens*? Jan and Hetta. They gave me a card but I have misplaced it."

There was a pause, then a voice that was clearly Rousel's said, "I do not know them."

"Oh, that is too bad. I was very attracted to that red-haired Texan." I rolled my eyes. I could just imagine Jean Luc doing an eyebrow jiggle at Rousel. "Is their friend, uh, Rhonda, here? Maybe she has a contact number for them."

"I do not know of anyone named Rhonda. This is a rental craft, and it must have been other people."

Jan and I both shot the finger in the direction of the boat. I mouthed, "Plan B."

I ended my call, Jan hit Jean Luc's number on her phone and handed it to me. We watched as it rang, then saw him reach into his pocket again, give an apologetic shrug at Rousel, and answer, "*Allô ma petite carotte.*"

My cheeks flamed on hearing his favorite nickname for me those many years ago: his little carrot. "*Va te branler.*"

He laughed and answered, "If I must."

"You must. Now, cut the crap and get inside that boat somehow and leave the bag under a cushion or something."

"Of course, my dear. I love you, too." Jean Luc hit the keypad, ending that call and reactivating mine. He coughed, then asked, "Could I trouble you for a glass of water? And I would love to see the inside of the boat. Maybe I will rent one for a weekend."

Without waiting for an answer, he pushed past Rousel who mumbled something, but at least didn't shove him back outside. There was a rustle of movement, Jean Claude said, "*Merci*," and we heard the distinctive gurgle of him taking a long hit from a plastic water bottle. "Ah. There is a fine layout to this vessel, I must say. Even the settee around the dining table is comfortable. Do you mind—"

Rousel cut him off. "I do not wish to be impolite *monsieur,* but I have an appointment I must attend, so if *you* don't mind...."

"Oh, of course. Sometimes I forget my manners. You have been very nice. I must go as well. That call, you know. Thanks for the water. I shall visit the boat rental office one day soon and perhaps get a contact number for that Texan."

We watched as Jean Luc stepped onto the quay and waved back at Rousel, who slammed the door shut. But then a curtain moved.

"Jan! Hit the deck! Rousel is watching Jean Luc."

I threw myself across the backseat and Jan doubled over on the passenger side so when Jean Luc opened the door and the interior light came on, Rousel couldn't see us.

"Jean Luc, can you get out of the parking lot without him seeing your license plates from the boat."

"Is there a baguette in France?" He smoothly maneuvered the car out of Rousel's line of sight without turning on his headlights and stopped. "Now what?"

"Already on it." I texted Rhonda: **Call me. Now! No text, need to talk**.

The phone rang, but it was Jenks. I told him to call me on Jan's phone.

Both phones rang at the same time, so I took Rhonda's call while Jan quickly filled Jenks in on what was going on.

"Rhonda, listen to me. Rousel is *here* on the boat. He's not going to show up at the airport."

"W-what?" she screeched. I held the phone away from my ear. "How can that be? H-he," she blubbered. "W-why would he? Are you sure?"

"Absolutely. He's on *Trebés* right now, right here on the Canal du Midi. I don't know what his game is, but do you have any money at all?"

I let her sob for a minute or two while listening to Jan's end of her conversation with Jenks. "Jenks, you know better than to run off and leave Hetta. What did you think we were gonna do, sit around playing tiddlywinks?"

Jean Luc was now on his phone speaking with his friend at Air France, filling him in on the situation and asking him to find and help Rhonda.

"Hetta?" Rhonda hiccupped.

"I'm here. Obviously the cousin never showed up, so we are arranging for someone to pick you up, okay? Do you have any money?" I asked again.

"Y-yes. I keep what Mom called mad money pinned in my bra."

"Good. Just stay where you are until we sort this out. Worst case, you can take a cab to a hotel, okay?"

"How can I get a hotel room without my credit card?"

"We'll take care of it by phone if we have to."

"Thank you, thank you. What a mess. And why? And what'll I do with Rousel's bags?"

I wanted to reach through the phone and throttle her. "The very last thing I'd be worried about right now, if I were you, is what to do with that bastard's crap. And, as soon as you get somewhere to access the Internet, you need to report your credit card stolen. Goodness only knows what he's charged to it. Look, just sit tight. I'm putting Jan on. Tell her what you're wearing." Not that it mattered. Finding a frumpy, hysterical, American woman sitting on a stack of luggage shouldn't be that hard.

Trading phones with Jan, I said, "Hi, Honey, as you can tell we have a situation here."

"Of course you do, Hetta. Couldn't just visit a few museums, huh? Or maybe take a painting class?"

"Very funny. Look, I'll call you back as soon as we figure out how to deal with Rhonda." I lowered my voice. "I cannot believe she's been dumped at the airport by this lowlife SOB and *she's* worried about what to do with *his* luggage? Give me a freakin' break."

"What?"

"My sentiments exactly. Some cousin of his took Rhonda to the airport, dumped her there and said he'd be back, but nope, never did. Betcha he knew Rousel wasn't gonna show. Nice family, huh?"

Jean Luc was signaling he needed to talk with me. "Stand by, Jenks."

Jean Luc said, "My friend Claude is with security for Air France, and he's at the airport right now. He couldn't find your friend on any passenger list for tonight, but I told him how her boyfriend had abandoned her, so he will find Rhonda and make sure she gets to my apartment in Paris."

I gave Jean Luc a thumb's-up and said to Jenks, "Did you hear that? Looks like our problem's solved, thanks to Jean Luc. Once Rhonda's settled in, she can sort out this mess for herself."

"Yes, I did hear that. Who's Jean Luc?"

Crappola. "An old friend."

"Put him on."

Double crappola. "Jean Luc, Jenks wishes to speak with you."

"Who is Jenks?"

Double, double, toil and trouble.

Chapter Twenty-nine

Not feeling warm and fuzzy at all with the situation of Jenks and Jean Luc talking on the phone, I was tuned into Jean Luc's end like Po Thang sighting in on a standing rib roast. It was hard to hear everything, however, because Jan kept yelling at Rhonda on my phone.

I tried to shush her, but she growled at the distraught woman, "Listen to me, you ninny. Calm down and shut up." Jan's compassion has major limitations.

Unable to eavesdrop with Jan hollering, I snatched my phone from her and heard Rhonda squalling. Holding the phone against my chest to muffle her, I went back to eavesdropping on Jean Luc's end of his conversation with Jenks. He was mostly listening very intently, and had gone quite pale in the phone's glow.

My heart sank. Did Jenks somehow surmise Jean Luc was more than just an old friend and was threatened him with great bodily harm? That's not Jenks's style, but still...

Then Jean Luc said, "Yes, I understand," and handed me back Jan's phone and punched a key on his own phone.

We played musical phones, with me stabbing a warning finger at Jan not to yell at poor Rhonda again. I was about to say something to Jenks when Jean Luc let loose with a string of agitated French even I had trouble following, but as it registered, I whispered, "Oh. My. God."

"Claude, listen to me very carefully," Jean Luc told his friend at the airport. "You may have a possible terrorist threat in the main terminal. The woman I asked you to assist, Mademoiselle Rhonda, is in possession of bags not packed by herself. We have reason to think there may be foul play. She is on the telephone with a friend here, so what are your instructions?"

Instructions? Was he kidding me? I took the bull by the horns, threw the phone Jenks was on into Jean Luc's lap and took mine back from Jan. "Rhonda, leave the bags, all of them, and your purse and coat right where they are and get as far away as you can from them. Right now!"

"Why? Oh, no! There are—" I heard shouts, screams, rapid multiple footfalls, a scuffle of some kind, and the phone went dead.

"Jean Luc, is Jenks still on the phone?"

"No."

"Rhonda's gone as well."

With the frantic phone conversations ended, gloomy silence settled in the car, as though we'd run out of anything to say after all the excitement in the last few minutes. I was certain Jan and Jean Luc felt as helpless as

I did. Finally, I said, "Well, good grief. Will Claude call back and let us know anything?"

"I'm certain he will when he can. Right now he'll be very busy."

Jean Luc turned on his radio, just in case a news bulletin came on, then we all activated our phones and looked for social media chatter, breaking news, anything about a situation at Orly Airport, but there was nothing so far.

"Now what?" Jean Luc asked. "This Rousel. What shall we do about him? We don't have any proof he's done anything illegal."

"Oh, I do believe he has," Jan said with a broad smile and a wink.

We all said, at the same time, "Plan B!"

Jean Luc dropped Jan and me at the Harbor Master's office and stayed in the car to make his phone calls while keeping an eye on *Trebés*.

I knocked on the Harbor Master's boat hull and he stuck his head out the slider. "Hey, I remember you," he said, then spotted Jan. "But haven't met your friend."

I introduced Jan, then said, "We were out for a drive and I wanted to show her the marina and maybe have dinner at the restaurant. Then the funniest thing happened."

"Yeah? What?"

Jan did a little dippy thing she does when she's flirting. "Well, I don't want to cause any trouble, but I was walking down the quay and I saw this man sneaking around that boat there." She pointed at *Trebés*.

"Sneaking?"

"Yeah, like this." She executed a perfect Pink Panther sneak walk. "And…" she hesitated and chewed on her thumb, "he had a *gun*."

"A gun? Are you sure?"

"Are you kidding me? I'm from *Texas!*"

I guess he's been there. He picked up his phone, hit speed dial, and gave Jan's information, calling her a passerby, to someone on the other end. With his alert given, he told us, "It's probably nothing, but better safe than sorry these days. I suggest you're not here when the police arrive. They can be a real pain."

"We're gone! Nice meeting you," Jan said.

We rushed back to the car and Jean Luc sped away, then doubled back and parked where we were, out of the way but with a view of the marina, and more importantly, *Trebés*.

"You're sure he's still on the boat?" I asked.

Jean Luc did that eyebrow thing he uses when his competency is questioned. "Unless he jumped off on the other side and swam away, *absolument*."

Jan checked her tracker. "Yep, he's there."

Within minutes, the distant nee-uh, nee-uh of sirens closed in, and then whirling lights played off the boats as various vehicles screeched into the parking lot. Too late, we realized all avenues of escape for us were blocked.

The people Jean Luc had shared a wine with on their boat parked behind *Trebés* came out on deck to check out the commotion, but were waved back inside by men in riot gear. The Paris attack was fresh enough that the local police were taking no chances.

Rousel also slid open his door and stuck his head out. A spotlight painted him with white light, making him raise his hand to cover his eyes. A bullhorn order was given for him to step off the boat, but he ducked back inside and slammed the door.

Jean Luc said, "Uh-oh," which is French for, "Uh-oh."

"I gotta feeling le Roué is headed for the slammer," Jan said. "Couldn't happen to a nicer guy."

"Poor Rhonda. I hope she's all right."

Jan turned and looked at me. "Poor Rhonda? This," she waved her hand in the air, "is all her doing."

"Oh, come on. She's been duped. Rousel's the bad guy here. I hope they give him thirty years in the electric chair."

We were so intent watching the action near the boats, we were surprised when, seemingly out of nowhere, we were surrounded and ordered out of the car. Just as we exited, hands on head as ordered, the Harbor Master and party boat crew were being ushered to what I figured was a staging area for marina evacuees, and they all pointed out Jean Luc, Jan, and me.

"That's him!"

"That's them!"

Zut, alors!

Chapter Thirty

After being ordered out of Jean Luc's car and fingered by six people, we were frisked and then marched several yards away while dogs sniffed the car.

They also brought the dogs over to give us a sniff, and one of them showed great interest in my pocket. The pocket that once held the gun we'd planted on Rousel's boat. I held my breath while they ordered me to remove the jacket, but they were evidently convinced I wasn't a suicide bomber so they gave it back.

After the search-and-sniff exercise unearthed nothing incriminating in Jean Luc's car, they herded us into what seemed to be a gathering area for witnesses, and asked us to sit on the pavement. We joined the Harbor Master, partiers, and a smattering of others caught up in the dragnet.

A loud pop startled us, and as one we turned to see the glass shatter on one side of *Trebés* and a cloud of teargas erupt. Within seconds, Rousel stumbled out on deck, gasping and cursing.

Jan hollered, "Yee Haw!"

"Jan! Shush. You'll call attention to us."

"Sorry, I'm just glad they got the SOB."

"Seems a little extreme, if you ask me," one of the French partiers said. "I wonder what he did."

The Harbor Master said, "That one," he pointed to Jan, "said he had a gun."

I nodded and murmured, "And, he messed with Texas."

The others didn't hear me, but Jean Luc did. He leaned over and whispered in my ear, "Your idea of planting the gun on him was quite clever. I had no idea you could be so devious."

My ear, tickled by his breath—which somehow always smells like licorice— twitched.

"Just keep that in mind, DooRah."

He broke out in a guffaw at me using my pet name for him to his face for the first time. "Oh, I shall, I—look, they have him."

Rousel, who was gagging and struggling for breath, was handcuffed, roughly pulled away from the boat and hustled to a vehicle that looked like a giant metal armadillo. Before they tossed him inside and slammed the door, they splashed water into his face.

The marina restaurant, which had been *FERMÉ* (what a surprise!) was opened by the manager, who, according to the Harbor Master, lived locally and was rousted out by the authorities. Before we were allowed to go inside and out of the cold, however, all of our cell phones and personal belongings were confiscated. They gave us a card with a number on it, and then put a sticker with the same number on all our stuff.

Besides Jan, me and Jean Luc, the harbor master, and the six partiers from the boat behind *Trebés*, they'd rounded up another five people who had the bad luck to be in the vicinity. I recognized two guys who had been working on a boat in the small dry dock area and an old woman with a poodle who was out for a walk.

While we waited to see what happened next, a man who was evidently the local mayor showed up and vouched for the old lady and she was taken home. Then they called the Harbor Master over, and I put my legendary hearing abilities to work.

"He keeps pointing at you, Hetta," Jan whispered.

"Shush. I'm trying to hear what he's saying."

"You can hear them from this far?" Jean Luc asked.

"I could if you two would shut up."

A uniform appeared next to us. "We prefer, *monsieur*, that you do not speak among yourselves until after your interviews."

Jean Luc looked like he might challenge this, but then with a head and eye-roll, nodded assent. "Well, then, could you turn on the television. We want to know more about the evacuation at Orly."

The man looked surprised, then said, "*Monsieur*, how do you know anything about that?"

Jean Luc, busted by his own blooper, was momentarily speechless, so I stepped in. "We heard something on the radio just before you arrested us."

The man sighed. "You have not been arrested, *mademoiselle. S'il vous plaît* just wait quietly until we call you."

I'd only caught snippets of the conversation between the Harbor Master and his interrogator, but there was no doubt he'd buttonholed us as "persons of interest." Why, he was not sure, but it was obvious we had seen something, at the very least. And the man on *Trebés*? The Harbor Master told them the marina records were at his office so there was a lull in the questioning while they escorted him there. They were back in a few minutes carrying a clipboard, which he tapped and then pointed at me.

Jean Luc pulled a napkin from a holder, a pen from his pocket, and wrote a quick note while our keepers weren't watching. He slid it to the edge of our table and knocked it off into my lap. WE MUST TELL THE WHOLE TRUTH FROM THE BEGINNING. TRUST ME. EXCEPT FOR THE GUN.

Trust him? The last time I did that, I ended up brokenhearted and practically suicidal in my hurt and angst. But I figured, it's his country, he has the pull and we need all the help we can get, so I nodded and passed the note to Jan, wondering if we even knew *how* to tell the truth anymore.

Of the three of us left in the suspect's room, as I now called it, I guess I was deemed the most suspicious, as they chose me to go first.

"*Mademoiselle* Coffey," a dour man said, handing me my cell phone, "you may make one call. Choose carefully, and you must put the conversation on speaker. And, do you wish for an interpreter?"

"You have one here?"

"*Non*, but we can arrange for one within an hour."

The very first thing you learn when speaking a second language, no matter how good you think you are, when accuracy matters you'd better call in a professional. Even during my courses in Brussels, I was allowed to take most exams in English.

"Will the interpreter be a lawyer by any chance?"

He raised an eyebrow. "Do you think you will require *un avocat*?"

I was about to say, "Maybe," but the nee-uh, nee-uh of police sirens and then flashing lights distracted me. Several vehicles slid into the restaurant's dimly lit parking lot. Within a few seconds, the door flew open and in bounded Po Thang and Charles, followed by René, André in full chauffeur's livery, and two men I didn't know but who looked mighty important.

Po Thang made a beeline for me, causing my interrogator to slide his chair back in alarm, but my dog only had eyes for me. After a hugging and whining session, Charles joined in for an ear scratch until called back. Po Thang reluctantly followed, and I turned to ask the man if I could use René as my interpreter, when an aide of some kind trotted up and handed him a phone. A little impatient with all the interruptions, he grabbed it and huffed, "*Maintenant ce que?*"

Evidently his "what now" received a strong answer, as he went very quiet and a little pale while listening and finally said, "*Mais monsieur le Ministre de cours!*" and handed the phone back to his aide.

"Minister of what?" I mouthed at Jan.

Jean Luc, who had rushed to meet the group of men who'd arrived with such fanfare, bear-hugged one I recognized from his photo on the Internet as d'Ormesson, the elder. "Papa, this is all a complete misunderstanding. You did not have to—"

The other man with them, a formidable-looking sixty-ish, deepened what I figured was a permanent frown and commanded, "Jean Luc, do not say another word, except goodbye to all these," he made a wide sweep of his arm, "people." He said it like, "peasants."

"*Monsieur le avocat*, I cannot leave Hetta and Jan here."

René patted Jean Luc on the shoulder. "Of course not. They have been vouched for. We all leave together."

The Austin Princess, a seven-passenger vehicle, now contained seven humans and two dogs, as the authorities absolutely insisted that Jean Luc's vehicle remain at the scene of the crime. What crime, we still didn't know, but I had a pretty good idea.

After Jean Luc introduced Jan and me to his father and his father's lawyer, we surveyed the chaos in the marina. There were now military boats involved, probably fifteen official vehicles, sniffer dogs, a bomb squad, a fire truck, and two ambulances.

I whispered to Jean Luc, "Obviously they've found the .380. I've heard of some pretty strict gun control laws, but don't you think this is a little extreme? It was only one little pistol."

He chuckled and said, "Text only. Just stay silent and let me do the talking, all right?"

Jan mumbled, "That'll be the day."

As soon as we pulled away, two motorcycle cops fell in with us, one behind, one in front. I texted Jan, who had landed the passenger seat in front but had to share it with our furry friends. **See if you can get a photo or two**. I know, I'm not using proper texting acronyms and shortcuts, but for now I remain an AFZ: Acronym Free Zone.

My phone vibrated, announcing a text from Jean Luc: **Is the you-know-what traceable to you?**

I thought about that. I didn't have a concealed carry permit in California, but I bought the Taurus in Texas at an estate sale from a friend of a friend whose father who owned it had died. I certainly didn't register it anywhere. **Maybe, but it will take a lot of doing**.

He nodded his head. I texted, **Ask about Orly**. He shook his head. **Wait**.

René opened the bar. "Anyone care for a drink?"

"*Yes!*"

"*Oui!*"

"*Absolutment!*"

 "Is there an armadillo in Texas?"

"*Certainment!*"

"I am driving, but yes."

"*Yip!*"

"*Wouf!*"

Chapter Thirty-one

By the time we were dropped off at the boat in Castelnaudary it was after eleven, and all the restaurants were closed—if, in fact they were ever open—but we had plenty of snacky stuff in our larder. The Frenchmen declined the suggestion they join Jan and me for crackers and cheese, opting instead to continue on to Gruissan and probably much better wine and cheese.

Po Thang, delighted to be back home, immediately searched for his swan friends, but evidently they'd found someone else to steal bread for them. Fickle fowl.

It was good to be back on the boat, especially since the French feds kept our luggage. Jan and I always carry travel kits, leaving our toothbrushes and the like at home, wherever that may be. Not only that, we have emergency bags in our vehicles so we can hit the road in case of, well, an emergency. It has held us in good stead over the years, as we have a tendency to get run out of Dodge.

We showered, put on warm jammies, and had a glass of wine before turning in. I think I was asleep before my head hit the pillow but was awakened by a menacing rumble I first thought was thunder but quickly realized it was my guard dog. He headed for the main cabin, where he set to menacing the quay-side slider. Jan arrived about the same time I did.

"And me without my gun," I whispered.

"Dang. I'm gonna take a peek, so don't turn on a light."

For lack of a better idea, I grabbed a metal mooring stake as a weapon.

Jan moved the curtain a tiny bit and peered out. "Two men, no uniforms, in an unmarked car."

"Just sitting there?"

"Yep."

"What do you think? Friend, foe, or fortuity?"

"After the past day, I don't think we have the luxury not to be paranoid. And, we do *not* believe in coincidence."

"So, they're either here to hurt us or guard us? Guess we better find out which and deal with it so we can get some sleep. Saddle up the dawg."

I put the critter cam on Po Thang, we tested the signal and loosed the hound. He made a beeline for the car, jumped up with paws on the window of the driver's side and set up a furious, saliva-slinging attack certain to ruin the paint job. I've *got* to remember not to let him watch *Cujo* again.

Lights flicked on in the buildings across the street and a couple of people came out on their balconies to shout obscenities at Po Thang.

Fearing Po Thang would hurt himself, I hit a button that sends out a high-frequency signal only dogs can hear, his command to cease and desist. He immediately shut up, backed off and sat glaring at the driver, giving us a good camera angle.

"Well, good grief." I hit the button twice and Po Thang returned to the deck, looking quite pleased with himself. I pulled on a sweatshirt and tromped out to the car and the men I recognized from the interrogation room back at the restaurant in Port-Lauragais. They seemed mighty miffed at being outed by a dog and two women.

The driver rolled down his window. "My apologies, mademoiselle. We thought to wait for a decent hour before disturbing you, but your dog had other ideas."

"Well, now that we're disturbed, you might as well come in for coffee."

They were sent, they said, to return our bags but were in no hurry to leave once they placed our luggage on the boat. They gratefully accepted bowls of hot coffee and cookies, commenting on the fact they'd never had an Oreo but liked them. I hope to shout they did, because those stupid cookies cost me a fortune when I bought them in the imported section at the Super U. Okay, the stupid one is me for buying packaged cookies in *France*.

"So, can you tell us what happened after we left Port-Lauragais?" I didn't ask what I wanted to, like what happened to Rousel, but I wasn't ready to admit to anyone in authority that I actually *knew* him.

The guy had to be a mind-reader. "Mademoiselle, we are not at liberty to discuss the events of last evening at this time, only that we are now aware that you are acquainted with the man we arrested, monsieur Rousel Badiz al Bin Jasseron."

Rats.

Chapter Thirty-two

Jan and I exchanged a look when the cop said *they* knew *I* knew Rousel Badiz al Bin Jasseron. Jean Luc's lawyer had warned us not to talk with *anyone*, especially the authorities, about the situation, but the way they said they knew I was "acquainted" with Rousel le Roué hinted they thought we were *much* more chummy.

I couldn't let that slide. "Yes, I did meet Rousel, but I cannot say I liked him."

Jan, bless her heart, jumped in. "Like him? We think he's a despicable gigolo. We're pretty sure he was using a friend of ours, trying to get to her money."

He looked at a notebook he took from his pocket. "Your friend, mademoiselle Rhonda Jones?"

We'd received a text from Jean Luc telling Rhonda was in "protective custody" and was not allowed to communicate with us for the moment. Claude had assured Jean Luc that although distraught and confused, she was safe.

"Yes, she was romantically involved with Rousel, but we did not trust him."

"Her passport was on the boat, along with her credit card. Do you know where she is at the moment?"

"Paris. I'm sure she will be happy to get them back."

"Have you talked with her since last night?"

Uh-oh, trick question. "Uh, let's see." I pretended to think, stalling for time, not wanting to admit I knew a danged thing about Orly.

He switched to English, "And you, mademoiselle Simms, you have not talked with her?"

"Can you tell me something?" Jan asked, cleverly answering a question with a question.

"Perhaps."

"Why did you storm that gigolo's boat. All he did was steal a passport and credit card, right?"

Sometimes Jan is a genius. We were all tiptoeing around the elephant in the room, and it was time to break out the peanuts.

The men exchanged a glance, then the one who said almost nothing focused on Jan. "There was a report of an intruder with a gun. Made by *you*, mademoiselle. And, I might mention, mademoiselle Jones was in possession of a cell phone you bought in Mexico."

Oh, man, are these guys fast, or what? If they didn't know yet, I figured they'd nail me for said gun soon enough. A little chill ran down my spine.

Jan, however, isn't one to be cowed easily. "So what? Do you usually call in the entire freakin' French Foreign Legion to round up one guy with a gun?"

I thought she side-stepped that fairly well, but these guys weren't a couple of dummies.

"*Mademoiselles*, I think we *all* know there is far more to this story, *n'est-ce pas?*"

In for a penny... "The gun thing aside," I said, trying to duck that issue, "we thought Rousel was just a roué who was gonna take our friend to the cleaners, but in retrospect, if he planted a bomb in his luggage and sent her off to Orly? Call me crazy, but if you ask me, if you're planning on cleaning out someone's bank account, blowing her up seems counter productive."

Jan, never one to be left out of *anything*, piped up. "Yep. Here we just thought he was a gigolo and he turns out to be some kind of terrorist? Right?"

By now, unless they wanted something from us, they should have beat feet, but even though they'd evidently both lost their ability to speak, they sat still. If we hadn't been deemed off-limits by someone on high, they probably would have happily broken out *le* waterboard. Finally, they stood as one. "Please excuse us for a few minutes," one said. As they headed for their car, they were both on their cell phones.

"Uh, Hetta, now that you let the cat out of the bag, ya think we oughta make a run for it? It's four in the morning! Who the hell are they talking to?"

"You're reading my mind. Call Jean Luc."

"Me? He's *your* boyfriend."

"Not. Besides I'd have to say "merci" to him, and I'm not ready for that."

"Get over it." Then she broke into the chorus of Paul Simon's "50 Ways to Leave Your Lover."

She was right. I'd "Jump on the bus, Gus," and set myself free.

Jean Luc sounded wide awake when he answered. "Hetta? What's wrong?"

"Not sure if anything is. Sorry I had to call so early, but we might have a situation here. Two French feds from the roundup at Port-Lauragais showed up here to return our suitcases, or so they said. I get the feeling they're really here to get more information."

"Like what?"

"That's just it, they really haven't asked many questions. I sort of put them on the spot and they hightailed to their car to call someone."

"Oh *merde*, what have you done?"

I felt my blood pressure bump up a notch but chose not to verbally flip him off. "Well, they kept beating around the bush, trying to find out how well we knew Rousel, so I told them we knew him only casually but we felt the man was a gigolo trying to take advantage of our friend, Rhonda."

"I'm quite sure the authorities know you befriended Rhonda. No problem there. What's the *bombe?*

"How do you know there's a bombshell?"

"Because I have gotten to know you quite well the past few days. You are not one to *laissez le chien dormir*."

He's a fast learner; I rarely let sleeping dogs lie. "Okay, so I got tired of them pussyfooting around and told them we'd thought Rousel was just a roué who was gonna take Rhonda to the cleaners, but if he planted a bomb in their luggage and sent her off to Orly to go boom, that doesn't make any sense. If you're planning on cleaning out someone's bank account, blowing her up seems pretty stupid."

Jean Luc burst out laughing. "Yes, I suspect that could take the romance out of a relationship, *n'est-ce pas*? Do not worry. By now they will have talked to Claude and realized that I was the one who raised suspicions at Orly. We were on scene at Port-Lauragais and even though they do not think we are suspects in any kind of terrorist plot, they are, as you say, connecting the dots."

"I wish *I* could. When will we hear anything about what *really* happened at Orly?"

"We already know that Rhonda is fine, Rousel is under arrest for the moment, and there was no explosion at Orly."

"Then I guess—uh-oh, here come the fuzz. I'll leave the phone on so you can hear what they say."

The two were smiling, something new. Either they were delighted they'd gotten permission to rough us up a bit, or they had good news. I was hoping for the latter.

Po Thang only growled at them a little this time, but I still finger-tapped his head and he settled onto the settee with a small gnarl. He always has to have the last word.

Jan, ever the hostess, put down the length of rope she was fondling and offered more coffee. The men passed on it, but the one who did most of the talking said, "We cannot divulge more than the fact that your friend in Paris is safe and the man from the boat in Castelnaudary is in custody. However, we were told to thank you for your assistance in this matter. So, thank you, and good day."

As they hustled back to their car I told her what they said and then remembered Jean Luc was still on the phone. "Did you hear what they said? Did I understand that correctly? They were *thanking* us for our assistance?"

"It would seem so."

"Assistance when? What we did? Or what they want us to do. You're French, was there an innuendo there that I didn't catch?"

"Good question. I will call the lawyer as soon as it is polite, since there does not seem to be an emergency. Have you heard from your friend, Jenks?"

"No, but he's, uh, not always at liberty to call."

"He is in prison?" He sounded hopeful.

I had to laugh. "No, but he is the man I *love*. He happens to work in security and is not always able to use certain phones." *Or be around when I need him.*

"You are in love with a spy?"

Am I? "He's not a spy. And even if he were, it's none of your business."

"*Au contraire*, Hetta. It was on his advice that I alerted my friend Claude of a possible threat at Orly. They evacuated the airport, no small matter. If there was in fact no danger, I could possibly lose my credibility."

"You *have* credibility?"

He sighed. "I am resigned that you are not interested in reigniting our...*liaison de coeur,* but can we be friends?"

"Don't you mean our *liaison amoureus*?" I spat. Evidently my resolve to let bygones be bygones was very short-lived as I rejected his term, love affair, and threw back the French street talk for a stressful illicit affair with a married man.

"I was not married," he protested.

I ended the call, not willing to even discuss such a lame defense.

"Why do I get the feeling that didn't go well?"

"He was about to launch the French *cherche la femme* defense. It really means that he got in trouble trying to impress me and is a convoluted way of saying if a man has a problem, there must be a woman involved.

We can thank Alexandre Dumas for coming up with that one."

"Men! They try to justify their bad behavior with semantics."

"So do we."

"Yep, but we get away with it. I say we get back to our vacation, how about that? Where do you want to go next?"

"Mexico."

"Cut and run, huh?"

"Sounds good to me. Well, it would if we had not been told to stay put in France until our lawyer says we can leave."

"Oh, yeah, like that's gonna stop us."

"Let's sleep on it. We're exhausted and not in any condition to make decisions."

She grinned. "Like a few hour's sleep will keep us from making our usual bad ones?"

Chapter Thirty-two

At noon the day after chasing Rousel along the canal and setting off a chain of events that ended with Rhonda being taken into protective custody in Paris and Rousel arrested for we knew not what at Port-Lauragais, we treated ourselves to a long and lavish lunch on the Canal.

The weather had warmed some and the wind calmed, so a quay-side outdoor cafe that is dog friendly was just the venue for deciding our future in France.

We were, as usual, unfashionably early, and so had the place to ourselves. We'd barely settled into our chairs and opened our menus when Jean Luc called.

"Where are you, Hetta?"

"Castelnaudary, where I was the last time we talked...like eight hours ago."

"*Non*, I mean, where *exactly* are you?"

"You writing a book?"

"*Amusant*. We are at your boat and you are not."

I stood up and peered down the street, where I spotted the Austin Princess with René, André, Jean Luc and the lawyer dude standing nearby. About that time Po Thang, who had been half-asleep under the table, what with no diners to beg from, suddenly sprang to his feet and took off running down the quay. Half way to the boat, Charles met him for a wag fest.

"Follow the dogs," I told Jean Luc, and hit the whistle button to recall my dog.

The waiters, who had pretty much ignored us, fell all over themselves when the four men entered, and the chef came out of the kitchen to jaw with René. One waiter snatched the menus and waited for the chef and René to choose our lunch. I so love being in the "in" crowd.

Tables and chairs were rapidly rearranged, this time in the area with the best view and obviously reserved for Frenchmen. We had no sooner been seated again when a Jeroboam of Vueve Clicquot La Grande Dame arrived.

"Holy crap, what are we celebrating?" I asked. Once upon a time or two I'd been treated to Clicquot on someone else's expense account. Even in France, I figured this magnum, which is a three-liter bottle, had to run nearly five hundred bucks.

"*Un moment, s'il vous plaît, Hetta*," Jean Luc said as the waiter filled six tulip glasses.

"A toast!" René stood and proclaimed.

All the men jumped to their feet, grinning like the *chat* who ate the *canari*.

I started to stand, but was waved back into my chair.

Jan and I were wondering what was going on when Jean Luc's lawyer said, "The government of France salutes you!"

Jean Luc, René and André raised their glasses and repeated, "*Á nos amies américaines!*"

Not having any idea what the proper response would be, I raised my glass and made a toast of my own. "*Vive la France*!"

That brought smiles and raised flutes. After we all took a sip—mine was more of a glug—and we were reseated, I quipped, "Hey, I'm not one to turn down a salute, although now that I think of it, I don't recall that ever happening."

Jan drawled, dilettantes Ain't that the truth? Most times Hetta's given the boot, not a salute."

More chuckles and lifted glasses. At the rate we were toasting, that jeroboam wasn't gonna last long.

"Okay, are you going to tell us what this is all about?"

The lawyer nodded at Jean Luc, evidently pre-chosen because of his command of English.

"Have you ever heard the term, 'dry run'?"

I had to think a moment. Of course I'd heard the saying, mostly remembered from a dreaded debate class in college. We'd do dry runs ad nauseam, practicing our rebuttals in front of a critique group before going into an actual debate.

"Yes. It means a practice run. Someone once told me it came from the bootlegging days of Prohibition. The rum runners would make dry runs, with no booze in their vehicles, to learn the roads so they could outrun the revenuers.

I should have picked a better example, as I now had to explain Prohibition to a bunch off Frenchmen, who found the concept not only unfathomable, but downright uncivilized.

"How very strange," Jean Luc said, but then shrugged that French shrug and pulled a face that says, "But then again, it was the *Americans*."

The Frenchmen all nodded in agreement. Actually, so did Jan and I.

"Anyway, where was I?"

"Dry run," I prompted.

"Oh, *oui*. Dry run has taken on a whole new meaning in these troubled times and, thanks to you lovely ladies, one has most probably been unearthed."

"Orly?"

"Yes. Your friend Rhonda was never in danger, as there were no explosives in any of those bags. The entire set up has been deemed a dry run, perpetrated by someone who wanted to observe whether an American female tourist, waiting alone in a busy passenger terminal would raise suspicion."

"And it didn't," said Jan, who was starting to slur a mite.

Luckily food arrived in the form of that wonderful hot brie on toasted baguette that I dearly love. Being French, they served only one per person, but when Jan and I—the Barbarians at le table—devoured ours in one bite, they got the hint and went for more.

"No, not until I called Claude. Had it not been for your...diligence in trying to protect your friend from what you perceived as a gigolo gold digger, they would have succeeded."

"And who is *they*?"

"That is unknown for certain. It is suspected that Rousel Badiz al Bin Jasseron is affiliated with at least one of many militant groups here in France."

René spat, "*Beurs*." He said it like a curse.

Both Po Thang and Charles also softly rumbled.

"Obviously this was well planned out, but why did he come back to the boat?"

"Because it worked once."

"What does that mean?" Jan asked.

A light went off in my head. "He was in Paris during the November fifteenth attack, then returned to the boat and went cruising. No one was looking for him down here, but had he stayed in Paris, he was certain to be on the radar if he's a known militant. Right?"

"There was no paper trail to the Canal du Midi. The boat was rented by mademoiselle Rhonda Jones, her credit card was used for the rental. He was invisible to authorities. We suspect he planned to lie low on the canal, then perhaps make his way to Marseille and disappear."

"How?"

"He had a rental car stashed at Castelnaudary and from there to Marseilles is a short drive."

"Let me guess, the rental car is in Rhonda's name."

"Yes, her passport and credit cards were on *Trebes*, but also her driver's license."

Food arrived again, this time a poached sea perch, so talk of Rhonda and Rousel was suspended temporarily. One does not discuss un-pleasantries while eating in France; it is bad for the digestive system.

My mind evidently did not get that memo. While we ate, my brain was in overdrive. Breaking all protocol, my fork stopped in midair as I blurted, "The November attack was by ISIS!"

Jean Luc nodded slowly.

Jan and I stared at each other as reality settled in like a bombshell.

"Oh, hell."

"Dang!"

Not to be left out, "Ruff."

Chapter Thirty-three

When the reality that we had been messing with ISIS hit us, Jan and I suddenly lost our appetites.

The group is well known for retaliating against *anyone* they deemed the enemy, which is just about everyone. They go after the families, friends, and pets. Just how far would they go to retaliate for a foiled dry run? We'd stalked Rousel and were responsible for his arrest! This is no way good.

Po Thang must have picked up on my panic and began to whine. Tears flooded Jan's eyes. I was just in shock.

The lawyer waved his hands in the air and said, "*Non, non, non.* Do not worry. Your names have never been revealed to anyone. All your names, including that of mademoiselle Jones, have been erased from any reports."

He said this in French, so I let Jean Luc translate. Jan relaxed some, but then she said, "Rousel won't put two and two together?"

"Think about it. When was the last time he actually saw you?"

"The day he and Rhonda left for Paris."

"Exactly. He has no way of knowing you were in touch with Rhonda at Orly, *n'cest-ce pas?"*

I saw where he was going with this line of reasoning. "But what about Rhonda? She'll tell the feds about the phone, and how we told her to leave the terminal in a big hurry."

"Yes, that is so." He looked at his watch, and asked the waiter to turn on the television. "Just wait a few minutes, and all will be revealed. Anyone for brandy and coffee?"

Four hands and one paw raised. Charles was too polite to beg.

Just as our coffee arrived, the unmistakable notes of breaking news came from the television, and a man materialized behind an official looking podium. Camera clicks sounded, bulbs flashed, and everyone behind the man looked very solemn. Talking heads informed us of the topic to be addressed: the recent evacuation of Orly airport.

The spokesperson, who delivered his address in French, was talked over by a translator because the restaurant had tuned into one of the English-speaking business channels found where foreigners gather. Normally, the voice-over was annoying, but not when I didn't want to miss a word of what the man said when my precious self might be involved.

Basically, he said that as everyone was aware of by now, the Orly airport had been evacuated as a matter of caution, and he wanted to reassure the French people there had never been any danger to anyone in the area.

It was a short conference with a brief Q and A session afterwards. We were all glued to the image, hanging on every word. When the regular program returned—a weather report for all of Europe—the lawyer asked the waiter to turn it off.

"Feeling better now, Hetta?" Jean Luc asked.

"Well—" my phone chirped and I glanced at it. "I gotta take this, it's Jenks!"

I walked away from the group to talk with him, although I was bouncing off the walls with excitement after that press conference.

"Hetta, did you by any chance just see that press release?"

"Yes, I did! They covered our butts! According to the powers that be, there *was* no emergency. Security simply reacted when a female tourist left luggage unattended in the terminal while she went outside to look for her boyfriend, who was late for their flight."

"Nice spin. Works for me."

"Hey, how did *you* see that on television? Where are you?"

"Lille. I'll be back on the boat by tomorrow afternoon."

"Yee haw!" I yelled, catching the attention of my fellow diners, and Po Thang, who came on the run to share my excitement with yips and whines.

After I talked with Jenks, I returned to the table and grabbed my glass. "Jenks is coming back. Tomorrow!"

Jan, who was in her cups by now, slurred, "Well, hell, there's *my* eviction notice."

"Yep."

We all wove our way back to the Austin Princess and were saying our goodbyes, with promises to visit René and Charles once Jenks returned.

Jean Luc, before he joined the others in the car, asked me for a word in private.

We walked a few feet away from the car, and he said, "So, I have to ask, or I'll regret it the rest of my life. What about us?"

"We'll always have Paris."

Epilogue

Jan was long gone by the time Jenks arrived at the boat, hightailing it for Paris where she'd been invited to stay with Rhonda in Jean Luc's apartment. Any qualms she had at being in close quarters with Rhonda were immediately assuaged; she bombarded me with snapshots and videos of DooRah's "guest apartment"—all five bedrooms of it. Her suite, a one-bedroom with a view of the Eiffel Tower, included a sitting room and kitchenette.

She also reported that Rhonda was still heartsick, but not over Rousel; she was furious with herself for being such a dupe. I'm sure Jan would reassure her with tales of *my* previous cockups—you should pardon the expression—in judgment. However, if Rhonda was expecting a sympathy sister's shoulder to bawl on, she was sooo very wrong. Jan is a great bully to have around at times. And I suspected Rhonda was in for a massive makeover by a cadre of expensive Parisian experts. Like I said, Jan dearly loves to spend OPM, and Rhonda has plenty of loot.

Even had I not been glued to the window, Jenks's arrival would be hard to miss. The minute he stepped from the cab, Po Thang, who was lounging on deck, went bonkers. As did the swans.

All the honking, hissing, yipping, and sobbing—that would be me—would have sent a lesser man back into that taxi, but Jenks is a man's man, with enough *sangfroid* to weather such an emotional onslaught.

I had the boat stocked with his favorite foods, and spaghetti and meatballs on the menu for lunch, which also met with Po Thang's hearty approval. He wasn't so happy, however when, after lunch, we locked him out of my cabin.

During cocktail hour, Jenks shared news he had of Rousel. I suspected he wasn't telling all he knew, for Rousel had disappeared into the clutches of GIGN— pronounced, *jhay jhin*—the *Group D'Intervention de la Gendarmerie Nationale,* a seriously badass French counterterrorism organization, probably never to emerge. After all, with no crime to report to the public—if you don't count some silly tourist inadvertently leaving unaccompanied luggage in the terminal building—there was no crime to officially punish. No suspect to arrest. End of story, *n'est-ce pas?*

"So, where does that leave Rhonda? Or, more importantly, Jan and me?"

"Again, with Rousel gone, there is no connection to you or Jan."

"Okay, then, what about that cousin who dumped Rhonda at the terminal building?"

Jenks smiled. "Rounded up sitting in his car in the parking lot. Sang like a bird. He was not a cousin and had been promised a hundred bucks to say he was. Believe it or not, the so-called cousin was to pick her, and the luggage, up and take her back to that apartment where she'd been staying in Paris."

"What? You're kidding. Wait, let me guess. After assuring Rhonda that he was sincerely remorseful about the missing the plane thing, maybe using an excuse like a sudden death in his family, he would accompany her to the States, and right to her big fat bank account?"

"That's my take."

"Well, for crying out loud."

"You probably saved her life."

"There were times when I wanted to kill her myself."

Jenks chuckled and gave me a hug, only to get his arm nosed. "Hey, you've had Hetta to yourself for too long. My turn."

Po Thang stuck out his tongue.

"Better watch it there, Po Thang. This man is gonna get us back home, and unless you want a long and lonely ride in a baggage compartment cage with the lesser dogs, you'd better be nice. Speaking of, when and how *will* we get back to Mexico? Not that I'm all that ready to go. We still have to visit with René, cuz I promised."

"We have three weeks, then duty calls. And Air France, in appreciation for your assistance in a matter of security, will get you, Jan, Rhonda, and Po Thang back home."

Planning the next three weeks included another ten days on the canal, plus a two-day stay in Gruissan where we'd dump Po Thang with Charles while we bopped, dog free, around the South of France.

Jenks asked if I wanted to go back to Paris, but I gave that an emphatic, "*NON!*"

To paraphrase Edith Piaf singing "*Non, je ne regrette rien,*" I have *no* regrets for the past because from now on, "…my joys, today, they begin with Jenks."

Oh là là!

FIN

A note from Jinx

If you have enjoyed this book, please tell your friends about Hetta, or post a short review on Amazon. Word of mouth is an author's best friend, and is much appreciated.

I have editors, but boo-boos do manage to creep into a book, no matter how many people look at it before publication, and if there are errors, they are all on me. Should you come upon one of these culprits, please let me know and I shall smite it with my mighty keyboard! You can e-mail me at jinxschwartz@yahoo.com

And if you want to be alerted when I have a free, discounted, or new book, you can go **to www.jinxschwartz.com and sign up for my newsletter.** I promise not to deluge you with pictures of puppies and kittens.

You can find me on Facebook at https://www.facebook.com/jinxschwartz That puppy and kitten thing? No promises on FB posts :-)

Oh, and no swans, dawgs, boats, or French citizens were actually harmed in the writing of this book.

Thanks for reading my books! jinx

36224972R00160

Made in the USA
San Bernardino, CA
17 July 2016